ABSENT FRIENDS

ABSENT FRIENDS

Geoffrey Wheatcroft

HAMISH HAMILTON · LONDON

HAMISH HAMILTON LTD
Published by the Penguin Group
27 Wrights Lane, London W8 5TZ, England
Viking Penguin Inc, 40 West 23rd Street, New York, New York 10010, U.S.A.
Penguin Books Australia Ltd, Ringwood, Victoria, Australia
Penguin Books Canada Ltd, 2801 John Street, Markham, Ontario, Canada L3R 1B4
Penguin Books (N.Z.) Ltd, 182–190 Wairau Road, Auckland 10, New Zealand

Penguin Books Ltd, Registered Offices: Harmondsworth, Middlesex, England

First published in Great Britain 1989 by
Hamish Hamilton Ltd

Copyright © 1989 by Geoffrey Wheatcroft

1 3 5 7 9 10 8 6 4 2

British Library Cataloguing in Publication Data
CIP data for this book is available from the British Library

ISBN 0–241–12874–9

Printed and bound in Great Britain by
Butler & Tanner Ltd, Frome, Somerset

TO SELINA

CONTENTS

PREFACE

This book was written in the winter of 1988–9. It was written because I was stuck at work on another, more complicated book; because I was resting, as actors say, from my journalistic career; because I had been excited by re-reading books like Isaiah Berlin's *Personal Impressions* and Alan Watkins's *Brief Lives*, to which this book bears certain resemblances; and because, for one reason or another, the people whom I have written about were on my mind. They are all people whom I have known, they are all now dead.

The word 'friends' in the title has been used elastically. The subjects range from an American writer whom I met once, to a couple of my closest friends. There was an obvious temptation to include the famous with whom I had had fleeting contact to balance the obscure whom I knew well, but I have tried to apply certain tests. All the people have affected or influenced my life, as friends, as teachers, as colleagues, as writers. For many of them I might have borrowed another title, 'Debts of Honour', but that would not quite apply to all of them. Anyway, in the end they selected themselves. If not all illustrious, most of them are older than me, which is a relief. Plenty of books tell of the generation which was at school or at university in the first decade and a half of this century, and what happened to them; it became something of an English obsession, those photographs of cricket teams of eighteen-year-olds taken in 1910, only one or two of whom survived until 1919. Nothing like that has happened to my generation, born immediately after the World war and now in their forties. Most of my friends who are contemporaries are mercifully still alive.

That some are not is what was on my mind when I began to write these impressions; and why they are not; the nature of death. 'Natural causes' used to be a phrase more popular than it is now, when medicine has encouraged us to think ourselves almost immortal. And indeed, in once sense, death is not natural. In another sense, nothing is more natural; the one completely inevitable truth of all our lives. The goal of life is death, as I quote Mozart on another page. And yet the goal comes in a disconcerting variety of ways. Some of my friends died in old age, when their bodies had reasonably given up. Some died too young – at thirty-seven, forty or forty-three. Some died of diseases which few of us would contemplate with equanimity, some died suddenly. Two died by their own hands, one when his heart was broken by bereavement, one more drastically when a cause célèbre in which he played a leading part had thrown him off balance. Two died in accidents, completely unforeseen. There is no pattern and, I think, different degrees of grief or loss are appropriate. One of these friends used to speak of the uncanny way in which almost all great composers seem to enjoy an especially sublime phase towards the end of their lives, whether they died at thirty-one like Schubert, thirty-five like Mozart, fifty-six like Beethoven or eighty-seven like Verdi. But there is no such consolation in the cases of whose who have been removed just as they were coming into their own, when fate snaps its fingers.

The randomness of death is what has selected these portraits; I could have chosen another score of people who were close to me and who have influenced me. But, as they

2

have fallen into place, they form a sort of autobiography (I am not sure what sort), not that I ever wanted or want to write such a thing. There is no one here from my childhood, though I might possibly have included a friend who died when we were both eleven, or my mother, or either of the two grandparents whom I knew; or one or two family friends. There is no one in fact from the first twenty or so years of my life, growing up among a professional family in London where I had been born: and I met all my subjects at university or afterwards.

When I left Oxford, where Gareth Bennett taught me, I had no idea what to do. I had not done much work (or much else) as an undergraduate but had acquired a love of books and typography. At one moment I thought I wanted to be a bibliographer, an ambition which was not encouraged by the British Museum to which I applied. I vaguely thought of several careers (as I had vaguely thought of several different subjects to read at university) such as the Bar or even academic life: not quite such a far-fetched idea as it now seems, in that boom period of the 1960s when practically anyone who got a reasonable degree, whether deservedly or as in my case by luck, at least contemplated 'doing research'. Some of those who did more than contemplate it are now in middle age stuck in the grooves of academe, in places which bring them little joy, and it is one of the blessings that I count that I did not follow them. If nothing else is clear to me, I know I was not meant to be a don, or for that matter a lawyer.

Instead, I studied typography and went into publishing as a production assistant. I have occasionally wondered what would have happened if I had stayed there, designing and producing books. But, although what I learned has been very useful to me in newspaper life, typography is a happier hobby than trade for me. As it happened, I was whisked aside into publicity and then, even less successfully, editing, from one firm to another – Roger Machell was a colleague at one, Anthea Joseph at the other – and then to a third, where I met Michael Dempsey. Then after six and a half not very fruitful years my publishing life drew not very peacefully to its close. I had already started writing for papers, to begin with book reviews, and oddities like pieces on sport for the *New Statesman*. While, as I kicked or cooled my heels after being sacked, I bumped into Alexander Chancellor. He had just become editor of the *Spectator* in that summer of 1975 following its purchase by his friend Henry Keswick and in a moment's absence of mind hired me as his assistant. George Hutchinson joined us quite soon. There followed more than five happy years, four of them as literary editor when among others I asked Hans Keller and Stephen Koss to write for the paper. Jenny Naipaul was a colleague at 56 Doughty Street, and Shiva became a drinking companion as well as a contributor. Margaret FitzHerbert came to *Spectator* lunches and parties and it was through the magazine that I first met Philip Larkin.

In 1981 I left the *Spectator* to write a book, published as *The Randlords* four years later. As I mention later, Hugh Fraser disliked that title, though he encouraged me to write the book. The book had a chequered publishing career in London, and also New York but at least on a visit there I was able to meet Dwight Macdonald and write about him. Shortly before my book was published, I joined the *Evening Standard* to edit the 'Londoner's Diary' for eighteen exhausting and exhilarating months. One pleasant task was to take my colleague Sam White to Lord's when he was in London, renewing a friendship made years before.

Through the 1970s I lived a peripatetic existence before settling in Islington but my life in London had two spiritual (or spirituous) centres. One was Fleet Street. In El

Vino I drank with Philip Hope-Wallace and Willi Frischauer, across the road with Peter Utley. The other was
Soho, the Dean Street of the French pub and Muriel's. I
think of Goronwy Rees when I go into the one, Liz
Smart, in the other. The Groucho Club did not appear
between the two until the mid-eighties; I still associate it
with Mark Boxer, as I associate the rather different Beefsteak Club with Iain Moncreiffe. All of these are London
memories, and among other things putting these memories on paper has been a way of exorcizing the city where
I was born, where I have spent all my life, and which I
have come to dislike very much.

Looking through these portraits, I detect a sharp, I
should not like to think disparaging, note in some of
them. That was far from my intention. Voltaire said that
to the living we owe respect but to the dead we owe
nothing but the truth. I have tried to honour these old
friends with a little of both, respect and truth. These were
all people whom in some degree I knew, liked, loved,
admired, and of whom I could say that their liking for
me made me think better of myself. Those were the words
used of his friendship with Orwell by A. J. Ayer, who
died while this book was in proof and who is my last
portrait.

As these sketches were done from memory, with no
assistance and scarcely any research, even what passes for
it in a newspaper office, I have only to acknowledge that
some of the pieces were first written in different form
for the *Spectator*, the *New Republic*, and the *Independent
Magazine*.

I am grateful to Messrs Weidenfeld & Nicolson for
permission to quote from the *Letters of Evelyn Waugh*
and to Messrs Faber & Faber and the Marvell Press for
permission to quote from Philip Larkin's poems. On page
142 there are quotations from 'High Windows' and

'Annus Mirabilis' from *High Windows* (Faber & Faber), and on page 143 from 'Talking in Bed' and 'Wild Oats' from *The Whitsun Weddings* (Faber & Faber) and 'Reasons for Attendance' from *The Less Deceived* (Marvell Press). The photograph of Gareth Bennett is copyright Hugh Newsam Film Services; those of Sam White, Philip Hope-Wallace, Willi Frischauer and A. J. Ayer, the Hulton-Deutsch Collection; Anthea Joseph, Michael Joseph Ltd; George Hutchinson, Barnet Saidman, by courtesy of Mrs Hutchinson; Hans Keller, the BBC, by courtesy of Mrs Keller; Stephen Koss, A. McCaughey; Shiva Naipaul, Jerry Bauer; Margaret FitzHerbert, John Murray (Publishers) Ltd; Philip Larkin and Iain Moncrieffe, Camera Press Ltd; Dwight Macdonald, Mariette Pathy Allen, by courtesy of Mrs Macdonald; T. E. Utley, *The Times*; Goronwy Rees, *The Sunday Times*; Mark Boxer, *The Tatler*. For other photographs I am grateful to friends: to Michael Parkin, for Michael Dempsey and Muriel Belcher, to Rebecca Fitzgerald, for Hugh Fraser, and to Christopher Barker and Jeffrey Bernard, for Elizabeth Smart.

Although it should normally be otiose for an author to thank his agent and publisher for doing their jobs, on this occasion it would be churlish for me not to thank Gill Coleridge and even more Christopher Sinclair-Stevenson for encouragement, generosity and tolerance beyond the call of duty.

Widcombe, St James's Day, 1989

I

GARETH BENNETT

Men reading Modern History at New College in the 1960s were lucky in their tutors. There were three. The eldest, P. H. Williams, was old enough to have seen the tail-end of the war before coming up to New College and then lecturing at Manchester for several years before returning to the college as a Fellow in 1964. He was a specialist in the Tudor period, later an editor of the *English Historical Review* and author of a forthcoming volume on the sixteenth century in the new Oxford History of England. Eric Christiansen had also just returned to the college from exile in Manchester, still in his twenties, as mediaeval history tutor. The third history tutor taught me what I know about early eighteenth-century England and was a Fellow of a very different sort. G. V. Bennett was a clerical don, already an endangered species; he was not a New College man, or an Oxonian; he had not been to a public school. He was college chaplain and only in the second place a tutor. His position at the college was in some respects awkward. His career was unhappy, though how unhappy no one realized until his death at the end of 1987 when he enjoyed a brief and terrible season of fame.

Gareth Vaughan Bennett was born in Essex in 1929 into a lower-middle-class family; his father was a City clerk. The family lived for a time in East Horsley and Gary went to the Royal Grammar School at Guildford. When they moved back to Essex, he went to the Southend High School for Boys, to which he was always afterwards attached. Gary was an only child, a devoted mother's boy, solitary and inward-looking and, as he believed, over-protected in childhood. His upbringing was unintellectual and un-churchy. His father had been raised as a strong Evangelical but the parents were not regular church-goers. Gary became an avid reader, though not of 'the books the real middle-class read: Beatrix Potter and A. A. Milne I never knew. The *Magnet* and the *Gem* and Percy F. Westerman were my mainstay.' As a boy he became pious, attracted by the High ritual of a nearby church.

He missed National Service as Grade III unfit but won a place at Cambridge, to Christ's where his tutor was J. H. (Sir John) Plumb. Plumb found Gary clever but uneducated, 'a mind historically tabula rasa'. Bennett worked very hard at Cambridge, which was not surprising, coxed one of the college eights, which might surprise those who knew him later, and, what was in its way least surprising, became acutely class-conscious. English life being what it is and the universities being what they are, it would have been hard for an introspective, unattractive, plebeian boy not to be aware of the gulf between himself and those who had come from public schools, or in those days from public schools by way of 'good regiments'. This had a bearing on Gary's life.

Because of his educational backwardness he made a slow start in the Tripos but ended with a starred first in History Part II and began work for a doctorate, supervised by Norman Sykes, later Dean of Winchester. He had decided to be ordained and had chosen church history as his field, especially the short but riveting period from the Restoration to 1740. His dissertation was on White Kennett, the attractive clergyman who was Bishop of Peterborough from 1718 till his death in 1728. Attractive, but disappointed: Peterborough was an impoverished backwater where Kennett hoped not to end his days but

did. It was a coincidence of which a Freudian might make something that the human subjects Gary Bennett chose were studies in failure.

Bennett went to be trained for the priesthood to Westcott House at Cambridge. It is worth remarking that the phrase 'trained for the priesthood' is odd in England, or would have been not long ago, and that theological colleges are a recent innovation. Candidates for ordination were expected once to have learned something at university, including a modest grasp of moral and pastoral theology, without further technical instruction (just as, not so long ago, English schoolboys were not instructed in 'English language and literature' but were expected to master the grammar of their own language and to read its literature for pleasure). This is not a sentimental plaint: the change from educated clergyman to technically instructed but ignorant priest is a significant one in English social history, and one on which Bennett's career cast a sombre shadow. The vice-principal of Westcott in 1954–6 was Dr Robert Runcie, whom Gary was to know well for the next thirty years.

Bennett taught for a time at King's, London; his dissertation was awarded its doctorate, won the Thirlwall Prize and was published in 1957; he applied for the chaplaincy of New College and was elected in 1959. His position at the college was not anomalous quite, but it was complicated. Although Oxford colleges had ceased to be religious institutions they still had chapels – at New College a famous one, with one of the three permanent Oxford choirs singing evensong daily – and chaplains, despite the hostility of militantly atheist dons. There were several of those at New College; one used to ask every candidate for a Fellowship only one question: 'Are you a Christian?' and if the answer was affirmative vote against him irrespective of academic record.

The chaplain had not long since been one clerical don among several; now he was on his own. It was harder to find someone in holy orders who had any sort of scholarly distinction and a man like Bennett who was both in orders and had the right array of Firsts and doctorates was a catch. He was not taken on as a tutorial Fellow but the fact that he could teach an important slice of the history syllabus was much in his favour. The college gave Gary a further mark of approbation by nominating him to one of the two Wiccamical prebends or canonries at Chichester Cathedral which were in its gift. He was henceforth usually known as Dr or Canon Bennett; when I sent him postcards, chucking tutorials or whatever, I addressed them, correctly I thought, to 'The Revd Prebendary G. V. Bennett'.

By the time I went up to New College six years after his election, Gary was a fixture, and an oddity, and in some ways an embarrassment. It might be said (though he never began to see this) that he had gone out of his way to make himself unpopular. He did not ally himself with any of the factions in the Common Room but antagonized all of them at one time or another. As a young man, Gary had been a Conservative but he was turned slightly leftwards (as has been recorded) by Suez and (as is less well-known) by the constituency affairs of Southend, where he had belonged to the Conservative Association.* So, Gary did not have much time for the

---

* The seat had once been held by Lord Elvedon, whose daughter Lady Honor Guinness married Sir Henry (as he later became, but always known as Chips) Channon. When Elvedon succeeded his father as Lord Iveagh and head of the greatest dynasty in the beerage, his wife succeeded him as Member for Southend, followed by his son-in-law. When Chips died in 1958, the nomination for the seat went to his son Paul, then aged twenty-three and fresh from Eton, the Blues and Christ Church. One of his kinswomen unhelpfully said, 'They may not know the horse but they know the stable'; and several years later

patricians (nor they for him); and yet he never became a radical, in fact was dead against the radicals on every vital issue, above all the admission of women.

His lack of aptitude for making friends and influencing people did not stop Gary Bennett devoting a large part of his energy to college politics, or simply to intrigue. When he subsequently turned to church politics, many of his colleagues assumed, as Eric Christiansen has put it, that this 'was simply the result of his usual inability to mind his own business; a sort of hobby which occupied his own mind, and satisfied the sense he had of his own importance'. This temperamental trait was combined with his capacity for being, as Dr Runcie described him to me, 'an angular colleague on committees; there were those who did not enjoy being chairman of a committee on which he sat' – and indeed there were those who did not much like attending college meetings when he was present.

Of course he should have devoted more of his energies to his work. 'Unfulfilled promise' is a tiresome and often misleading phrase, but Gary became a Fellow of New College and a Canon before he was thirty, having published one book, and in the nearly thirty years he remained at the college published only one more. It is true that he wrote essays and articles and preached sermons, but they only reinforce the sense of wasted opportunity. He was an excellent scholar and writer. His second book, *The Tory Crisis in Church and State 1688–1730*, is a life of Francis Atterbury, leader of the extreme High Church party under Queen Anne and Bishop of Rochester from 1713 until his trial for treason as a Jacobite and his exile

in a review of Chips's wonderful diaries, Randolph Churchill related the story of Southend and concluded, 'Never has it been so truly said that Guinness is good for you'. Principled or chippy as one chooses, Bennett did not think Guinness was good for the party.

to die as a chaplain at the court of the Old Pretender. It is a marvellous book, racily told and reading like a thriller. Rereading it today is also eerie, because of the pre-echoes of Gary Bennett's own life. For, along with his exiguous literary production and his restless intrigue, the third strand in his career was a sense of disappointment. To repeat, he was a Fellow of New College for almost thirty years, when no preferment came his way.

Many people dislike their work, but in Gary's case resentment of it came to eat him up. When I was taught by him, he had not been in Oxford for ten years but he already made little secret of his disaffection. He was short with pupils who were unruly or unpunctual – on one occasion when I was maybe ten minutes late for a tutorial he told me to go away with words to the effect that if he could be on time, so could I – as well as acerbic about inadequate work. And yet he was a very good tutor. He was not inspiring, as some teachers are said to be, but you learned from him. If his pupils paid attention, they received better marks on the paper than they deserved. That was notably true in my case in 'Costin and Watson', the paper of constitutional documents, which appealed to Gary's legalistic mind and logic-chopping and love of pernickety, perverse argument, and also my own. Whether he loved history in a fuller sense I was never quite sure at the time. He once asked me how far I thought contemporary literature illuminated a period and I said that imaginative literature had always to be treated with caution; after all, it is by definition an exaggerated version of life rather than life itself. Gary said that, Yes, it was a great waste of time, wasn't it? in a way which made me smile: I had not meant to say that reading Swift or Pope was tedious in itself. This mild philistinism applied to most of the arts: as far as I knew, Gary found little enthusiasm for the music in chapel where he was one of those responsible for the hideous new organ frame put up in the 1970s, and he had a frightful kitsch painting of the Crucifixion hanging in his rooms. But I now realize that he had a deeper love of and feeling for history, especially for the history of the Church of England, than I saw at the time. His posthumous collection *For the Church of England* has delightful essays on Anglican worthies, Laud, Ken, Tillotson, Tenison, which get inside their skins and inside their times.

He remained ill at ease in the college, sensitive as a friend has written to both 'the barbed comments of self-conscious non-Christians and to what he perceived as the superciliousness of some of the wealthier members of the college', meaning, I take it, undergraduate bloods rather than upper-class colleagues (despite his High Church-manship, Lord David Cecil can have felt very little in common with the chaplain, but I doubt whether he was supercilious towards him). It is true that Gary was a figure of fun and a butt for the young gentlemen, though it was not he but his predecessor as chaplain who had been crucified with croquet hoops on the lawn by the First VIII; as ex-officio treasurer of the Boat Club, Gary had merely to sit through rowdy dinners wearing a fixed smile while the dirty jokes were told.

There was no way of avenging these humiliations, not against their perpetrators. His touchiness and, sometimes, resentfulness, showed in other ways. I said once I had to go to London to listen to the maiden speech in the House of Lords of a friend in the college – admittedly a quite absurd thing to say and to be doing – and Gary snapped at me, 'Sycophant,' not quite ironically. This may have sharpened Gary's appetite for political machination, large enough in any case. He schemed assiduously for what seemed to others the pettiest of ends. He was college librarian, and became obsessed with the need for a special room for rare (or as he insisted on calling them 'anti-quarian') books, away from the unlovely 1930s college library, in what would have been an even unlovelier new building on Longwall. I daresay that a colleague had shrewdly bargained, hoping to get this edifice built to house more postgraduate students and offering Bennett a sop in return. That is how college politics go, with lamentable results. People complain about the conservatism of dons but a stroll round Oxford to see what has been inflicted architecturally in the last thirty years suggests that they are in some ways nothing like conservative enough. No doubt some such mutual back-scratching led to the building of the notorious organ case.

Gary's finest hour came in 1973 when he was made one of the two University proctors. The last embers of student rebellion smouldered when a mob seized the Indian Institute building at the corner of Holywell and Broad Street. Most of them were post-hippies who were not members of the University, but the police refused to eject them. After other remedies had failed, Bennett hired a gang of roughs from the town and directed them when they set up ladders to break into the upper windows at dawn while the slothful and sybaritic revolutionists were still asleep. The coup de main was completely successful. The rebels were routed and, as even dons unsympathetic to Bennett ruefully admit, Oxford has never seen troubles of the same sort since. Few had thought of Gary as a man of action; in his daydreams had he seen himself as some churchman militant, a mediaeval prelate riding armoured and caparisoned into battle?

But that was his last public triumph. Disappointment took over once more. The portrait of Bennett's second study in failure, Atterbury, did not appear until he had been at New College for almost twenty years and if the echoes of his own frustration in *White Kennett* were unconscious and prophetic, they were surely conscious by the time he wrote his book on Atterbury. Both these men became bishops, though of two of the poorest sees in England. Kennett never escaped from Peterborough. In Atterbury's case, indigence was mitigated by the custom that the Bishop of Rochester was simultaneously Dean of Westminster, with another and handsome income. But his fall when it came was further and harder. At all events, Gary Bennett might have been writing about himself: 'At each vacancy of a bishopric he seemed to have been full of expectation.'

Many of those who knew Bennett were surprised at his ambition and did not share his own estimate of his suitability to be a bishop. And after his death his qualities or lack of them were discussed. The Archbishop of Canterbury thought that Gary had 'a pastoral heart', others that this just was what this reclusive, sharp-tongued bachelor don lacked. In another age his intellectual distinction would have been enough. After all, how many of the present bench of bishops have written any books of academic excellence? If not bishoprics, deaneries have been a traditional appointment for scholarly clerics. Gary's hope for preferment rose again when the Bishop of St Albans, his old friend Dr Runcie, became Archbishop of Canterbury. But although several deaneries came up – Winchester, St Paul's, Westminster, Canterbury itself – none was offered to Bennett, not under the new Archbishop or under the prime ministership of Mrs Thatcher, with whom Gary was at least more in political sympathy than were many contemporary clergymen. Again, he knew what he was writing about when he described Swift in his Irish exile who 'received the shattering news that all three of the deaneries had been filled'.

His hopes rose once more in 1984, when the bishopric of Durham fell vacant, and Professor MacManners retired from the Regius Chair of Ecclesiastical History and the accompanying Canonry of Christ Church. Bennett believed he was proxime accessit for Durham when Dr David Jenkins was appointed. He intrigued clumsily to succeed MacManners. At a reception at St Benet's he cornered Richard Cobb, who was also retiring from his Oxford History chair, and asked who the runners were and what his chances were and whether Cobb could help. This struck Cobb as an example of Bennett's naïvety, in believing that he of all people would have any weight: 'It made me think at the time that he would make a very poor courtier.' In the event the Regius chair was frozen, as part of Oxford's cutting off its nose to spite the face of Thatcherism, and no appointment was made. These promotions of others 'seem to have produced a great despondency ... he was, he told the Archbishop, "a forgotten man".' That was Bennett describing White Kennett, but it might have been himself; if, that is, he had been as frank enough to speak so to Runcie. They were often in touch. Runcie was Bennett's guest several times at New College, and they saw each other also when Bennett became a well-known figure in the General Synod. 'I would appeal to him for help when confronted with an address which called for some historical reminiscence or allusion,' Dr Runcie told me. 'He was always very generous in his response.' The Archbishop also says that 'I have always considered that he could have been a distinguished Dean and so he might have been if he had lived.' Dr Runcie also said, 'I cannot comment on whether he was considered for a bishopric since I am a member of the Crown Appointments Commission and their consultations are strictly confidential.'

And so Gary was stuck at New College. His dislike of teaching was stronger than ever, especially of teaching women once they were admitted to the college. I began with the words 'Men reading Modern History . . .', which is correct until women were at last admitted in the 1970s. But then again, despite the fact that he had originally come to the college as Dean of Divinity he managed to escape that responsibility, also increasingly irksome, and arranged for another chaplain to be appointed while he remained a Fellow.

In calling him clumsy, I may have underestimated his talent. The trouble was that his skill was negative, less formidable for advancing himself than for blocking others. There were two remarkable examples of this latter at New College. Gary conducted a long vendetta against an inoffensive clergyman called Canon Jones who for obscure reasons had dining rights at the college which Gary wanted to end. Then in 1985 Arthur Cook retired as Warden. There was a strong internal candidate to succeed him in Penry Williams, who had been at the college for a quarter of a century and, as I innocently thought, had no enemies. In fact, Gary Bennett determined to thwart his fellow historian, a colleague with whom he had worked every day for so long. Enlisting first of all the help of two regular allies, he succeeded: enough Fellows were persuaded to vote against Williams and then to make the surprising choice of Harvey McGregor, a successful barrister who also taught Jurisprudence.

When some of the details of this bitter election were told to me I was taken aback. Anyone who has set foot in a common room knows that spite and malice are the heart and lungs of academic life; or, as Henry Kissinger once said, academic politics are so much more savage than any other kind because there is so little at stake. Journalism has a reputation for ambition and treachery, but most Fleet Street offices might be temples of brotherly love compared with many colleges and the New College election was venemous by any standards.

These were locust years for Gary in his private life also. In the 1970s he bought a house in Moody Road in the Oxford suburbs and moved his elderly parents there. His father died and Gary went to live there with his mother until she too died in 1981. Some time later he wrote in his diary, 'The nights have been rather long since mother died'. He became more withdrawn and dined in college less often, to the relief, it must be said, of some of his colleagues.

His energies were now diverted to church politics. He was elected to the General Synod, the governing body which the Church of England had unwisely created to include lay members as well as the ecclesiastics of the old Convocations of Canterbury and York. When I had first known Gary he had not been strongly identified with any church party and I was not the only one – so clerical colleagues of his have told me – to be surprised when he became publicly identified as an Anglo-Catholic. Indeed I used to doubt whether he was a man of strong religious convictions; many present-day parsons and even bishops, after all, have discovered like Mr Prendergast in *Decline and Fall* that there is a species of person called a Modern Churchman who could draw the salary of a beneficed clergyman without professing any religious beliefs. My view was shared by others: there is an undecided bet between Freddie Ayer and Eric Christiansen in the New College Betting Book that the Chaplain would not know sixteen of the Thirty-Nine Articles. But however that may have been it was not true that Bennett was without strong convictions. His turbulent waters ran deep, as events showed. He joined the general purposes sub-committee of the Synod and frequently spoke, becoming known as a voice of traditional, non-extreme Anglo-

Catholicism and as someone who could be called on to give a judicious statement of the intelligent conservative position whenever some fresh squabble broke out in the church.

That was just why he was invited to write the Preface to *Crockford's Clerical Directory* in February 1987. *Crockford's* is the Church of England's Who's Who, published biennially and by tradition containing a Preface, anonymous but it is to be supposed by some eminent personage in the church, commenting freely on ecclesiastical matters. Gary Bennett was in some ways an obvious choice for Derek Pattinson, Secretary-General of the Synod, and James Sherry, Deputy Chairman of the Church Commissioners, who chose the authors of the Prefaces. Bennett accepted on two conditions, that the author's anonymity would be strictly observed, and that what he wrote would be published unaltered. Unfortunately, with hindsight, this was agreed upon; and so, as with Atterbury, 'a train of events had been set in motion which was to involve him in utter disaster'.

These echoes from nature to art, past to present, are not as it were an accident. Gary's mind ran to conspiracy, intrigue, blackguarding; and one of the reasons why he was such a good historian was that his chosen period really was like that. From Charles II to George II, above all the reign of Anne, was the heyday of the plot, the anonymous pamphlet, the denunciation, who's in, who's out, who's doing whom down, all of this at least as much in the politics of Church as of State. It is not fanciful to suppose that Gary Bennett identified with his characters. Now, like Atterbury before him, 'with the verve of the born journalist he was', he set to work on his polemic. Looking back it is easy to see that he was carried away, took the bit too hard between his teeth. So absorbed was he that he forgot himself in more ways than one. Ironically in the

light of subsequent events, one colleague remembers Gary
that spring grumbling that he had to rush away from
dinner to get on with that wretched Preface. And, at the
same time, he forgot his tone of voice, shielded as he
thought he was by anonymity.

He delivered the Preface at Ascensiontide. 'It was not
difficult for a writer of Atterbury's' – or Bennett's –
'incendiary talent to make out that the condition of
religion in England required an urgent remedy', and two
years later the Preface is as lively and startling as it was at
the time of its publication. One writer, far from unsympathetic to Bennett, has spoken of his not inconsiderable
waspishness and of 'just how bitchy the attack' on Runcie
was. Another said in answer to the question put by Dr
Habgood, the Archbishop of York – 'why did this donnish
and predominantly negative analysis of the state of
Anglicanism arouse such a response?' – that it 'was simply
because we are not used to hearing a clergyman tell the
truth'. These two descriptions are not mutually exclusive:
perhaps Bennett was both bitchy and truthful.

He was unthinking in another sense. After his death
there was some rather pointless discussion as to how far
he could be called naïve, an innocent abroad. There may
have been an element of misjudging his effect, though
there is no doubt that he wanted his voice to be heard,
was quite happy to cause a minor sensation. He did not
expect the Crockford's story to be taken up by the popular
press as it was, but would have been disappointed if no
one had noticed it at all. Where he miscalculated was in
the degree to which he thought he was covered. He may
have remembered one of his phrases about Atterbury's
famous pamphlet 'A Letter to a Convocation Man' of
1697: 'Its publication caused an immediate sensation', as
Bennett like Atterbury wanted. 'It was read in common
rooms ... and episcopal palaces ... There was intense

speculation on the anonymous author.' What he forgot, but should have remembered, was how difficult such anonymity is to protect. Two friends in Oxford, both clergymen, knew of his authorship, the Revd Philip Ursell, Principal of Pusey House, and the Revd Geoffrey Rowell, Chaplain of Keble. To Ursell Gary said, 'It's anonymous and they'll never know for certain that I wrote it', which was true and innocent at once, as he was to find.

Gareth Bennett's last week began on Sunday 29 November 1987 when he went to the High Mass at Pusey House, the Oxford headquarters of the ritualist High Church. The preacher and celebrant was the Archbishop of Canterbury, from whom Gary took communion for the last time in his life. They had known one another for almost thirty years, been on friendly terms, worked together. Subsequently Dr Runcie has said that the Preface contained little in the way of criticism of the conduct of the Church that Gary had not said before in public and still more had said to him in private, which is doubtless true but charitably overlooks the tone of voice of the Preface.

We might picture the scene at the altar rail of Pusey House chapel. Archbishop gives Sacrament to Prebendary. Bennett knows what he has written about Runcie, what will be published in four days' time: 'It would therefore be good to be assured that he actually knew what he was doing and had a clear basis for his policies other than taking the line of least resistance on each issue. He has a major disadvantage not having been trained as a theologian, and though he makes extensive use of academics as speech writers, his own position is often unclear. He has the disadvantage of the intelligent pragmatist: the desire to put off all questions until someone else makes a decision. One recalls' – actually, one misquoted – 'a lapidary phrase of Mr Frank Field that the archbishop is usually to be found nailing his colours to the fence.' 'Academics as advisers and speech writers' was a beautiful touch coming from one of them; while composing the Preface, Gary told a friend, he had wondered whether to lay a false trail by referring to himself as an obscure country parson, but he thought better of that.

He continued with an attack on the Archbishop's approach to Church appointments. 'His clear preference is for men of liberal disposition with a moderately Catholic style which is not taken to the point of having firm principles ... One thing cannot be doubted: the personal connection of so many appointed with the Archbishop of Canterbury himself. A brief biographical study will reveal the remarkable manner in which the careers of so many bishops have crossed the career of Dr Runcie: as students or colleagues at Westcott House or Cuddesdon, as incumbent or suffragan in the dioceses of St Albans or Canterbury, or as persons working in religious broadcasting at the time when he was chairman of the Central Religious Advisory Committee of the BBC and the IBA. There is indeed no more fertile recruiting ground for the new establishment than Broadcasting House. Though one may accept that an archbishop should have an influence on appointments, it is clearly unacceptable that so many are the protégés of one man and reflect his own ecclesiastical outlook.'

What is remarkable about this is not how malicious it is, but how transparent and revealing. It took no psychic gift to guess that the author was expressing some personal resentment. Another clergyman was described by Bennett as 'bitterly disappointed at his neglect by the new regime after his considerable efforts'. That same bitterness and disappointment speak at every sentence of his words on Dr Runcie. He, Bennett, could well be described as a man with a moderately Catholic style; and so it must have been his firm principles which had thwarted him. He too had a personal connection, a close one, with the Archbishop whose career and his had crossed early; it must have been his lack of 'a good appearance' or of articulacy over the media, or some other irrelevance, which told against him, or which his enemies used as an excuse when speaking against him.

How far these hints gave Gary's game away, or his authorship, is hard to judge after the event. Several people seemed quickly to have guessed after the storm broke on Thursday 3 December. Copies of the Preface had been circulating for a week or two and in building up its story of a 'remarkable personal attack' on the Archbishop of Canterbury, *The Times* cleverly solicited the opinions of various prelates and ecclesiastical dignitaries. The newspaper was not disappointed. Runcie himself made no comment and in fact behaved with silent dignity throughout the affair. It was because of that, Dr Habgood, the Archbishop of York, later said, that he felt constrained to denounce the Preface: 'there is a sourness and vindictiveness about the attack ... which makes it clear that it is not the impartial review of church affairs which it purports to be.' There was something in that, though Dr Habgood might have pointed out that this attack on Dr Runcie was by implication and a fortiori an attack on himself, the real leader of the 'liberal establishment'. Dr Habgood later told me that he had not known for certain who wrote the Preface. He thought it might possibly have been one of a number of people but that there were strong hints, 'evident mostly in the use of language'. It is significant that in dismissing the 'scurrilous' charges he said that the church would be wise to regard it as 'an outburst from a disappointed cleric'. That was temperate compared with the Bishop of St Albans, who denounced

24

the author's 'anonymous, gutless malice', or the Bishop of Peterborough, who said that 'the piece has all the hallmarks of a disappointed clergyman'.

In the Preface Bennett had discussed ecclesiastical appointments. Since James Callaghan's concordat in 1977, the Crown Appointments Commission had recommended two names on each occasion, and 'Mrs Thatcher had acted in complete conformity with the terms on which the Commission was set up. If anything, her office has been over-ready to co-operate with the archbishops and disinclined to challenge the names proposed even in the face of constant complaints that the system was producing an unbalanced episcopate.

'Only in a few instances where the Commission overreached itself and would have brought in the House of Bishops one of the shriller exponents of the opinions of Dr Spaceley-Trellis had the second name proposed been preferred'.* If not the opinions, then the tone of Bishop Taylor of St Albans was pure Spaceley-Trellis: 'The Church of England has shot itself in the foot. My phone has been warm since this happened. Already the vultures are circling round this man.' There speaks the voice of the modern bishop.

That week Gary Bennett's own telephone warmed up and scarcely stopped ringing for several days. He had deluded himself into thinking that the Preface would be a storm in a vicarage tea-cup, no more. He had deluded himself about his anonymity. The Archbishops were not the only ones, foe or friend, to make an informed guess. Two ecclesiastical journalists guessed: Clifford Longley of *The Times* who asked Bennett directly, and the Revd William Oddie of the *Daily Telegraph* who presumably

---

* A small illustration – not the only one: Denis Healey once referred to 'Rentacrowd' – of the way in which Michael Wharton's 'Peter Simple' column in the *Daily Telegraph* has entered the language.

wrote the paper's leader that Friday in defence of the *Crockford*'s Preface. And, to another friend, Bennett was 'the only man in the Church of England who could have written it'. That was Dr Leonard, the Bishop of London, whose examining chaplain Bennett was and who rang him on Thursday, as leader of the Catholic party in the Church, to congratulate him on a splendid piece of work (despite its characteristically waspish aside about Dr Leonard's 'predilection for popish outfits').

He was puzzled rather than dismayed when Gary denied his authorship. That evening Gary told Ursell of this conversation and said that he had very nearly decided to admit his authorship. But he did not, and continued flatly to deny it to friends like John Cowan, the German tutor at New College, as well as to the press. He was later criticized for this, but what else could he do? The greatest of Anglican moralists, Samuel Johnson, said that a man is not required honestly to answer a question which should not properly be put, and anonymous journalism provides a nice illustration. The bargain having been struck, it must be kept by both author and publisher. Cowan was only upset later because of what he might have said to Bennett if he had known the truth, and what he did say after he heard and believed Gary's denial, not least words to the effect that the identity would come out in the end: it always does.

Earlier I said that Gary forgot himself. He did not imagine what the press is like when its blood is up. As Robert Runcie says, 'Although he was a sophisticated scholar he was not at all used to media attention, especially from the tabloid press. I find it difficult to believe that he foresaw the scale of the controversy.' And Dr Habgood goes so far as positively to blame 'an extraordinary campaign of vituperation by some sections of the popular press. They were looking for an opportunity to continue their campaign' – against Dr Runcie, that is, and Dr Habgood himself as liberal villains. A journalist is parti pris, but although the press has its sinister as well as its comical aspects – we knew about other ecclesiastical journalists, but until then little had been heard of the Church Correspondent of the *Sun*, who emerged that week – it seems to me that the boys were doing their job. An exception perhaps is the reporter who assured Bennett (if he did) that Dr Runcie was going to name the author the next day. But even the offer made by the *Daily Mail* and forwarded to Gary by *Crockford's* of a fat fee in return for the author's story scarcely came into the same category of cheque-book journalism as payments to convicted criminals. The fact that the story was painful to some was very sad but too bad; as a former proprietor of the *Mail*, the appalling Northcliffe, truly said, news is what someone, somewhere doesn't want to see printed: all the rest is publicity. After all, the Preface was a real story, its authorship a matter of legitimate public interest: and moreover, Gary had made it so. Ferdinand Mount has perceptively said that if a culprit is needed it is anonymity. What the Preface said had been said before, if rarely so formidably, and many people thought it needed saying; but 'if the Preface had not been anonymous, Bennett would not have written as freely as he did; and if it had not been anonymous, the newspapers would have taken only a passing interest in yet another attack on the Archbishop of Canterbury'.

Gary Bennett forgot himself in one other way. His belief that his disguise was impenetrable was so foolish as almost to indicate a case of psychological repression. I have suggested that the attack on Dr Runcie was littered with obvious personal clues. So was the section on appointments: how could he not be thinking of – and betraying – himself when he wrote of 'the virtual exclusion of Anglo-Catholics from episcopal office' or reflected on 'the curious case of the appointment of Deans ... there is no more consistent body of liberal stalwarts than the inhabitants of deaneries ... One does not doubt that they were selected after the usual consultations and after advice was sought from the diocesan bishop and Lambeth. Indeed it cannot be said that most, or even many, deans are obviously the kind of people whom the present Prime Minister might choose'? (And whom might she not have chosen with a free hand but an intelligent, scholarly conservative?)

For close students of Bennett, there were further echoes of past and present. Dismissing the General Synod, he had remarked that its 'least persuadable part' is 'the House of Clergy. Over the past seventeen years it has consistently refused to consent to measures which would have changed the character of the Church; and it has merely become an irritation to the establishment ... Yet it can hardly be denied that the clergy would be even more troublesome to the liberal ascendancy if the House were more representative of the parochial clergy'. Had he forgotten – could he have? – his description of the church 250 years and more earlier, with 'a conservative clergy betrayed by a liberal episcopacy'? Above all he should have remembered his description of Atterbury's pamphlet: 'The very style of the writing, with its brilliant paradoxes, telling witticisms and smooth plausibilities, made it clear who the author was.' There were few men in the church who *would* have written that Preface, with its distinctive ecclesiastical position, its High conservative disapproval of liberal drift, its hint of personal grievance; there were even fewer who *could* have written it so well. Clergymen of intellectual ability and literary flair are all too rare today.

The siege by the press lasted through Thursday and

28

Friday. When Ursell rang him on Friday morning and said that he had agreed to speak about the Preface on the wireless that Sunday, Bennett was short with him. Four men had been planning to go from Oxford to Cambridge that day: Bennett and Cowan to a feast at New College's sister college, King's, Ursell and another clergyman, the Revd Stuart Dunnan, to a feast at Emmanuel. But Bennett was depressed and nervous now that his name had been mentioned in the press and said that he did not want to go, inconveniently for the others as he was the driver.

In the event he turned up at lunchtime and the four set off. It was that evening that Cowan remarked that the author's identity was sure to come out in the end as it always does. And although Garry, resplendent in his scarlet robes as a Cambridge D.Litt., seemed to enjoy the feast he was very upset the next morning. On the way from King's he bought the serious papers, John Cowan recalls, but when he reached Emmanuel he found Ursell reading the *Daily Mail*, which had a photograph of the Canon as chief suspect. Greatly agitated, Bennett said, 'I don't know if I can take much more of this. It's getting pretty close and pretty nasty.' He asked Ursell to come and see him that evening after evensong at New College which Gary did not propose to attend but which Ursell as singing chaplain would. They set off and drove back to Oxford.

And so around seven that evening Ursell drove to Bennett's house. The curtains were open, there were no lights on, Bennett's car was nowhere to be seen. There was a small garage, but Gary never used it whatever the weather. Without getting out of his car, Ursell asked a passing neighbour who said that he had not seen Bennett. After going home, Ursell rang Gary repeatedly that evening and on Sunday. There was no reply and he assumed that he had gone away to lie low somewhere and escape the reporters. On Sunday the Preface was discussed in newspapers and in broadcasts and denounced from some progressive pulpits but, for the experienced media-watcher, there were already signs that the storm was passing. It always does. One of the redeeming features of the press is that its attention span is so short.

On Monday Gary was supposed to be meeting the New College history tutors for the start of admissions week. This is the most gruelling week of the year for the dons, when candidates for the college are sifted; a year before, one of Gary's colleagues had facetiously said to him that if ever he chose to end his life it would be during that week. Gary had already shown symptoms of distraction. On the Friday, the last day of term, one of his pupils had turned up for a tutorial as arranged but found that he was not there and had left no note to say that he had gone to Cambridge.

When Bennett did not appear, Penry Williams rang John Cowan, who said he would drive over to Gary's house, where he lived alone with his cat Tibby. There was no answer at the door but a neighbour had a key and they went in together. The first thing they saw was the kitchen, 'in a terrible state', the floor covered with cat's excrement and there in the middle of the floor Tibby lying dead. A bottle of wine was sitting open with two glasses. Bennett's suitcase was at the foot of the stairs, unopened and with a newspaper still stuck in the strap. His coat was flung over the bannister. Cowan went into the garage and found the car parked there. He looked instinctively at the driver's seat and was relieved to see no one there. But then in the dim light he saw Gary sitting in the passenger seat. He was dead. The windows were closed except for one rear window where a hose pipe had been stuck in, attached at its other end to the exhaust. After two days of ringing Gary's number, Philip Ursell was finally answered, by the police whom Cowan had summoned. He straight away rang the Archbishop of Canterbury who, after a long silence as he took in the frightful news, said: 'I was sure he wrote it'. The next day, Tuesday 10 December, the news was on the front page of every paper. Although I had not read the whole Preface, I had like others supposed that it might be by Gary just from the extracts. My reaction on picking up the papers that morning was a mixture of shock, and recognition – so it was him – and bafflement. People don't kill themselves because their authorship of an anonymous article has been revealed, or even because reporters persecute them. What had happened?

Several months later I tried to find out for the sake of a magazine article. By then, Bennett's funeral had taken place and so had the inquest and the story had died away. There were still a number of wild theories floating around Oxford. Had Bennett been on the point of becoming a Roman Catholic? Had he killed Tibby before taking his own life? Or had someone else killed the cat? Had a visitor been waiting for Bennett on his return? Had the Archbishop of Canterbury telephoned him, or tried to, in the last three days of his life? Above all, were there what are called suspicious circumstances surrounding Gary's death? Did he simply take his own life when, as the misleading legal phrase has it, the balance of his mind was disturbed, or . . .

My desultory researches in Oxford unearthed no mysteries and pointed no fingers. There were odd discrepancies but, as an experienced lawyer once said, at the end of any long and complex case there is always a residue of unresolved and inexplicable problems. Most things said after Gary Bennett's death were proved wrong. The Archbishop of York said that a letter from the *Daily Mail* to Bennett offering him £10,000 if he would reveal his authorship had been found on his body, which was only partly true: the paper had written to the author of the Preface as such, care of *Crockford's*. The letter had been forwarded to Gary, had been collected by him at New College on his return from Cambridge, and was in his home after his death, but unopened. Gary had apparently driven to Carpenters the ironmongers, but not to the nearest branch, instead to one in Summertown. But then Summertown might be easier to reach by car than Headington, and parking is easier. Some were surprised that Gary knew the right hose and attachment to buy, but few of the most absent-minded dons are really incapable of small physical chores. The two wine glasses might be significant though not surprisingly Gary had steeled himself with drink: the equivalent of two or three large glasses of whisky was found in his body. Again, some have said that the disarray of his house was markworthy, but not to those who knew Gary and the habitual disorder of all his papers.

The Oxford coroner held a most unsatisfactory inquest which stimulated the suspicions of the conspiracy theorists. He speculated that 'some kind of foul play might have been involved', only to dismiss the speculation. All the conspiracy theorists were fascinated also by Bennett's diary which was quoted from at the inquest. Its tenor 'changes dramatically in the last days of his life', the coroner observed, which was scarcely surprising. It was in the diary that Gary had written, 'My God, what a mess ... basically my own fault ... I shall be lucky to weather this business through without some kind of public exposure. The more I think about it the more I think how bloody foolish I have been.' And so he had. The diary remains an object of mystery and fear: it has stayed in the hands of the Revd Geoffrey Rowell, former assistant chaplain of New College who is now chaplain of Keble, except when the coroner saw it, and some of Gary's former colleagues are happy that it should remain there. There have been odd hints here and there of its contents. I was, as I thought, reliably informed that it described how, on one of the last days of his life after the storm broke, Gary's telephone had rung, he had picked it up to hear 'that voice' – the Archbishop of Canterbury's – and had put the receiver down, but I have been subsequently and still more reliably informed that this is not so and that Dr Runcie never attempted to ring him.

If it could be shown that the Canon's cat had died other than of natural causes the plot might thicken but, although Tibby's body was disposed of with unseemly haste, I could not persuade myself that there was a mystery here. Gary might have killed Tibby before killing himself, but that would have been out of character. And the wilder theories about someone awaiting his return, someone else who bought the hose-pipe, someone who shared his last drink, fail for lack of motive. Are we really to suppose that the Archbishop of Canterbury was a Beckett in reverse, asking, Who will rid me of this turbulent Canon?

As so often, there is less to this than meets the eye; as an earlier prelate, Bishop Butler, said, things are as they are and not another thing. Close to the end of his tether and involved in a controversy which he had completely misjudged, Bennett returned home to find the one source of personal affection in his life dead: he snapped, and lucidly, with repressed panic and horror, arranged his own death. One of Tom Stoppard's characters wouldn't be seen dead with a suicide note, and in a sense the absence of any note from Bennett, which even level-headed observers found suspicious, is also in character. He was in a hurry; he was in anguish which he wished to end; what had he to say?

More to the point is the origin of his anguish. In his

33

last days and after, Gary Bennett was reproached by many people: publicly by the Archbishop of York and others for his attack on Runcie, unfairly by some newspapers for mendaciously denying his authorship of the Preface, privately by some who knew him for taking his life. The last is unanswerable, except by a Scriptural text which is good advice for devout and sceptic alike: 'Judge not, that you be not judged.' It is absurd to say, as some High Churchmen implied, that Gary had been hounded to his death by a liberal establishment; a more worldly man would have judged better the effect his polemic would have, a more resilient man would have weathered the storm.* All the same, some of the comments made after publication showed just how intolerant 'liberalism' can be. If anything 'killed' Gary it was his own incaution and lack of judgement, added, I am sure, to a sense that he had in one respect behaved badly. Dr Runcie has said that there was nothing in the Preface which Bennett had not previously said to him in effect, and also that he guessed the author. That does not alter the fact – one of the keys to the episode – that he and Gary Bennett were not strangers or even remote acquaintances but friends, and that whatever else may be said in its favour the Preface was a sharp personal attack, bred out of disappointment.

Was the disappointment justified? There is no question that Gary Bennett longed to leave New College, felt trapped there, hoped desperately for preferment, was crushed when it never came; and on any objective view he was entitled to hope, and then to feel crushed. His enemies or detractors have hinted heavily at Gary's

---

* It is as absurd, though endearing, to say as Richard Cobb did to me that if 'he had been the sort of person to look in for a pint every day in the Back Bar he would have got the whole thing in proportion': I can no more imagine Gary at ease, or at all, in the King's Arms than in the bar of White's, or at a disco.

undoubted failings of character and lack of 'pastoral qualities'. It is true that one cannot easily suppose anyone
finding him a deeply sympathetic counsellor, though the
word 'pastoral' begs a question about the modern Church:
what work is there for the shepherd when there is no
longer a flock?

In any case, he had other qualities. An important aspect
of the slow disintegration of the Church of England has
been the death of the Anglican intellectual tradition. The
English neo-Marxist Perry Anderson once observed that
English Protestantism had produced no Calvin or Kier-
kegaard, that our own last religious genius was Newman,
a Catholic. All the same, for several centuries the Church
to a significant extent incorporated the intellectual life of
the country, and its literary life. It is not so much a
question of asking, where are the Donnes and Hookers
and Berkeleys and Swifts and Crabbes of today: one can
scarcely imagine any of them in the present-day Church.
Gary Bennett was a very good writer and a first-class
historian. Part of his tragedy was that he did not write
enough and that he frittered his energies away in trivial
academic or ecclesiastical politics. Another part was that
his gifts were not recognized. He believed that he had
been passed over for Durham; he knew that he was very
able and gifted; he thought that Dr Jenkins who was
appointed instead was an intellectual buffoon; who will
say that he was wrong?

Who can say either that he was wrong more generally
about the Church? What surprised those who knew Gary
Bennett when they came to read his last testament, the
Crockford's preface, was not his asperity or waspishness –
they knew that anyway – but how deeply felt was his
lament for the Church. At the time of its publication the
Provost of Southwark, the Very Revd David Edwards,
had intuitively said that 'the writer is someone who

appears to be experiencing pain and anguish and feels that they are being driven out of their home'; at his funeral Geoffrey Rowell spoke of 'the pain he felt in belonging to a church which could seem ruled by trend and not the tradition handed on'; and what he wrote was written in anguish and from the heart. He felt betrayed, and he spoke for many others; we are not used to hearing a clergyman telling the truth.

He once described Archbishop Laud: 'a sad little man, embittered and tactless in a situation of great delicacy and danger', whose fate 'ought not to make him a theologically symbolic figure', another curiously apt though unconscious self-description. In the aftermath of Gary Bennett's sad life and sadder death, as the church he loved more than he could say continued on a course he abhorred, it seemed less a question of whether he might be a symbolic figure; more of whether, like Francis Atterbury, 'he may justly be judged a tragic figure: one who by defects of vision and a flawed personality hastened the events he most feared'.

2

ROGER MACHELL

Between the wars, London publishing flourished and
expanded. Several of the firms which began life then are
still famous today: Cape, Gollancz, Michael Joseph. These
houses had something in common besides the time of their
foundation. Each was created by a man of unusually
strong, if not always lovable, character. Not even Jonathan Cape, or Victor Gollancz, or George Weidenfeld –
the outstanding new name on the scene after the war –
had a more forceful personality than Hamish Hamilton,
who had worked for Cape before starting his own house
in 1931; a brilliant entrepreneur and publicist, dynamic
and shrewd. Another curious feature of the London publishing houses is how many of them have been run by
a double-act of the same kind. 'Nasty policeman, nice
policeman' would be making the contrast too sharply, but
again and again there is a second man, a gentler and more
studious foil to his pushful partner: G. Wren Howard
(who was 'too much of a coward, To be as big a rapist
As Jonathan Cape is') or Weidenfeld's Nicolson. In several
senses the best example of the species was Roger Machell.

Roger was slightly younger than Hamilton (whose
Christian name was really James but who adopted the
alliterative Gaelic form with his usual eye for a catchy
slogan). He was born in 1909. I knew little of his family
background though I asked him once if he was related
to Captain Machell who owned three Grand National
winners in the 1870s. He was. The one thing he could

remember was that 'Uncle Henry could jump onto what Nancy Mitford would call the chimneypiece in one bound'. (He was not, he agreed, related to President Samora Machell of Mozambique.) After Eton and Cambridge, where he acted with the Marlowe Society, Roger drifted into journalism, working for a time on the Peterborough column of the *Daily Telegraph*. When the war came, Roger served as a war correspondent. A friend of mine has a letter from his uncle describing Roger at the time. Someone had complained that a category of liaison officers was neither fish nor fowl nor good red herring; Roger said, 'Whereas the war correspondents are merely foul'.

It was, I imagine, his wit which caught Hamilton's fancy. The two met in the American Division of the Ministry of Information which Roger had joined after being invalided out of the army as a major. At the end of the war, he became a partner in Hamish Hamilton and remained a publisher for the rest of his life. Hamilton needed him. Readers of Evelyn Waugh's *Letters* will notice intermittent abusive references to Jamie Hamilton. The origins of this quarrel were obscure though I believe in part creditable to Hamilton: the two came to blows in 1940 shortly after Mussolini had entered the war, when Waugh arrived at a dinner party drunk and thought it amusing to address Hamilton's wife Yvonne, an anti-Fascist Italian, in you-speaka-da-lingo Wop-talk. But it must be said that Waugh was not alone and that not everyone loved Jamie. I had some inkling of this years later when I worked for Hamish Hamilton in my first job after Oxford, first as a production assistant, then as publicity manager. This sudden and youthful ascent was in itself interesting. After I had been introduced to him on my first day, he appeared not to notice my presence until one day several months later he stopped me on the

stairs and said with enthusiasm, 'I gather you're a friend of Margaret—' (a lady of title). I did not disabuse him as to the degree of intimacy, and was shortly promoted. That did not stop Jamie buzzing me, when I was trying to write and design the list single-handed at the last minute, to ask whether I could go and buy him some stamps as his secretary was out.

One should not make too much of these things but Jamie's brusqueness was not an incidental matter. He did not treat all of his colleagues with perfect delicacy, he was, some felt, both pushful and snobbish, in the end maybe even to his own undoing. Hamilton received no recognition from the sovereign. Not only would he very much have liked a knighthood, he deserved one. He was after all one of the outstanding publishers of his generation, with a really brilliant upper-middle-brow list, from Nancy Mitford and Simenon and Ed McBain to John Gunther and Alan Moorehead and A. J. P. Taylor. His distinction in his trade was greater than that of many other publishers who were honoured. He knew that, and it rankled. George Weidenfeld's knighthood and then peerage drove him to despair. And yet there must have been some reason for his neglect. He certainly had a habit of taking people up, lunching them at the Garrick or White's and dining them at Hamilton Terrace, and then dropping them. I have heard it said more than once that his somewhat casual treatment of others was reckoned against him in the circles where these things are decided.

True or not, it was the case that in Roger, Jamie had found someone with the exact opposite qualities, complementing his own. Roger was learned and cultivated, a lover of the opera and ballet as well as of books, whose flat in Albany was full of amusing things. He quite lacked Hamilton's drive, not only in later years when if you went into his room in the afternoon you would likely

find Roger dozing off his lunch, but generally: he liked
good books, which is to say books which he liked rather
than books which were going to sell. Many an author he
discovered did well for himself and for the list, but Roger
did not have that fingertip feel for the best-seller, the
visceral instinct for making money, which marks the great
publisher.

By contrast, he was a great editor. He had a faultless
instinct for what was right and wrong with a manuscript
and was unfailing with helpful advice to all his authors,
some of whom (like Alan Taylor) scarcely needed it,
others of whom surely did. Some publishers are authors
manqués, and a few in an obscure way avenge themselves
on more gifted writers for their own lack of talent. Roger
was the opposite of that. He had no wish to write a book
(though had he done he might have produced something
a good deal more graceful and amusing than some publishers' memoirs); or to put it another way he was an
engagingly lazy man. But he had the true gift for language. It was John Carter who said that only those who
have ever tried writing blurbs can have any idea how
difficult it is: distilling the essence of a complicated,
perhaps a brilliant book into two or three hundred words
which inform and entice the reader at once. Roger was a
master. Whatever it was for – a McBain 87th Precinct
story or an historical biography – he wrote the best blurbs
I ever read, far better than those I have written myself.
Jamie recognized this, as he recognized all that Roger
had contributed to the firm. Our correspondence was
circulated, some of it important, some trivial (I am not
sure into which category came Jamie's intrigues to get his
latest favourite author into the Garrick). One day there
was a note from Hamilton to Machell about a blurb
Roger had just written. 'You are marvellous.' And he
was. He was marvellous in his tactful and encouraging

dealings with authors as disparate as Nancy Mitford, J. D. Salinger, D. W. Brogan, and his favourites: James Thurber, Terence Rattigan, and Raymond Chandler.

He was marvellous also in the weekly editorial meetings, which was what made them occasionally bearable.* These were gruesome occasions, what with Jamie's bullying and the sales manager's nervosity and the production manager's crapulous bad temper. Then, a discussion would begin about whether A. J. P. Taylor's biography of Bismarck should be reissued as what publishers called a colour-plate, readers, a coffee-table book; this was the heyday of the fashion for remodelling old books in glossy format. After some minutes, Roger interjected, 'I'm not sure that a life of someone who represented all the least lovable Prussian qualities is necessarily right for a book to be *caressed*,' and that was that.

On another occasion, we were to publish Philippa Pullar's *Consuming Passions*. Someone had whimsically chosen for the back panel of the jacket a fossilized Roman loaf of bread of unambiguously phallic design, a long cylinder supported by two spheres. The sales manager, Jimmy Glover, was appalled: 'We'll never subscribe it in Dundee'. Someone else suggested that it really should be overprinted with an explanatory caption at the bottom. 'Or at least a knife and fork on either side,' Roger said. He was just as good at the seasonal but equally dejecting sales conferences. A new down-market list had been added to Hamish Hamilton and its editor was trying to excite the reps with the books he had signed up. One was to be called *What I Shall Tell My Children*, by Vanessa Redgrave: the views on life and love and art she meant to pass

---

* The world is divided into those, like Enid Starkie, 'who actually enjoyed college meetings', and those, like Richard Cobb who wrote that of her, adding, 'which is almost the worst thing I have ever heard said of anybody'. I am with Cobb rather than Starkie.

on to her various offspring (in the event never written). One of the salesmen asked, 'They're not by the same husband, are they?'

'No, that's why it's so interesting, you see. She had a kid by that film director what's-his-name, and then another by a man she wasn't married to and ...' when I caught Roger's voice saying quietly, 'Mm. What I shall tell my children: who their fathers were.'

In one other respect Jamie and Roger were opposites. Hamilton was attracted to women, and attractive as well, I suspect. He was also strongly homophobic, to use an expression then as yet unborn.* But as Roger once remarked – to a woman friend rather than to me – it was odd that someone who professed this prejudice should have as many friends and associates who were homosexual, like Roger himself. Jamie obviously knew something of Roger's personal life; indeed, a friend of Roger's was startled to receive a letter once from Hamilton thanking him for making Roger so happy. But if this was odd, it was not unique. Just as the curious thing about 'Some of my best friends are Jews' is that there are in fact people of anti-Semitic views who do have Jewish friends, so there are those who are fire-eating queer-bashers in conversation, but seem to surround themselves with those they profess to hate. If Hamilton was one example, Beaverbrook was an even more striking one.

In appearance, Roger was cherubic, a twinkly putto turning into a gargoyle. He was amiable in appearance and usually in manner, not always. Once he sharply rebuked me when I was being tiresome, and he had

---

* Now born, but still illiterate, as I am sure Roger would have pointed out. If it means anything at all from its Greek roots it can only be 'fear of the same'. Since the word describes something which exists, it is needed. Is there no exponent of Greek Love to give us an accurate coining?

enemies as well as friends. At the opera once, another publisher began an introduction, 'Roger, do you know Godfrey Winn ...?' to which Roger interrupted, 'Yes, thank you very much,' and walked off. He was not a large man, he took little exercise except the walk from Great Russell Street to Garrick Street for lunch, he became distinctly red in the face as the years passed, and somewhat frail. One year Roger and his friend David Wheeler came to the Wexford Festival. They, Rodney Milnes and I went for lunch at a country restaurant where Roger was as sparkling and droll as ever. We all had too much to drink and on our return Roger fell entering the hotel and hurt himself. This slight accident set him back more than it should have done.

I was always pleased to see him as I occasionally still did until his death in early 1984, partly because his good nature made me forget my undistinguished years in publishing, including the first two and a quarter years which had been spent at Hamish Hamilton. Years after I had left, and some years after I had migrated from the book trade to journalism, I wrote for the *Spectator* an informal obituary of Reynolds Stone, the great engraver whose several publishers' devices included the book and tree which can be seen on the title page of this book. A couple of weeks later I got a letter from Jamie Hamilton congratulating me on the piece: 'You were undervalued when you were here,' which was true though not entirely their fault. He had been away, he said; the cutting had been left for him by Roger with a note. I was touched.

3

ANTHEA JOSEPH

Women had to fight to enter the learned professions. Their struggle to enter trade was at once easier and harder. There were no legal or corporate restrictions on their entry, but the convention and atmosphere made business even more of a man's world. At the turn of this century there were no Elizabeth Garrett Andersons in the Yorkshire wool trade or in banking. Come to that, women could not join the Stock Exchange – dirty jokes and debagging and all – until within living memory.

Publishing fell somewhere between, a trade with the pretensions of a profession, an occupation for gentlemen in one ludicrous phrase; or, as Evelyn Waugh once put it with even more magnificent snobbery, one meets one's publisher like one's wine merchant for luncheon, not one's tailor. Because of this equivocal position, women had certain opportunities a generation ago in publishing which they did not have in other businesses. There was the usual male camaraderie, there was the Garrick Club, there were trade gatherings where men were boys. But publishing was not, in fact, a profession, it had no qualification for entry, anyone could get in in theory and anyone who did in practice could show what they were worth. By the time I worked in publishing in the late 1960s, the publicity departments of many firms had already become a female preserve and well before that women had been playing an important part on the editorial side also.* Quite often these women were not university graduates but there

* A different barrier operated then and still seems to: is there a woman sales director or production director in London publishing?

45

again they had advantages as well as disadvantages: it seemed ignominious that so many girls entered the trade as secretaries, but at least enter it they could, comparatively easily. People coming down from university found far fewer jobs than people looking for them.

Quite possibly, Anthea Joseph was the first woman to become chairman of the publishing company which she had joined as a secretary. She was born in 1924, the daughter of a successful lawyer who became a Judge of the Court of Appeal, Lord Hodson MC, received a conventional girls' education, and trained as a secretary. When did shorthand typing first become a respectable trade for girls of respectable family? I am not sure; perhaps after the Great war, when so many of the idle rich found themselves less rich and became less idle. She worked at the American Embassy during the World war and after it joined Michael Joseph as his, the eponymous founder's, secretary. He was another of the generation of new publishers between the wars, and a brilliant one. The two decades after the war saw a great bull market for books, sales restricted in the immediate postwar years only by the availability of paper and even after that holding up as prices remained artificially low. Joseph established a middle-brow list based on fiction, with a core of novelists whose names would turn any publisher today green: John Masters, C. S. Forester, Monica Dickens, Joyce Cary, H. E. Bates. Each of these would produce an annual novel which would then sell in numbers – scores of thousands, regularly – which would turn any author today greener. Joseph had learnt the trade as an agent, and knew how to look after authors with lunches and herograms (one of M.J.'s regular techniques was the laudatory telegram of congratulations after a manuscript was delivered but before it was read; like many great publishers, he read rather few books).

He had green fingers and he prospered. Four years after going to work for Joseph, Anthea married him, and became a non-executive director of the firm, which she combined with having a son and a daughter. This domestic interlude did not last long: Joseph died in 1958, eight years after their marriage. Although I did not know Anthea for another twelve years, I realized later that these must have been years which required all her resources of character. Like a number of others, the firm felt cool financial breezes as that book-trade boom approached its end. Books were still selling, but cash was short. Michael Joseph was taken over by one group, in turn swallowed by the Thomson organization which in consequence and inadvertently found itself a publishing concern for the first time. The tough and resourceful Peter Hebden became managing director and Raleigh Trevelyan joined as editorial director. But Anthea played a vital part.

It was not a part that she seemed cast for. She was a very type of English gentlewoman, with Home Counties written all over her (she lived in fact in Hampshire). You imagined her at the WI or the church fête, making jam and doing good works. This impression was misleading. Anthea was a Churchwomen – her faith sustained her at the end of her life – and in politics, I think, an unenthusiastic Conservative, but there was much more to her. Her directorship may have been non-executive but it was not nominal. From the beginning, she was an important voice within the firm, and a remarkably good judge. She was responsible for discovering 'Miss Read', pseudonymous authoress of charming tales of English village life, and she later made an even more lucrative discovery in the shape of James Herriot, also a nom de guerre, this time a Yorkshire vet. But Anthea had much wider sympathies. Michael Joseph became the London publishers of James Baldwin, the black American writer, thanks largely to her. His novel *Giovanni's Room* had difficulty, I believe, finding a publisher in New York, and 'MJ' himself had conventional prejudices against its theme and its author. Anthea had a woman's sympathy for homosexual men as well as an eye for a book and encouraged Jimmy Baldwin, who stayed with the firm for the rest of his life.

In 1968 Anthea became deputy chairman of the company, in 1978 chairman, but these years were not all easy, as I discovered when I joined the firm as a junior editor at the beginning of 1971, staying for three pleasurably futile years. Hebden had died suddenly and his replacement as managing director was the boy wonder Edmund Fisher, barely turned thirty.

As Edmund himself would I think now agree, this appointment was at the least premature. He had made his name in the firm of George Rainbird, also part of Lord Thomson's publishing équipe. Rainbird deserves a footnote in the history of London publishing for creating or commercially perfecting the coffee-table or colour-plate book: a book previously published by or sometimes newly commissioned from a well-known author – Nancy Mitford or Alan Moorehead – and dressed up with integrated black and white illustrations and four dozen colour plates. The book was then produced to order by a publisher who had to sell it with no risk to Rainbird; a philosopher's stone or goose which eventually laid too many golden eggs and withered away. The heroes of the operation were of course the production department. The sales department had to sell so many copies to an American, a German or a French, as well as a British, publisher from a well-produced dummy, and this was something Fisher was very good at, rather than running a general publishing list.

The firm of Michael Joseph still prospered, but personal

relations inside it were not ideal. I found myself a shuttle-cock between the warring factions, which I did not greatly mind (and it could scarcely be said that I had any other useful function in my three years there). There was Edmund with his boisterous manners, Raleigh, harassed and hating every minute of it, and, which impressed me most, Anthea serene above the conflict, though not impartial in it. Her judgement I have already mentioned: there were many more Baldwins and Herriots, not to mention Dick Francis, one of her favourites, and she one of his, in any number of authors who were loyal to Anthea as much as to the firm. She had an instinctive feel for a book, she was enthusiastic but objective, loyal but fair. Years after I worked with her I reviewed her stepson Max Hastings's book *Bomber Command* and said that though outstanding it could not be called elegantly written. When I next saw Anthea, she agreed on both scores.

And she could communicate her understanding of books, better than was always appreciated inside or outside the company. She was sensible in editorial meetings, and at sales conferences. At one, I remember her describing a novel and saying that the sex scenes were described 'from a woman's point of view, clinically'. One or two of the reps sniggered, but of course she was right. (Like many well-brought-up Englishwomen, in fact, she could be blunt and funny on the subject of sex; I remember her on the subject of the magnificent Ampthill inheritance case.)

In 1963 Anthea had remarried, to the author Macdonald Hastings, whom I had read as a boy in the *Eagle* and whom I used to meet with Anthea at the racecourse. Her charm and good humour were notably in evidence when coping with Mac, who sometimes needed coping with. And her courage and inner resources were in evidence when she contracted cancer and painfully died in 1981. She was a brave, likeable and admirable woman.

4

MICHAEL DEMPSEY

Friendship is more elusive than sexual love, and harder to capture in words. At least, I suppose that is why so few writers – Jane Austen and Turgenev are among them – seem to manage it. We have all had friends we could not resist, people who were engaging and charming, who traded on it, who got away with things as a result, whose visits were always looked forward to beforehand, always forgiven afterwards; but these butterflies shrink on the page. We understand the charm of a Charles James Fox – how thirty years after his death there were still elderly men at Holland House who would weep at his name – not because it can really be described but because we have known people like that. Michael Dempsey was like that. It may be that in thirty years' time some of us will still be around who remember him and weep, or laugh.

When did we first meet? It must have been towards the end of 1973 and must have been in the evening. We might have met before. Michael and I were contemporaries and although he had been to Cambridge, I to Oxford, we both had been working in publishing for several years though he much more prominently than I. I had just moved – marking though I did not know it the imminent end of my publishing career – to join Cassell as a commissioning editor with nothing to commission. Michael had also just arrived at Red Lion Square, after his more successful early spell in the book trade and in a more illustrious capacity.

As I learned from him later, Michael Cornelius Dempsey (he was fond of his middle name) had been born in 1944. His parents were both Irish; his father spent his life in the Royal Navy, ending as a Master-at-Arms, the Regimental Sergeant Major of a warship, though by the time I met him he had retired and was working as a probation officer. Michael had grown up in Malta and on other stations, and in Lancashire where he had been educated in the Irish tradition by the Christian Brothers. They taught him well enough to win a place at Trinity, where he blossomed, socially more than academically. He was conscious of this transfiguration, I think; although not chippy – that awful, indispensable English word – he could be touchy. In his first term at Cambridge he was called on by an undergraduate from the Fisher Society (the Catholic chaplaincy at the university). 'You're a Catholic, aren't you? Were you at Ampleforth or Downside?' 'I threw him down the stairs,' Michael told me, which probably was not the literal truth. He was not reconciled to official papistry, represented at Cambridge by the club-bable, beagling Monsignor Gilbey, and soon gave up the practice of his ancestral religion for good.

He read English, and never quite got free of the char-latanry of the Cambridge English school: all his life he displayed an excessive tenderness towards both Leavisite Eng. Lit. with all its sterility, and more extravagant mani-festations of literary pretentiousness. But I do not think he can have worked very hard: he rowed, he edited *Granta*, he drank, he chased girls: When he came down, he found a publishing job. I am not sure whether Michael could ever have become a great publisher. He was very bright, he had strong if erratic taste, he was highly energetic, even if the energy was dissipated by his habits. Before long, he was in charge of the New Authors list at Heinemann, and even found the odd new author. From there he moved

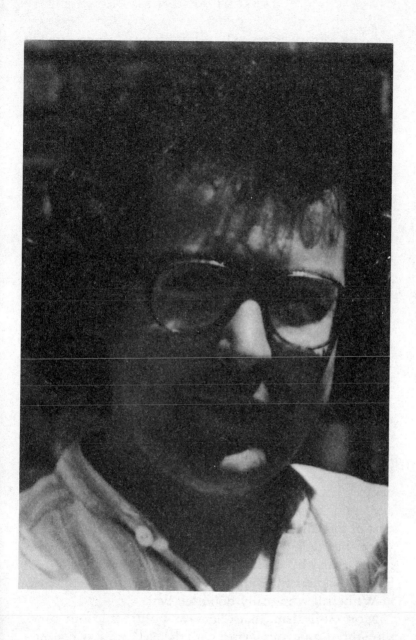

on in his mid-twenties to be a youthful managing director of MacGibbon and Kee. This was not quite as elevated an appointment as it sounds. London publishing was going through a phase of takeover and amalgamation, with small firms gobbled up by big groups. MacGibbon and Kee was one such independent which had been bought by a conglomerate, in this case by Sidney Bernstein's Granada group. Michael's imprint had directors – 'a Mickey Mouse board' – but very limited independence. Still, he was free to cut a dash and enjoy himself, enjoying the huge pleasure of spending someone else's money as if it were one's own. For a time Alan Brooke, a Cambridge contemporary and later managing director of Michael Joseph, worked for Michael as editorial director. 'I had to tell him he was letting me down,' Michael said. 'His expenses weren't high enough.'

This first brilliant career in publishing before I came to know him lasted several years. He also had political ambitions. For a time he kept a flat in Haringey where he became a Labour councillor, the source of many stories later both by and about him. He would have liked to go into Parliament, and was cleverer and a more plausible speaker than most Labour backbenchers twenty years ago or since, but he did not have the fanatical dedication necessary for attending endless meetings and moving references back. Michael saw politics in emotional terms, and in one way there is nothing wrong with that: the best part of the Labour tradition has always been an elemental warm-heartedness, a decent instinct to help the poor, rather than the desiccated calculating machinations of Fabian planners and would-be commissars and gentlemen in Whitehall who really do know best.

More still than that, he saw politics, I sometimes thought, in amorous terms, with the electorate as a beautiful bashful woman to be wooed and ravished by him. In the end he tired of this seduction, though not of other more literal ones. He ran through a succession of girls in his twenties, before briefly settling down with Emma Tennant. That is scarcely the word: little about Michael was ever settled or settling. Although they did not marry, partly because Emma had not extricated herself from her previous marriage when they met and partly, I imagine, because she thought better of it, they had a daughter, Rose, to whom Michael was devoted. Not very long after she was born, Emma tired of Michael's unreliability and intemperance and a taxi arrived at his office with a couple of suitcases containing his clothes. At much the same time, he and his firm tired of one another and he was between jobs when we met. By coincidence, just as I had absent-mindedly accepted a job at Cassell, so had he talked his way into opening a list of his own within the same company.

Whenever it was, our meeting was not auspicious. Michael was drunk and he was also conspicuously smoking a joint. A few days later I mentioned this to *Private Eye*, one of whose group of ill-paid informers I then was, to my shame. Once it appeared in print the source of the story became known to Michael. Many people would have taken this as grounds for enmity for life. Instead of which, when we next met, he grinned and said, 'Why did you write that about me, you bastard?' and said why didn't we go and have a drink.

We had a drink that day and on many days for years to come. Alcohol was not the only bond which united us, but it was a bond. In my memory I seem to have met Michael every day in one pub or another, which cannot be true, but there were months at a time when we spoke daily on the telephone. For a year and a half we were connected with the same firm. Michael did not have an office there and he did not come in daily, which was just as well. His presence was always disruptive and always noisy and always magnetic. When his large, slightly ungainly frame came through the door with a smile on his round face under his black curls, I knew I could not concentrate on any further work. I only hoped that if he was in high spirits, they were not too high. As was clear from the beginning, my own position there was pointless and potentially vulnerable, and as long as I was happy to settle for a quiet life Michael was a hazard. On one occasion, he playfully threw a typewriter across my office. It missed me and I am just as glad to say did not go through the fifth-floor window, as it might have done some damage to passers-by on the pavement.

Careless about others' persons, Michael was just as careless about his own. He had a little sports car, being driven in which I found bad for my nerves. One week I did not hear anything from him for several days. Then, for some reason, I was walking on the Sunday through Battersea Park where I ran into the literary agent Abner Stein who said obliquely that he was sorry about my friend. I asked whom he meant. He explained that Michael had crashed his motor and was in hospital. I sought him out there and found him with his jaw smashed and wired up, as it remained for several weeks, but laughing through the mesh. I saw him several more times in hospital. He described his adventures with the nurses and good-natured ex-girlfriends who had been to visit him, and on one occasion I nearly killed him. I had taken along a quantity of champagne and Guinness which we mixed and drank, too quickly and too copiously. Michael was suddenly nauseated; vomiting with one's teeth and jaws wired together is not funny and he only just managed to throw his head forward before choking.★

★ He later complained that he had a long-standing winning bet with Anthony Haden-Guest, the stake being dinner at an expensive

Was he still wired up when we went to the Isle of Man and Chester? On the first occasion I think he was. It was a sales conference, where Michael told the puzzled reps – who had grown up with the works of Churchill and Nicholas Monsarrat – that his list was aimed at middle-aged hippies. Then we went out and behaved badly. He insisted on giving me a little present of hash before I left, which I put in a matchbox. I had chosen to sail from the Isle of Man to Liverpool rather than fly and then, having remembered to post some kippers to Muriel Belcher as she had asked, I noticed that another boat sailed from Douglas to Dublin and decided on the spur of the moment to change my ticket and go and stay with friends for the Irish Derby at the Curragh that weekend. I had forgotten where I was, and what my change of plans might suggest to the CID men who stopped me (wearing a trench coat and felt hat, like an extra in *The Shadow of a Gunman*) at the docks. I thought for several minutes that they were going to search me and cursed Michael for dropping me in it again.

We went to Chester races and stayed in the flat of a friend of his, a sometime journalist who was running a press agency of sorts and was supposed to be writing a book for Michael's list. I could see why Michael had taken to this man. On the sitting-room wall was a brass plaque removed from a defunct Italian restaurant in Manchester: 'Here between 1.00 and 4.15 p.m. on 7 May 1957 — and — drank seven bottles of Chianti, because they were thirsty.' This was a word Michael often used. 'Why did you behave like that?' a girl asked him once; 'Why were you so drunk?' 'I told her I must have been thirsty that day' (he was fond of quoting his own repartee and laughing at his own jokes). On the other hand, he quoted with

restaurant, and that Anthony had suddenly agreed to pay up at the moment when Michael could take nothing but soup.

admiration another, thoughtful girl. 'We were having dinner at the Aretusa and I was just ordering a third bottle and she said, "Look, that's not necessary. I'm going to come back with you. You might concentrate on staying sober instead." ' Perhaps that was at the back of his mind later. An embarrassing anthology had been published called *You Always Remember the First Time* in which various well-known men and women described how they lost their virginity. Michael suggested that we should produce a rival volume for the drinking classes called 'You Never Remember the Last Time'.

In the late spring of 1975 my own paltry career in publishing came to an end when I was sacked by Cassell. That a number of others were 'made redundant' at the same time neither hardened nor softened this blow, which was not to me unexpected. Michael seemed more distressed than I was, saying that he could not have believed that it would happen. I could have. It had been clear to me for some time that there was nothing for me to do, that I wasn't doing it, and that anyway I had no aptitude for publishing, no love of the cut and the thrust, picking the right book and backing one's judgement. Michael had some of that. Apart from his charm and his intelligence – the former arguably more useful than the latter in the book trade – he was not like the publisher in *Put Out More Flags* who had never much liked authors 'except of course personal friends', or books, 'except of course books by personal friends'. Michael did like books and many authors, though his taste was erratic, sometimes esoteric, and geared to the tail-end of the 1960s, middle-aged hippiedom indeed. He would not have understood the Thatcherite England of the 1980s. But I felt in any case that he was running out of steam, and of enthusiasm. In order to justify his position and to keep his list going he promised grander and grander projects – books to be written by Anthony Burgess, whom he had once edited and who I think liked him – but in fact commissioned odder and sillier titles. He recognized this. At one point, when I was waiting for the end, we had a private competition for shlock titles. I was pleased with myself for commissioning a book called *How to Have a Baby and Stay Sane*, but I realized that I was not in the same class as Michael when he came up with *Is Your Cat Psychic?* and *The Wisdom of Kung-Fu* ('wisdom' was masterly).

We went different ways: I joined the *Spectator* in the autumn of 1975 after resting for a few months; in the following year, I think, his connection with Cassell began to draw awkwardly to its close. Whereas he had had more money than me, or at least given the impression that he had, now I had an income of some sort and he was beginning to tread financial water. He had bought a flat in Fulham, as I had in Islington. To be precise, his flat was in one of the least desirable situations in London, on Saturdays at least, in the Fulham Road between two gates of the Chelsea football ground. But it suited him: in a 1960s block, with a front sitting room catching the light, in which he hung his little collection of pictures, bought in the early 1970s. One was a sub-pop-art work called 'The Hundred Dollar Painting' which consisted indeed of a hundred dollar-bills stuck to a canvas and painted over with various words and images. Several of the greenbacks seemed to be missing and Michael claimed that he had peeled them off to buy drink, but this I think was a joke against himself.

He needed a source of income, but it receded further. He tried another publishing venture, but little came of it and his professional and financial scrapes became worse. He more and more resembled a cross between Savage as described by Johnson and Ukridge as described by Wodehouse, looking desperately for something to turn up. Even I was taken aback when he told me that he had had a problem in demonstrating for some purpose or other that he had a contract for typesetting, but had solved it by going into a legal suppliers in Chancery Lane, buying a contract form, and drawing it up and signing it with the company's name.

Before that I had become inured to his vagaries. In most of these indiscretions he led and I followed, anxious and occasionally resentful. There was the time he tried to burn down the Chelsea Arts Club because – but I forget why; perhaps we had been asked to leave, which was reasonable since neither of us was a member. I was still nursing my drink when he grabbed my arm and took me into the cloakroom where he had found a hurricane lamp whose fuel he emptied over some rags and struck a match, laughing triumphantly. Or there was the occasion of Andy Warhol's visit, to which we attached ourselves, an evening which became more and more rackety until Michael started hitting someone; I have little recollection, as the later part of that evening is hazy (Warhol's *Interview* magazine in New York subsequently recorded the evening accurately enough except for a mistake about my position: a long list of celebrities, 'and the editor of the *Spectator* who passed out'). At another party again, Michael insisted that he was going to hit someone who had displeased him and suggested that I join in: 'You kneel down behind him and I'll knock him over.' He was often high-spirited to the point of aggression at that time of the evening. Arriving once at another party later than Michael (which in itself was unusual), I asked if the joint was jumping. He replied in an authentic Cork accent: 'Sure 'tis grand. Dere's foitin' and fockin' and kickin' de Jewman,' indicating with thumb across shoulder a publisher neither Michael nor many others much cared for.

This boisterousness was partly aggression but partly an

obscure reaction to the difficulties of life. It took different forms. Michael was unstoppable, and infectious. His success with women was not because of classical good looks or even because of his charm, but because of his force of character. He could give the impression that he wanted someone very much (by impression I do not suggest affectation or insincerity: he often did want them very much) and from then on it was less war of attrition than blitzkrieg. These campaigns would be described in detail, or then again sometimes with a throwaway line. Meeting him one lunchtime I said that his companion of the evening before had seemed agreeable. 'Yuh, yuh, nice sort of girl. Does all the things in bed you ask her to.' He described other courtships laconically. After he had popped the question once, 'She said, "You're very nice, but I don't think I can handle a heavy relationship at the moment." I told her, "I wasn't talking about a heavy relationship, I was talking about casual sex."' Or, of another encounter, 'I think she might have changed her mind by then, but it was a bit late with thirteen stone of Irishman on top of her.' He had also an idiosyncratic vocabulary of interrogation – 'Did she drop 'em?' – and of description for different women: 'Was she a TYC or OMW [for tender young crumpet or other men's wives]?' Through all these infatuations and pursuits I believe I only once knew him to fall in love, with a highly intelligent, difficult and even unbalanced girl who had an attractive cloak of melancholy round her. That passion was unreciprocated and led nowhere, and Michael was downcast, but not for long.

It was around that time that he tried, Ukridge-like, to become an entrepreneur in the music business, as those who work in it call what used to be known as Tin Pan Alley or pop. I had not quite taken on board the arrival of punk rock, though the name of the Sex Pistols was not likely to be forgotten once heard; the *Spectator* surprised its readers by publishing an article on them. Michael was captivated by punk and soon became godfather to one or two bands. He admired their gusto and their depravity and disgustingness, as opposed to the mere more straightforward dissipation among rock bands of the generation before. He liked their noms de guerre – Johnny Rotten, Genesis P. Orridge, or, from one of his own bands, Laurie Driver – and their cult of drugs and cheap sex. He even affected to like their music. I could not follow him, more or less said so, and had scorn poured on my head. Punk was like country and western, he said, an authentic expression of working-class taste, which I did not dispute. When I grimaced he said, 'You're the sort of jerk who likes the Beatles' songs, aren't you?' and I said yes. 'Don't you realize that punk is the first pop music for sixty years that isn't based on the Blues?' which I didn't dispute either. Unenthusiastic as I was, Michael in effect ordered me to come and listen to his new band in some vile dive in Soho, and I weakly agreed.

Well like man was I going to go to a punk rock gig sober? No way. As it was, I must have exceeded the stated dose on the bottle and I was somnolent when I arrived in Wardour Street. Before I passed out, Michael introduced me to Jane Suck – the Madame de Staël of the punk generation – who subsequently gazed at me, he assured me, and said, 'I didn't fink they was like that when they growed older'. Wrong again, Jane. She had written a poem about herself, by the way – 'If you think you're out of luck, You should see Jane Suck. She couldn't find a dog to fuck, And wasn't run over by a truck' – which Michael quoted with admiration.

Sometimes his patience wore thin. The band were always expecting treats or tips, and proved fractious and intractable. He told me woefully of his attempt to have them interviewed by Polly Toynbee in the *Guardian* and presented as a socially important phenomenon. He instructed them on another occasion: 'People say that the punks are all fascists and National Front supporters. Well, we're going to show they're wrong.' 'Right Mike. Got any more speed?' 'Shut up. We're going to show we're a progressive Left band.' 'Right, Left, Mike.' 'We're going to play at the Rock Against Racism gig. Okay? Say it after me . . .' 'Rock Ay-gainst Racism.' 'Right Mike. But that don't mean we have to play wiv no niggers, do it?'

All of which would have mattered less if the punks had made Michael's fortune or saved his bacon, but they didn't. A record came out, 'Gary Gilmour's Eyes', whose donnée was the fact that a convicted murderer who was executed in Utah had his eyes or corneas or whatever removed for transplanting, and the song was sung by someone who woke up to find that he was looking through these eyes. It did not make it to number one. In the last two years Michael's predicament became more desperate. He was only one step in front of the dun or the bankruptcy notice or the repossession order. He was more erratic than ever and, as I was to write in an obituary for *The Times* in what seemed the right style, there were times when his conduct could exasperate his least censorious friends. He stopped off at my house once to use the telephone for a couple of hours while draining a brandy bottle at a speed which impressed even me. One evening I saw him in Soho and said that he looked a bit speedy, and he put his arm round me and said, 'My dear, I've taken enough drugs today *to kill a small horse*', and laughed noisily.

Does this give some idea of why I loved him? It was that infectious gaiety that was irresistible; the man who could laugh when opening a buff envelope or when hearing the worst news. To me this was especially attractive, the attraction of opposites: I low-spirited and highly-strung, Michael the reverse. He continually teased or even insulted me for my diffidence and inhibition, and I thought he was right. He was imperturbable in other ways. Michael was once asked to a *Private Eye* lunch by Richard Ingrams, who liked him. 'I loved your book on Chesterton,' Michael said enthusiastically. Ingrams explained that he had not written a book on Chesterton, and Michael went on with scarcely a flicker of a pause, 'I know, and when you write it for me it's going to be marvellous.' He was physically brave, or indifferent to what happened to him. On that occasion when he smashed up his car he went halfway through the windscreen. Small children can fall downstairs without hurting themselves because their limbs are so relaxed, and I think that Michael was likewise saved from worse injury or death because he was loose-limbed with drink. The prigs of today, by the way, will be horrified that he twice got off drunk-driving charges, I forget on what technicalities. He elected on at least one of these occasions to go for trial by jury: 'There was a platinum blonde on the jury. I made eyes at her.' Once he was arrested not in fact driving but slumped insensible over the wheel of his parked car. He revived when taken to Chelsea police station. In court a bobby solemnly read out from the charge sheet, 'He attempted to divert officers by doing animal imitations and playing peek-a-boo'. It may have been that case that had him puzzling one day as we stood over our drinks. I asked how he was going to get away with it this time; how was he going to plead? He looked grave, and then opened his eyes and pulled back his mouth not quite in a smile. 'I know. As an Irish republican in the tradition of Tone and Lord Edward and Pearse, I shall refuse to recognize the court!'

We did not see as much of each other in the course of 1981. At the beginning of the year I had left the *Spectator* to write a book about South Africa, and in the English spring I had gone there on the first of several trips. There had been a slight awkwardness in our friendship: I had lent Michael some money, more than I could afford, and thereby illustrated Evelyn Waugh's point that 'however great-souled & delicate-mannered people are, financial obligations between social equals are nearly always disastrous'. My soul is not great nor my manner delicate, and I was depressed at the prospect of a froideur with Michael, or of not getting my money back, or both. I managed more or less to forget the matter. Later, I was to remember ruefully the joke made about someone else: 'Truly it can be said that he left London a poorer place'. What upset me more was Michael's desperate state. Late one evening he had once put his arm round me and said as a bond of friendship: 'You and I ought to have a pact. Whatever happens neither of us is ever going to say: "I'm worred about you",' and he laughed. I never said it, but I was. It was not for me to lecture him; when an American friend said kindly, 'Okay, at home, but don't let them see you drunk,' Michael grinned and conspicuously did not take the advice. He had another scheme that summer and autumn, to start a publishing business in Ireland with a grant from the Irish government. This last desperate throw of the dice might have come off; I cannot know.

That December I left on a longer visit to South Africa. In Johannesburg a few days before Christmas I was reading in the evening when the telephone rang. My hostess Mary Hope said that it was for me, and Mary Kenny in London told me that Michael was dead. There was nothing for me to do except write to his mother and to the mother of his child, who replied truthfully that it was worse for me than her, and to send flowers to his funeral. The circumstances of his death remained somewhat mysterious. When I returned to London in March I felt rather

like Joseph Cotten in *The Third Man*. I knew that Michael
had had to flee the Fulham Road flat before the building
society seized it, and to avoid other creditors. He had
taken refuge in a friend's flat at the top of a large Victorian
house in South Kensington. There he returned one
evening after a day spent with friends in Putney; or had
he spent the evening at a Yugoslav club which he had
discovered as a convenient watering hole? Whatever, it
seems that he was trying to change a light bulb at the top
of the stairs. Either the ladder collapsed or he was struck
by electricity, just like Lord Finchley, and fell downstairs.
The precise cause of death was apparently a ruptured liver;
one can only pray that he died quickly. There was an
irony in Michael's dying from liver failure, but in that
particular way. A year or two later I quoted to Richard
West someone close to Michael who had said they kept
asking themselves, 'Why?' Dick said, 'I'm afraid where
Dempsey was concerned it was never a question of
"Why?", only "How?" ' The cycle of self-destruction had
anyway been working itself out in him; God knows what
would have happened if he had not suffered the accident.

When he was making fun of the quite numerous people
he disliked or despised, Michael used to say, 'He aimed
low and missed.' Where did he aim? In his twenties
he looked as if he might become rich and famous and
successful; he died at thirty-seven in sorry circumstances.
I thought after his death of Johnson's peroration: 'Those
are no proper judges of his conduct, who have slumbered
away their time on the down of plenty; nor will any wise
man presume to say "Had I been in Savage's condition I
should have lived or written better than Savage".' Nearly
ten years after his death I do not presume to say it. I miss
him.

5

GEORGE HUTCHINSON

'Well, Master Wheatcroft, we have done good work this morning and I think that we should reward ourselves with a drink at a somewhat earlier hour than usual.' It was striking how often George Hutchinson decided that the morning's work at the *Spectator* was better than usual, or superior as George would put it in his courtly way ('George called a column of mine "A superior article, most superior",' a friend of ours once said, 'as if he was a tailor feeling a bloody coat'). By this time we were working together: we had met before but scarcely knew each other until we became colleagues towards the end of 1975 in unforeseen circumstances.

The *Spectator* was, or rather is, one of the famous London weekly papers, a kind of journal which I do not think exists elsewhere though the two America weeklies, the *New Republic* and the *Nation*, have some resemblance. They used also closely to resemble one another in their tormented 'liberal' politics, and are now far apart, a microcosm of what has happened to the American liberal left, but that is another matter. In England the weeklies flourished at the turn of the century. A hundred years ago the two best-known were the *Saturday Review*, organ of intellectual Salisburian conservatism, and the *Spectator*. It had been founded in 1838 or if you like refounded, borrowing the name of Addison's and Steele's early-eighteenth-century squib with which it had no other connection. It was high-minded and strongly Liberal until the split of 1886 – calamitous in so many ways – when it followed the Liberal unionists. Between the wars the weeklies came and went, so that the *New Statesman* was at one time four in one, the *New Statesman and Nation* including the *Athenaeum*: the *Weekend Review*. The *Statesman* had a peculiarly strong emotional resonance in the 1930s, expressing in the emotional, muddled – to Orwell, corrupt – figure of Kingsley Martin all the contradictions of the left which hated both Hitler and war and, as Orwell again said, disliked fascism but not totalitarianism. The *Spectator* continued to speak for enlightened Conservatism (in A. J. P. Taylor's phrase, as though this was nearly a contradiction in terms) under the editorship of Wilson Harris. Harris was a remarkable man, one of the last independent MPs as well as a great editor, but he was a prig. For a time Graham Greene was literary editor of the *Spectator*, one of an extravagantly distinguished succession of people to have held that job (as well as some less distinguished), and conceived a great hatred for the editor. To mark Harris's birthday once, Greene gave him a French letter stuffed with Smarties chocolates (there is an echo of this in one of his novels, *The Human Factor*, written forty years later), rightly supposing that Harris would not recognize the present.

In the 1950s the *Spectator* changed once again when Ian Gilmour bought it. Gilmour was a rich young man with journalistic and political aspirations, under whose ownership the paper blossomed and prospered. He edited the paper himself for five years until 1959 when he appointed successively Brian Inglis, Iain Hamilton and, in dramatic circumstances, Iain Macleod in his place. At this time George Hutchinson was in his early forties and working at Conservative Central Office. He was a Shropshire lad by upbringing, though Scotch by descent: his father was from Kilmarnock. George was educated at the King

Charles School in Kidderminster; I was not sure what he had done in the brief interval between leaving school and the war, when he went into the Navy. He did not talk about the war, except by dropping unintentional hints – there was a strike in the 1970s by naval shipyard workers, or 'mateys' as George instinctively referred to them – but I believe he had a tough time on convoy duty in the Arctic and elsewhere. Dick West had a fanciful theory that the Russians had switched the original George for a plant of their own, carefully programmed with elaborate manners and thirsty tastes, but fancy this was.

After the war he entered journalism, on the Londoner's Diary of the *Evening Standard*. It is not pride and prejudice which make me emphasize how important this column has been to Fleet Street and London. As I write, three actual or potential newspapers are edited by former Diary editors, the successors of those who wrote for the Diary in early generations, from Bruce Lockhart to Malcolm Muggeridge, Randolph Churchill to Morris Finer. It is a wonderful column to write for, and always has been. I suspected when I was editing the Diary that it had become harder work, especially for the Diary Editor – I think his recent working day of 7.30 a.m. to 5.30 p.m. is a sadistic invention of Charles Wintour – and I cannot believe that Bruce Lockhart kept those hours; indeed, his diaries show that he did not. I could not imagine George even in his twenties working quite as hard as he would be expected to now, and in fact one of his obituarists wrote that his idea of news and deadlines was idiosyncratic when he was on the *Standard*.

That did not prevent his becoming Political Correspondent of the paper, then one of the most important posts on the newspapers in Beaverbrook's group and one which brought George into contact with the great, terrible man himself. More than the Daily and Sunday *Express*,

Beaverbrook used the *Standard* as his sounding board, the Diary and the political column in particular to fly his kites and settle his scores. For whatever reason, George did not stay there. Instead he had been offered the part of Diplomatic Correspondent on the *Standard*. He worked for stints at *The Times* and the *Daily Telegraph* and then went to Central Office where he served from 1961 to 1964. His position there was an important one: he was on the general purposes committee of the Conservative National Union and saw Macmillan daily. The two had something in common, both of them character actors playing a part. Macmillan's part was more calculating. Years later when I met the by then former prime minister in common room or club I was delighted by his cabaret turn but think that I detected the ruthlessness and perhaps the heartlessness beneath, the political realist (to put it gently) who sent back so many Russians to torture and death, who behaved so shabbily – and calculatingly – at Suez, and who presided so capriciously over an unstable country and society. Evelyn Waugh's explanation was that Macmillan had seen the light, at the time Ronald Knox became a Roman Catholic during the Great War, and rejected it. If he had followed Knox 'he would not be prime minister nor married to a Cavendish but he would have been a happy & virtuous publisher'. That theory may or may not be correct but Waugh was surely right to say that Macmillan had grown a carapace of cynicism to protect a tender conscience: 'the last Edwardian at No. 10' – the title of George's book on him, which neatly described the act – was a cynic and a lost soul.

George's own act was to play the stage butler, Jeeves to Mac's Wooster. He was not assiduous or over-zealous in the conduct of his duties. A friend who was writing a political column at the time (and still is) remembers George when telephoned for information: 'I shall let you have it within the hour and why do we not meet to take a drink?' They took the drink but no information was exchanged. Still, politicians and party officials are an unamiable lot and George's affability must have been a contrast to others and earned him his CBE which he was awarded – or, as he might have correctly said, to which he was appointed – when he left Central Office. Gilmour still owned the *Spectator*; he knew George, of course, and asked him to join the magazine as managing director. As it proved, this was one of Gilmour's last appointments. Three years later, in perhaps the one reprehensible act of his life, he sold the magazine to an obscure businessman who very nearly destroyed it in the next eight years. George played some part in the sale, I believe, as did Peter Walker the Tory politician and his associate Slater. In the following years our hero the *Spectator*'s fortunes sank very low as it came to be written with an astonishing vulgarity. George did not remain with the paper throughout this unhappy episode. He wrote his book on Macmillan, he began to write a column on *The Times*, he pottered. He had by now perfected his act, and an entertaining one I found it: the tweed suits, the hat, the lunches at the Carlton.

In 1975 the *Spectator* changed hands once more, bought happily – for its own fortunes if not for his – by Henry Keswick of the Hong Kong trading company Jardine Matheson. He appointed as editor Alexander Chancellor, a childhood and school friend and the only journalist he knew, who was then working as a reporter for Independent Television News and who before that had been with Reuters. In a fit of absence of mind Alexander took me on as associate editor. Neither of us had any experience of magazine journalism or much idea of what to do and it was if not in despair then in perplexity that Alexander turned to the wiser, older counsel of George. And so for the next five years I saw George daily. His contribution to the paper was unusual. Several years later he and Kingsley Amis edited together an anthology of pieces from the *Spectator* and the *New Statesman*, incongruously. One evening after they had worked together all afternoon, I found Kingsley alone in a room otherwise full of empty bottles. He asked me, 'What does George actually do here?' and it was tempting to say, Si monumentum requiris, circumspice. But George did more than that. Before long Alexander and the rest of us had learned enough, more or less, about running the magazine. George thereafter provided moral support, or perhaps he enjoyed, like the constitutional monarch in Bagehot's phrase, 'the right to be consulted, the right to encourage, the right to warn'. He did not write much for the paper, and even in his editorial contributions he held back, sometimes resisting the temptation, I felt, to compose a good headline in case it might look too flashy, or perhaps in case a good headline might be required next time. When Harold Wilson resigned in 1976 a leader had to be written to mark the event – by me? I forget; in those days we kept up the tradition of most potent, grave and reverend leading articles – and it came to George's hand. I watched him as he thought for a while and then wrote in at the top a headline of masterly ambiguity: 'A very moderate leader'.

On another occasion he was required to write a piece, the *Spectator*'s Notebook from Brighton during the Conservative conference. It came over, more or less, but much too short to fill the page, by several hundred words. I was at the printers and rang Brighton with urgent but unavailing messages asking George to ring me back. At last I tracked him down, clearly in fatigued condition, and asked for another paragraph. 'There is no need for it, Master Wheatcroft. You must place further space between the items.' I think it may have been that week also that George began his *Times* column by deploring the fact that Julian Amery, a local MP moreover, had not been called during the defence debate. However, George continued, he was able to make amends and to bring to publication what Amery would have said; and the column then took in the bulk of this undelivered speech.

At this time the deputy editor of *The Times* was Charles Douglas-Home, who did not see the funnier side of things. Not long afterwards he fired George from his column, an event which Auberon Waugh lamented in terms of cosmic woe and not wholly ironically. I missed the column also. Though George's pose as a flâneur, as well as his natural indolence, sometimes got the better of him, he was an original, a salty and well-informed writer whose column even at its most inconsequential was more worth reading than most of many ponderous prize-winning commentators'. Otherwise, George put himself into the social side of journalism rather than writing. Our local at the *Spectator* was the Duke of York in the mews opposite. Some London pubs do not open until half-past eleven (Gaston of the French pub once told Jeffrey Bernard that he did not want to cater for the sort of person who actually needed a drink at eleven, which is why Jeff now patronizes the Coach and Horses two streets away). The Duke opened punctually at eleven; at five to I would often look up from my desk to see Dick West or Jeff Bernard standing in the doorway of my office looking meaningfully at his watch.

Or it might be George, saying that he had to go out to get a packet of cigarettes, and would I like to join him. I would. The cigarettes were bought – Players' untipped – and the tinctures or cocktails. George liked other people who shared his tastes. He was fond of Patrick Cosgrave, as not everyone was, and they talked together. Or rather, they both talked: I remember finding them once in the Duke of York and observing them Grouse in hand for some time. As each delivered a monologue, the other made no pretence of listening. He waited with benign indifference until the speaker opposite came to a temporary pause, and then took over, when the first could enter his own reverie. George took a shine also to Michael Dempsey as not everyone did and they conspired together. George had established a friendship with the Palestinian-born publisher Naim Attallah many years back; I believe that he was one of the first to show the young immigrant kindness when he arrived in England. Later, when he had made his money, Naim returned the kindness, granting George small favours. When Michael was looking for a backer – his perennial condition in his last years – George effected an introduction, when for some reason I was present also. We met at Attallah's office near Knightsbridge at around five. Our host offered us drinks, saying correctly to George that he would know where to find what he wanted, and asked Michael what he would like. Dempsey thought for a fraction of a second before saying, 'If that's mint tea you're drinking, could I have a glass?' This pleased Naim, as it was meant to. He replied in words I still remember exactly: 'I see you are non-alcoholic like me.' At this, George spoilt the effect by spluttering with laughter, almost coughing out the whisky he was sipping. 'No, no, Naim, I do not think that Michael Dempsey could be called that,' and chortled to himself, to Michael's understandable irritation.

By this time George was already in visible decline. Things had taken their toll; he did less work, frittered more, sometimes, I felt, contradicted whoever's advice it was and drank because he was sad, not because he was happy. This made me sad also because he was no mere figure of fun but, when he wanted to be, an entertaining

75

companion and even an original mind with an instinctive understanding of how politics, or at least the Tory party, worked. Like several other commentators, journalistic and academic, he Brayed successfully in the second half of the 1970s, switching sides to Mrs Thatcher with enviable agility. Of Patrick Cosgrave that could never be said: he was an early Thatcherite, backing her for the leadership before she won it, not that this prescience did him much good.

Nor in the end did it help George. He was cynical and sneering about his former friend Heath (who had asked for it) and might have joined Mrs Thatcher's weird court. But he did not live long enough to enjoy the fruits of the new regime. In the winter of 1980 we heard that he had been visited with cancer. I went on a little holiday somewhere warm that March, and wrote to him in hospital with something I thought might amuse him. It might have done, but when I returned it was to learn that he had died, and a letter from his kind and loyal wife Pam told me that mine had not reached him in time.

6

HANS KELLER

In the early 1960s there were few serious programmes about music on television; come to that, there are not many now. Watching one when I was still a schoolboy, I found myself looking at and listening to someone very serious, though using irony and humour of a sort to make his points. One of these was that 'modern' or contemporary music was nothing like as difficult to understand or to play as people supposed. Twelve-tone music had a bad name (as well as a long one, 'dodecaphonic') but was perfectly simple. Anyone could whistle a tone-row, 'especially if like any dog you have perfect pitch'. And to illustrate the point, he whistled the tone-row from Schoenberg's Piano Suite.

Coming as I did from an unmusical home, struggling with (I am sorry to say) the trumpet, and more knowledgeable about jazz than the string quartet, the precise argument was lost on me as I dare say it was on most of the audience. But the speaker was hypnotically interesting, a thin, intense man in his forties with hooded eyes, beaky nose and moustache. He spoke with an audibly non-English intonation; years later he told me why he had never quite lost his 'Viennese lilt'. I forget his explanation; it seemed to me to require none. Accent in second languages is a function not of intelligence or personality but of a mimetic gift or lack of it. It has nothing to do with command of language as such. Thomas Szasz has lived in the United States for fifty years and writes marvellous

English, but still speaks with an agreeably thick Hungarian accent.

Lilt or not, the speaker had a formidable, even frightening command of the language which he used like a musical instrument, or like a weapon. I had not then heard of Hans Keller, but over the next twelve years or more he came to fascinate me almost to the point of obsession. That was before I met him; I occasionally saw him again on television; I heard him more often on the radio, where he would have been unmistakable even if he had written the script – though, as he often pointed out, he always spoke without one – and it had been read by an actor; I read him in various magazines, but especially in the *Listener* where Karl Miller gave him his head.

And so before I met Hans in 1976 I had learned a good deal about him. He was a musician, of course – and not a critic or a musicologist, he always insisted – but he had other interests besides, psychiatry for one and sport for another, especially an absorbing interest in football about which he wrote often. I learned also about his own story, which he related in occasional autobiographical pieces, part of his huge output of articles, reviews, lectures, broadcasts, as yet to my knowledge unanthologized.

He was born in Vienna in 1919, just as the city's great intellectual and artistic flowering was beginning to fade. It was there that Hans had his roots. Not in a lyrical sense, of course; he was as far from the carefree Viennese boulevardier of operetta as it is possible to be, but even when he had become British an invisible umbilical cord led back to the Vienna of Mahler and Musil. All his life, in fact, his spiritual father-figures were Schoenberg and Freud; he disliked and despised Karl Kraus. Like many Viennese Jews of the time, his father came from Bohemia, but the family, Hans said, was emancipated psychologically as well as physically, meaning that they had left

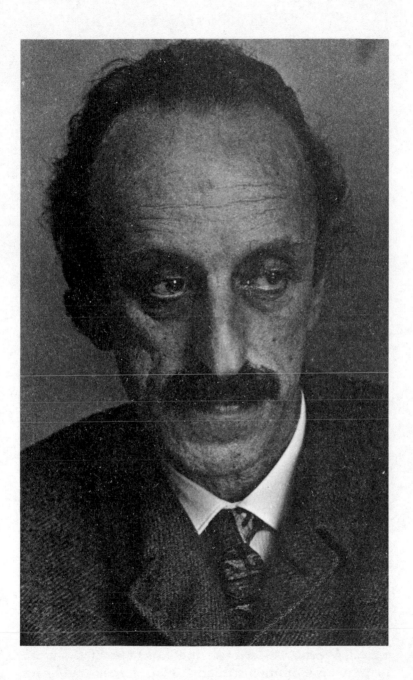

the ghetto behind in spirit as well as fact. Between the wars, his father's brother, Hans's uncle, edited the famous liberal German-language paper in Prague, the *Prager Tagblatt*. Hans's grandmother was still living in Prague in her nineties when the National Socialists came and murdered her. His father grew up poor, but made good as an architect and the family lived comfortably off in Döbling in the XIIth district, 'the Hampstead of Vienna' in Hans's phrase. He was the only child of his parents' marriage though he had an elder half-sister who, luckily as things turned out, married an Englishman.

It is not easy to imagine Hans as a child. He was immensely intelligent and highly musical, tapping out 'Mit dem Fuss . . .' from *Hansel and Gretel* (which he was later to describe as the one true post-Wagnerian opera) when little more than a baby. When can his formidable personality have begun to be shaped or rather to give itself expression? He described being thrown out of two of three schools where I dare say he had begun to show towards fellow-pupils and masters that icy disdain which was later to be so marked. The family circle was musical. Hans grew up playing the violin, and had detailed memories of musical Vienna: of Huberman playing the Beethoven concerto, and also the Mozart 'Concertante' with Arnold Rosé, leader of the Vienna Philharmonic who would walk over from his desk to take the viola part, a piece of musical versatility which was to be a touchstone with Hans; perhaps most of all of the cellist and composer Franz Schmidt, whom Hans recalled as the most musical person he had ever met, with a faultless memory for Bach cantata, Mozart concerto, Schubert song, even if he had only heard it once.

Whatever else formed Hans, the trauma of 1938 was critical. Vienna was feverish and violent throughout the 1930s, with Communists and Fascists demonstrating on the streets, and even right-wing Zionists, followers of Jabotinsky, who, Hans recalled, 'used to go Nazi-bashing' in uniform. There was open anti-Semitism in shops and newspapers and ski-clubs; and in schools. A master read out an essay by Hans and said, 'It is high time for Austrian culture to be rescued. We must have reached a low point in degeneration if it is possible for a Jew to write the only outstanding German essay.' Hard though it may be to imagine what Hans was like when young, it is harder to grasp the psychological effect on him – or on anyone – of such episodes.

The Germans entered Vienna on 12 March 1938, the day after Hans's nineteenth birthday, and consummated the Anschluss. Did I once see Hans grimace when I used that word, with its suggestion of legitimacy or satisfaction in 'joining'? But then he knew very well how satisfied most Austrians had been, as he witnessed the spontaneous outburst of rejoicing, and of cruelty, which followed. His next few months were described by Hans in a magnificent broadcast, subsequently printed; one of his most successful pieces, he later said with irritation, meaning that it had given the wrong sort of satisfaction to people, the satisfaction of thinking how much better we are here or, unconsciously, how much better we would have behaved. He was right, but the reaction was characteristic.

His mother had left for London, his father was dying; a death which was potentially calamitous as it meant that the authorities would not release Hans. After Kristallnacht he was imprisoned for a week as he tried every ruse to escape. He was beaten up, saw a man shot and another kill himself. What impressed him most was the behaviour of the orthodox Jews, their completely calm acceptance of suffering and refusal so much as to ward off a blow. One boy of his acquaintance, beaten to an unrecognizable state, said that 'we've had a few thousand years training,

haven't we?' and that another episode like this made no
difference; you can't blame them as 'they haven't reached
the stage where they know what they're doing'. And
'then he told me a Jewish joke appropriate to the occasion.'
By luck as much as anything Hans was released and was
able to reach London, having vowed that if he escaped he
would never be in a bad mood again, a promise which
amused some people when he mentioned it thirty years
later.

In his early years in London he did not pursue a formal
musical education but he played the violin intermittently
in orchestras and quartets. He was presumably interned in
1940, though I never asked him. He met the beautiful and
gifted Milein Cosman, also a refugee, from the Rhineland,
and married her. After the war Hans was living with his
mother in south London but he and Milein later moved
to Hampstead.

Hans gave his own reasons for not becoming a professional musician. He disliked corporate life, and he had
no time for many other musicians. When he did play in
orchestras he had to dose himself with Veganin against
the headaches produced by so much out-of-tune playing
all round him. He gave recitals with one quartet, in which
his mother played the cello, and he was asked to join
another by someone whom he desribed as subsequently
leading a famous quartet but declined. Hans would not
have enjoyed spending his life literally playing second
fiddle. And he began to write, endless articles (at twenty
shillings per thousand words when he was young) for
musical journals, drawing on his enormous self-taught
knowledge of music. He and Donald Mitchell began a
magazine together, *Music Survey*, combative and icono-
clastic, laying about the stuffy and conventional English
musical life of the day. Hans had several bêtes noires,
especially the music critics of the London newspapers, like

Frank Howes of *The Times*, who thought that Bruckner symphonies would never be regularly performed and did not regard Schoenberg as a musician at all. The young Keller made himself unpopular in various ways, not least by attending performances and recording in his magazine who the respective papers' – then anonymous – critics had been.

It was I suppose these years of musical guerilla warfare that finally hardened Hans's character and stimulated his aggression. It was not much weakened in his twenty years at the BBC (not, he would quickly say, 'his BBC career': 'I don't have careers'). He was a wonderfully disruptive presence in what some older people still called the Corporation; not in his successive jobs in charge of music talks, chamber music, orchestras and new music, where he was conscientious and industrious and even – what sounds surprising – encouraging to work for.

He encouraged new music also, but his position was sometimes misunderstood. Although Hans battled hard for the music of his time against English conservatism – polemically asserting in print that Schoenberg was the most important composer since Beethoven – it was only for music which he thought any good, not for 'advanced' music per se. In fact, he saw right through much such advanced music in the 1960s and 1970s, when the avant-garde became a bandwagon for ambitious mountebanks to ride on. He was sceptical of Boulez and of Stockhausen. He warned musicians and musical writers of the danger of over-reacting to past blindness: because from Beethoven onwards undoubted masterpieces had been dismissed by those who first heard them, it was tempting to be indulgent to anything new and obscure, but the temptation should be resisted. He and a chum organized a spoof, the 'first performance' on the BBC of a composer called Zak. A number of percussion instruments and other bits and pieces were arranged about the studio where Hans and his friend whacked them at random, and then awaited the puzzled but respectful notices in the press.

One of Hans's best asides was to the effect that, in Haydn's and Mozart's time, everyone had been avant-garde so that no one had to worry about it, and the living composer to whom he was most devoted was Benjamin Britten, who was far from being a member of the avant-garde. Hans's relations with Britten were sometimes sticky – as they were with most people – but in their way they were loyal friends. Britten's wonderful Third, and last, Quartet which was written not long before his death was dedicated to Hans, as he quite often reminded us.

In 1976 I had for the first time some little journalistic patronage at my disposal as assistant editor, shortly to be literary editor, at the *Spectator* and tried to put some of our space and some of Henry Keswick's money the way of people I admired. I rang Hans at the BBC to ask whether he might like to write for us. 'This is telepathic,' he said (or was it psychic?): he had been thinking of approaching the *Spectator*. That was not mere politeness. Karl Miller had left the *Listener* two or three years before and, as I subsequently learned, Hans had tried the *New Statesman* without success. We met for lunch and I found what I had hoped for, perhaps at more than one level of consciousness. He was courteous, odd, intense. I was exhilarated, fascinated. We talked about psychology, about Thomas Szasz, who had recently broadcast on Radio 3; I said that Szasz struck me as possibly more a figure in the history of moral philosphy than of science, to which Hans replied, surprisingly in retrospect, that the same might have been said of Freud. We talked about sport – I forget what footballing event was on at the time, though I remember asking him inanely if he had ever acquired any interest in cricket.

And we talked about music. I was not disppointed. He was stimulating and, as far as someone can be over lunch, profound. We established a sort of rapport. I said that I had found a recent performance of *Moses and Aaron* conducted by Boulez distressing. Hans agreed and explained as he was later to do in print that Boulez essentially could not phrase, which made his conducting of Schoenberg as inadequate as of Wagner. I confessed – the word is apt enough – another problem I had, with Brahms, to which Hans comfortingly said that I had no need to worry: 'Most great composers have had neurotic personalities, but Brahms was the only one whose music was itself neurotic.' This was my first experience in person rather than on the printed page of Hans's aphoristic gift (he would have detested that phrase), his ability to illuminate a whole question, a composer's whole work, in one sentence.

Over the next five years we met often, spoke weekly, wrote regularly. My letters from Hans delighted me, as they would have enraged many people, but then I like to think that I had got the point of him, in public and in person. He could be kindly in private. He once asked me to give a Radio 3 talk and I did so on a subject which I knew was near to his heart, the absurd cult of 'authenticity' in musical performance; he could not have been a more sympathetic and helpful producer. But at the same time, even in private relations, he made no secret of his conviction that he was in the right: 'I disagree with you because you are entirely wrong and I am entirely right,' was an utterance in a broadcast discussion which Neal Ascherson later remembered when he wanted to sum Keller up.

None of Hans's letters to me ever contained quite those words: but one I remember was headed, in handwritten, red-inked capitals over the typescript: 'This letter is supposed to be, not a pain in the neck, but incidental amusement.' It contained a slightly bullying paragraph about business, wishing to know where he stood with the *Spectator* (he had some reason for perplexity, as will be seen), before embarking on the discussion of words. 'Charlatan. No, if you want to discuss the question of consciousness, you should not examine the word "apart from its etymology" ... its denotation was proportionally narrower, to the extent of excluding George Steiner ...' (this must have been a reference to an earlier conversation, or a letter of mine). '*Hochstapler*, only a step or two behind, is about to be thus visible.' And then he continued with a dissertation on *Song-Lied-Song-lied*, an interesting example of reciprocal borrowing. Having conquered the English language – the military metaphor is apt – he had strong likes and dislikes, disliking especially the English tendency to borrow foreign words and phrases.

This willingness to impart information or to correct error was always couched in studiously courteous tones: 'Not a terribly important note, just curiosity: "the two A-major duets". Do you mean the hyphen – because of the adjectival key? You'd contradict long-established, arranging practice – deliberately? No – unless I hear from you.' This was a reference, by the way, to the only occasion on which I scored off Hans, though without trying and it would have been a brave man who tried. In a piece for me, he mentioned a couple of bars' music at the end of the first movement of Mozart's A major (no hyphen) piano concerto, K.488, which also appears identically at the beginning of a duet in the same key in *Così fan tutte*; or rather, as Hans wrote, 'the A major duet in *Così* ...' I corrected this to '... duet "Fra gli amplessi" in ...' which Hans queried with icy politeness. I pointed out that there were two duets in that key in the opera ('Guarda sorella' in the first act as well). There was an audible pause on the telephone before he said: 'Yes, that is so. It is an unusual key for Mozart. I wrote an article comparing those two duets. It must have been published before you were born.' (It probably wasn't. Hans was vague about dates. He once asked me if I had been at the première of *Peter Grimes*, which did indeed take place before I was born – though not before I was conceived – in 1945.)

Until now I have tried to express my admiration for Hans, but it has perhaps become clear why others, even if they could not deny admiration, had no love at all for him. He was greatly disliked by not a few people. Naturally music critics and the London musical establishment of his youth hated him. Inside the BBC, there were a few colleagues who enjoyed his esteem: William Glock, Mischa Donat, Deryck Cooke whose *The Language of Music* he properly revered and the memorial meeting for whom after his untimely death Hans turned into an attack on the BBC's management. Otherwise he did not suffer fools gladly, which saying covers many forms of aggression. In Radio 3 meetings he did not bother to conceal his contempt for the idea of catering to the audience – the happy days to which he later looked back when listening figures were never discussed – or for that matter for many of his colleagues, and this did not make life easy. It was a fault on his part. A man like Hans may be very much cleverer than most other people, but most other people cannot be expected to enjoy being reminded of this so regularly. It was a fault less of manners – as I say, his manners were outwardly scrupulous; one colleague who esteemed Hans was Gerard Mansell who ran the External Service of the BBC, and who remarked to me once that the way Hans never lost his temper in meetings provoked others to lose theirs – than of humanity and of communication. His style was the man, but it got in the way of his message.

This was true of his public performance. I was far from the only one to have noticed Hans in the 1960s. *Private Eye* tried to turn 'Hans Killer' into a figure of fun, a ludicrously teutonic intellectual – 'O mein Gott …' – dilating incomprehensibly on music and sport.* I am sure this hurt Hans, who was much more sensitive than his aggressive carapace allowed. In the course of his sticky relationship with the *Spectator* he once threatened to withdraw entirely when the lads at the paper published two letters attacking him, headed 'Keller in English' and '. . . und auf deutsch'. This, he told me, suggested an atmosphere in which he was not happy. He also once asked in a veiled way if I knew of the reputation which the *Spectator* was acquiring. By this he meant a reputation for anti-Semitism. I had of course to defend my own paper on the charge, and not hypocritically. It was true that an informal connection had grown up between the magazine and *Private Eye*. The *Eye* itself had, as James Fenton once put it, in the name of ignoring all the polite conventions kept the anti-Semitic joke alive in print (or, you might say, that's not anti-Semitism, just Jew-baiting). It was true also that in the *Spectator* the *Eye* men Richard Ingrams, Christopher Booker and Auberon Waugh held forth on the Jewish question as on other sensitive questions with various degrees of breezy insensitivity.

In fact, had Hans known how he was viewed at the *Spectator*, he would have been pricklier still. I had my own territory which, I was told, I filled with middle-European names like Keller and Szasz who were mocked sometimes publicly and sometimes privately by the rest of the paper. It was bad enough that things always seemed to go wrong with Hans's pieces, in unconscious reaction as it were to

* It was astonishingly thick-skinned of the makers of a television programme about Hans shown after his death to call it *The Keller Instinct*.

his own attitude. Headlines displeased him, spelling corrections also (why could not each contributor spell '-ize' words with an s or z as he wished?), and when I corrected his phrase 'Schubert's brother-in-art Haydyn' to 'Haydn' it appeared as '... brother-in-law ...' But he was right: there was an atmosphere of hostility to him. For two or three years I published a monthly article on music by Hans, usually pegged to a forthcoming broadcast. The editor did not pay much attention to these for a time. Then Alexander Chancellor, a very intelligent as well as amiable man and musical besides, but who suffered to an acute degree from the English upper-class dread of being thought too clever, read a batch of these pieces in a sitting and summarily put an end to them. It was not so much their content he disliked so intensely as Hans's style. It is quite true, as Chancellor perceptively put it, that native English-speakers tend to use the language in speech or writing in a rough, impressionistic way and that the ferociously exact command of the language of those who have learned it later – Conrad, Nabokov, Keller – can be headache-inducing.

And, although I thought Alexander's reaction exaggerated, he was not alone. I later heard from the editor of another weekly, Anthony Howard of the *New Statesman*, that he had met Keller and been greatly put off. Even those who did admire Hans sometimes found him hard to take. He published a book with the lamentable title *1975 = 1984–9*, a collection of pieces which he pretended were connected: his memoir of Vienna in 1938, an account of a different species of totalitarianism met on a visit to Prague, pieces on psychoanalysis, music and football, all compulsive reading to me. They were respectfully reviewed by the poet Peter Porter, who also got Keller's point, but who remarked that some of his arguments – such as that the symphony orchestra was an anti-musical institution – were perverse, and noted ironically that promise Hans had made in the hands of the Gestapo about never being in a bad mood again; so far was that from the case, Porter said, that Keller's very style had become a by-word for hectoring didacticism. Two more books were published after Hans's death, the dazzling work of instruction on *The Great Haydn Quartets*, and a polemic against *Criticism*. This was reviewed not very respectfully by Michael Tanner, who also recognized Hans's stature but said in effect that the book was pretty insufferable, not least because of the author's fondness for thrusting unfunny jokes in the reader's face. These, as I say, were sympathetic critics.

There was indeed something alarming about Hans's vanity and didacticism. He was vain rather than ambitious; someone more calculating in the effect he made on others would have made a display of modesty. Two of Hans's books have pictures of him on the front cover, admittedly a tribute to Milein who drew them. In the Preface to the Haydn book, he quotes Oskar Adler's opinion that he did not know what would become of the boy Hans, 'but one thing I can tell you: the world will hear of him', and Britten's opinion that 'Hans Keller knows more about the string quartet, and understands it better, than anybody alive, composers and players included', which, Hans remarked, may have been why Britten dedicated the Third Quartet to him. Elsewhere he quoted the psycho-analyst Willi Hoffer saying that Keller had an 'unequalled knowledge of psychoanalytic literature'. Sometimes his self-importance was merely comical, as when he described a lecture tour of South Africa. He made trouble by insisting on only speaking to integrated audiences, but 'I wasn't even deported, apparently because they knew I was going to leave anyway'. Or just possibly because lectures on Schoenberg to the comparatively few Xhosas and

Tswanas interested in him did not represent a serious threat to the apartheid system.

All of which is in a sense by the way. Hans cannot be understood without this background of his overbearing manner and the 'notorious aggression' which he himself recognized but which he persuaded himself was 'essentially sunny'. In the foreground was his original genius, and a man of genius was what I believe he was. He was right, and what he had to say on most subjects was true and important. He was right about psychiatry, recognizing despite his reverence for Freud what a closed society Freudianism had become. He was right about football, his passion for which struck some musical friends like Donald Mitchell as deplorably trivial. He watched football, and tennis, with the same fanatical intensity as he gave to everything, analysing each match in statistical detail, the number of free kicks and corners. What he liked in sport was individuality, Greaves or Best or George or Brooking.* He hated regimentation and uniformity and team spirit: everything in fact which was represented by official English football in the 1960s, above all by Ramsey's World Cup-winning side of 1966. It was a sad year for football, and a correspondingly good one came four years later when the World Cup was won by Brazil, the best side most of us could ever hope to see, a whole which was as great as the sum of the parts, from Pele to Jairzinho, one of Hans's special favourites not least because he was said to smoke sixty cigarettes a day. Hans himself smoked heavily but with his background, it scarcely need be said, he did not drink much: the occasional glass of beer or whisky. Just how much such habits are the products of

---

*His comparison of Trevor Brooking's midfield play with the closing passage of 'Là ci darem la mano' in *Don Giovanni* delighted one journalist so much that he reprinted it ironically without further comment.

immediate environment he both knew, and did not know. He remarked once on the rarity of both alcoholism and homosexuality among Jews; I pointed out that although this might be true of the Jews – educated Europeans – we immediately thought of, he would find a different story if he went to New York.

Although he seemed to like England – and thought that English suited him better as a language than German – he remained in many ways an outsider here. Again, he both knew this and did not, did and did not want to belong. Many immigrants, notably refugees from Hitler's persecution, are deeply anglophile, cherishing the foibles and peculiarities of their adopted country, despite its reputation – not always unjustified – for prejudice and insularity and exclusivity. But as has been observed by one immigrant, George Weidenfeld, who should know, anti-Semitism in England tends to be ad hominem rather than a blanket rejection; and as another, Lewis Namier, once said, there are few hurdles in England which cannot be cleared by money and charm. So has been shown again and again not only in the eighteenth century of which Namier wrote, but in the last fifty years as those who came here from Germany and Austria have made good not merely in material but in social terms, popular and accepted everywhere.

Hans was not among them. It is not enough to say that he had no social as he had no professional ambition. He appreciated being asked to Buckingham Palace garden parties and to the *Spectator*'s sesquicentennial dance in 1978 and he enjoyed more than I suspect he realized the recognition of the great, like Edward Boyle when he wrote to the paper about one of Hans's pieces. But he remained wonderfully Central European in his argumentativeness and lack of compromise. His feelings about his native Viennese were mixed, for obvious reasons:

fifteen years ago he wrote with irritation near disgust of the taxi driver of his own age, taking him from Vienna airport who made the usual platitudinous noises about 'that madman': no doubt, Hans said, he had been an enthusiastic Nazi then; they all were. But some Viennese chords still tugged at him. A friend remembers how a few years after the war the famous recording of *Die Fledermaus* arrived, and Hans and his family listened to it with rapt pleasure. His contempt for Kraus I have mentioned; Kraus the tormented, unhappy satirist of Vienna; despising his contemporaries, renouncing his ancestral religion, and denouncing the Viennese liberal press and the psycho-analytical movements as Jewish rackets; maybe a 'self-hating Jew' (though the phrase should be given a rest): it is not hard to see why Hans disliked him. And yet they had more in common than Hans could have recognized.

Above all, Keller was right about music. The influence which he had on English musical life was immeasurable but huge. His Haydn book will be studied as long as string quartets are played, not only by the many quartets he coached. His influence for that matter runs through anyone who has ever read or heard him on music – in words or music. He created 'functional analysis', a system of wordless discussion of music by rearrangement. I only heard one example, his analytical arrangement of the Mozart G minor String Quintet. He trailed this in the *Spectator* with a piece asking what we would think of a discussion of *The Critique of Pure Reason* written in music. I suspect that this analogy does not stand up, and that verbal analysis of music is with us for some time yet. All the same he was certainly right about the vapidity of much writing on music, including most programme notes, which are either meaningless or pleonastic. If you know that an A minor first subject is followed by a second subject in C major then you don't need to be told and if you do not know then being told is no use.

He was right in his ceaseless attacks on 'authenticity', a battle which he looks more like winning than seemed possible fifteen years ago (as I write, Andras Schiff is again playing Bach in London on a modern piano, and playing it far better than most harpsichordists). That was Hans's point when he said somewhat sweepingly that he had never heard an authentic performance which was really musical (though that was in the mid-Seventies; he could not have said it after hearing Simon Rattle conduct the Orchestra of the Age of Enlightenment). He was profoundly right about the gramophone record which 'with its repeatability represents our age's most potent anti-musical force'. We are breeding or have bred a generation in whom musicality is almost impossible: they hear but they don't listen. It is as grave a problem as that of canned music which plays everywhere – the 'better' music the 'worse' – to the lament of anyone musical. He was full of insight on any number of musical topics, from the meaning of key, which he alone adequately explained to me, to the fact that there is no 'correct' speed for any piece of music ('tempo is a function of phrasing'), to the genius of Gershwin, to the inadequacy despite their technical proficiency of most Japanese performing musicians, in Western music that is, whose background they could not hope to know by instinct. From anyone else, that might have seemed almost racist, but Hans was convincing and, I think, correct.

And he was right on individual composers, from Bach where it all began to Britten, whom he acclaimed as the greatest of all living composers when still in his thirties. Even now, when I think of a composer I am likely to think of something Hans said about him. Brahms's neuroticism was one insight, another his lifelong unhappy love for the gypsy idiom, unconsummated except for one brief rapturous moment in the slow movement of the Clarinet Quintet. Hans understood the kinship between Haydn and Schubert, and that the lack of personal performing virtuosity they had in common was why neither had been able to write a great opera or concerto or concertante piece – unlike the virtuosos Mozart and Beethoven – and which was why their greatest music is essentially private. He had his blind – or deaf – spots, but then I shared some, such as his lack of enthusiasm for Debussy.

He pointed out that 'romantic individualism' is a delusion: it is much harder to distinguish between two contemporary pieces by Mendelssohn and Schumann than between Bach and Handel or Haydn and Mozart. And yet he recognized the greatness of Mendelssohn, and of his Violin Concerto, the greatest in the whole genre (not excluding Beethoven and Brahms, that is). This led to a violent attack on Saul Bellow who had disparaged the Mendelssohn concerto in his book on Israel. Hans devoted a whole review to denouncing Bellow in turn, then devoted part of his book *Criticism* to reprinting his review with a long description of the circumstances in which it was written and published with minor editorial changes, an example of Hans's insistence on matters of principle, or lack of sense of proportion, or both. He announced that in response to Bellow he would write a book on the Mendelssohn concerto, to be dedicated to the State of Israel. I believe that it was written but is not yet published.

Bellow's book touched two nerves, Hans's love of music and his Jewishness. He would have said that he was not blind to what was least open or humane in Israel, disliked the regressive nationalism he observed there. But he was defensive: 'Why has the *Spectator* got its knife into Israel and Jeremy Thorpe [this must have been early 1979], not that there isn't a lot to criticize in both?' In the end, as with so many other Jews of his generation, I believe, his instinctive love of Israel was a sort of boyish pride, which was the stronger for following on shame and horror. Hitler had exposed the Jews' powerlessness: now they had shown their power. A Zionist uncle of Hans's had dreamed of a state 'where even the policemen would be Jews', and in Israel, Hans admitted, that was part of his own reaction of delight. This was understandable; less so his insistence that Israel's existence was 'an answer to extermination'. What he meant was clear enough and, although the point is dismissed as irrelevant by more rigorous Zionists, it is one of the deep emotional arguments for Israel. It is a less good intellectual argument: 'answer' has two senses: 'reply', which Israel is, and 'solution', which is another matter.

'A highly conscious Jew' was Hans's description of himself, and he was indeed highly sensitive, prickly, difficult (could even *Private Eye* call someone touchy in this matter who knew the circumstances in which his grandmother, cousins, friends had died?). He despised evasive Jews, lambasting in print someone who had changed his name from 'Mandelbaum', for which I reproached him. What is a 'Jewish name', anyway? There are no Mandelbaums in the Book of Kings. And as I have suggested, his prickliness on the subject took several forms. That did not distinguish him from others; what did was his originality. The fascinating case where his musicality and his Jewishness both impinged was Wagner. Of course Hans recognized his towering genius and, as much to the point, the superiority of his later work, the *Ring* and especially *Tristan* and *Meistersinger*. His love for the last was unaffected by memories of performances where the end of Hans Sachs's hymn to the 'Deutsches Volk und Reich' had been greeted by shouts of 'Heil Hitler!'. He detested the ban on Wagner's music in Israel and wrote for me a brilliant article on the subject. Listening to a rehearsal by the Israeli Philharmonic in Jerusalem he recalled, there was an interval when he suddenly realized that the cor anglais (or English horn, as he insisted) was playing on his own the most beautiful passage ever written for his instrument, but which he could never play in public, from the opening of Act III of *Tristan*. More than that, Hans claimed that Wagner was not only a genius but a 'thoroughly nice man'. This made me smile when I published it. Hans insisted that the received attitude was an example of mediocrity fearing greatness. Wagner's music frightens us (in a different way from Brahms's) by speaking directly to the dynamic unconscious. We react by denigrating his personality. Even Wagner's Jew-hatred, Hans most strikingly asserted, was irrelevant and in any case entirely the result of his infection by Cosima (he asserted it wrongly, as I now know better than I did then).

An enemy of Hans's might have related his 'persecution mania on Wagner's behalf' to himself. Wagner was not 'thoroughly nice', he was beyond niceness in the conventional sense, and so was Hans himself. Was Hans happy? He would have sneered at the question. 'Happiness is a depressive concept,' he once said, perhaps the most characteristic of his utterances I can recall. I think the answer is that he was also beyond happiness. His own self-mastery was shown at its most striking in his last years when he contracted the awful, wasting Motor Neurone Disease. It gradually incapacitated and paralysed him, but he chose in effect to ignore it, as that posthumous television programme showed. The results of this self-possession were evident all his life, not only at its end, and often disconcerting to others, but that was what he wanted. He was half-ironical about 'Thanatos', 'Freud's PPB on behalf of the death-wish', but also used to quote Mozart's saying that the goal of life is death. His own death in 1985 could fairly be said to vindicate this. I would certainly say of Hans as he said of Schmidt that he was the most musical person I have ever known; in fact, I have rarely met a more remarkable man.

7

STEPHEN KOSS

If the English vice is hypocrisy, the American disease is surely anglophilia. It is a morbid affliction, striking down the most boorish tourist doing Stratford-upon-Avon and Bath or the cleverest Rhodes scholar. It affects by heredity those would-be English, East Coast, Ivy League Wasps with suits from Savile Row and accents from somewhere on the way to Oxford, a class of people rightly mistrusted in their own country and not liked quite as much as they may think in England; we prefer New York Jews. But then again, those are almost more susceptible to the complaint than anyone else. The most extreme case I ever saw was Sid Perelman, the comic writer who wrote the Marx brothers' scripts; you might have thought a distinctively American humorist, but who felt he had to spend his declining years in London wearing tweeds.

The disease might be expected to afflict particularly those professionally engaged in English life, letters and history, critics like Richard Ellmann (though his was the related syndrome of hibernophilia) or historians like Stephen Koss. For a man who devoted himself to nine-teenth- and twentieth-century British history, Stephen had preserved his immune system to a surprising degree. His attitude to the country where he spent so much time and which was his subject was ironic and semi-detached. He could be critical and sharp, but he had all the same an intensity of interest in and affection for England which was part love affair, part amused friendship.

By the time I came to know Stephen he was in his late thirties. He was born in 1940 in the generation of hard-working and ambitious Americans whose grandparents had arrived as immigrants and whose parents had clawed their way out of the slums into suburban prosperity by way of trade: the children were to be doctors and dentists, publishers and journalists and academics. If many Americans have a romantic idealized and fantasized idea of England, few Englishmen really understand the complexities of American society with its own subtle class system and strong if elusive snobberies. Until the World War, the Ivy League universities were almost as exclusive as Christ Church, which did after all take in the odd working-class boy like A. L. Rowse. The first generation of New York Jewish intellectuals went to City College, not to Columbia, let alone Yale. Between the wars, it is said, Harvard was forgetting its contempt for the Irish only to discover anti-Semitism; and Lionel Trilling's had an uneasy teaching career at Columbia.

Columbia was Stephen's university also, in easier times. He went there from Long Island, where he had grown up, to a university more hospitable to the upwardly-mobile than it once had been, in 1958, during that long hiatus in middle-class, and especially academic, American life between the tensions of the McCarthy years and the upheavals of Vietnam and student rebellion. While he was an undergraduate he met and married Elaine, who was at nearby Barnard College. The 1960s were a boom time for universities throughout the English-speaking world. Even in 1968 most people leaving Oxford with respectable degrees at least contemplated going on to do research, however unsuited they would have been to it. As Stephen's colleague Isser Woloch has said, 'it was easier to embark on an academic career at that time than it had been before or is likely to be again'. The 1980s by contrast

have been locust years for the universities, something which their faculties have tended to blame on the malice of reactionary governments. As much to the point is the fact that they simply, and recklessly, over-expanded twenty years before and the natural contraction with the passing of years would always have been painful.

After skipping through MA and Ph.D. oral exams, Stephen came to England for a year as a Fulbright scholar, to work on his dissertation on Morley at the India Office during the Liberal government of 1905. He was astonishingly industrious, with a capacity for reading and for working through archives that I have scarcely seen equalled, but at that time he had not found himself as a writer and the first draft of his dissertation was severely criticized for being too long and clumsy and ill-organized. He rewrote it quickly and more or less successfully. The next stage on this academic ladder, or rat-race, was to have the work published but Stephen then suffered an all too common setback. It is curious how often a researcher chooses an apparently recondite topic which has never been covered before, only to become aware that someone else has been working in the very same field. Sometimes the researcher finds out in time to drop his work, or (what is in some ways better) waits until the other one is published, to take a view. Stephen adroitly switched track to Morley's contemporary Haldane and in fact published not one but two monographs before he was thirty. This was the beginning of his remarkable fecundity which produced eight published books – no slim volumes, but weighty scholarly works – in fifteen years. He went to teach at Barnard, where he spent several happy years before things went wrong. Quite why he fell foul of a group of colleagues there I am not sure. Things were very difficult for several years while he taught at both the Upper West Side colleges, Columbia as well as Barnard, until he managed to escape completely to his old home. Perhaps the painful intrigues at Barnard can be explained, perhaps they are inexplicable, except by Kissinger's apophthegm quoted earlier.

If Stephen enjoyed visiting England, it may have been in part because he could remove himself from these petty but painful squabbles. Or rather could observe others' intrigues and betrayals with disinterested amusement: Stephen was never averse from gossip, but gossip which does not directly concern us is more pleasurable than contemplating our own worries. By the time I came to know him he was moving smoothly in English life, which is to say in several of its channels, from Fleet Street to Oxford. The annual research visits to England were crowned with a visiting fellowship at All Souls. When he asked me to dinner there he was clearly revelling in the foibles of Oxford life and the benign or malign eccentricities of his colleagues. And even the most puritanical anglophobe might admit, you would have to be odd not to enjoy staying in that beautiful building. He understood Fleet Street – it was his subject, after all – and became a sought-after reviewer. John Gross first introduced him to the *New Statesman,* and then to the *Times Literary Supplement.* It is a measure of Stephen's industry that in 1975, he wrote for them and a couple of other British papers (he scarcely ever reviewed for American papers) at least fourteen reviews, most of them of large, scholarly books. It must have been in 1979 that I first asked him to review for the *Spectator,* which he added enthusiastically to his roster: I never heard him complain (as most of us sometimes do) about the imposition of book reviewing. His relations with us were happy, I think, though complicated at first by something which amused both him and me. My assistant on the books pages was Clare Asquith, who was prickly towards Stephen on account of his biography of the prime minister, her great-grand-father. I should say that they soon warmed to one another.

Stephen himself could be prickly and sharp, over important matters of scholarship, or matters as unimportant as they could be. On one occasion I gave him lunch and we walked back afterwards from Garrick Street, he to catch a bus to the British Museum, I to go shopping in Soho. I said we would go down Cranbourn Street and through the alley with Chinese shops, he insisted that another way would be quicker. When we reached Shaftesbury Avenue he said almost with asperity that he had been right. Did the two or three minutes matter, or was he pleased to be demonstrating a superior knowledge of the topography of London to someone who had lived there for almost forty years?

He certainly prided himself on his knowledge of England and things English. At the time I may not have taken him to be afflicted with that sort of anglophilia but I now think that others saw it differently. Isser Woloch remembers that 'strangers or children would think Stephen English, and I wondered that did not reflect some sort of affectation.' No one English could have thought that, though a New College don did once ask me, 'Is your friend Koss an upper-class Yank or just a Jew?' Isser Woloch (who has written that Stephen 'earned and savoured his membership of the Reform Club in Pall Mall') worried also that Stephen seemed less interested in American politics than he ought to have been and seemed more at home with *The Times* (of London) than the *New York Times*. But then, it is not thought reprehensible if one says that Richard Cobb is more at home with *Le Monde*, Raymond Carr with *El Diario*, than with *The Times*. And Stephen was not oblivious to American politics. Just before Christmas 1980 I flew to Kennedy airport and bumped into Stephen waiting for his children off the same flight. Taking a lift off him into Manhattan, I asked what he thought about Reagan's victory. He gave a wry half-smile and said, 'It's pretty appalling, however you look at it.'

I have said little of Stephen's work, but it was a remarkable achievement and not only in scope: eight books published in fifteen years, culminating in the two monumental volumes of *The Rise and Fall of the Political Press in Britain*. They are two intensely enjoyable books, full of, yes, gossip of the kind that journalists and politicians both relish. Whether the work had a real theme I was not so sure — whether, that is, there had been a rise and fall rather than just a beginning, middle and end. It is true that newspapers do not 'carry weight' politically today, to the chagrin of some self-important colleagues. No one now reads *The Times* leading article for guidance, not many read leaders at all. In the late 1970s when I doubled as leader writer for the *Spectator*, I was not sure for whom, if anyone, I was writing, and the views I expressed, such as they were, were my own and not the voice of some collective unconscious. Indeed, the *Spectator* suspended its leader in 1981, a significant event which Koss noticed in the last pages of his book. Today, the only national paper whose editor has strong and distinctive ideas of his own is the *Sunday Telegraph*, and Peregrine Worsthorne signs his leaders. That something has happened can hardly be doubted; but I wonder if the 'fall of the political press' is not a reflection of a wider social change. A political press only makes sense within a system of aristocratic or at least bourgeois government, not when there is a mass electorate: *The Times* had enormously more influence eighty years ago when its circulation was below 40,000 than it does today when it is almost half a million.

The *Rise and Fall* proved to be Stephen's last book. I cannot remember whether I saw him after the second volume was published, or whether we last met in London or New York. I think it must have been a year or two before that – I had dinner with Stephen and Elaine on the Upper West Side, which I remember because I had recently been in South Africa and their son, then in his teens, disapproved of something I had written from there. The rest of the story I heard only later. In 1976 Stephen had begun to be unduly tired and been informed that his heart rhythm was irregular. Shortly afterwards he told a friend that 'the medical storm has lifted and I feel absolutely perfect'. He could, he was assured, 'live with the "condition" for the next eighty years, suffering no inconvenience unless I aspire to become an Olympic athlete'. This optimism proved to be misplaced. He returned from his annual trip to Europe in 1984 with alarming symptoms of short breath and slurred speech. He now learned that his heart was gravely impaired, and its condition was deteriorating. There was only one hope: a heart transplant. This was offered to him as though it were that or nothing. Isser Woloch who saw him at this time speaks of an inner calm and serenity which seemed to take over Stephen, and that his ironic view of life which he had cultivated had struck deep roots. He was no doubt appalled at the prospect of this weird operation, and detached himself from the events in which he was the leading player. This was just as well. He died during the operation.

Perhaps Stephen never entirely worked out his feelings about England. What is for sure is that he was mourned there as much as in his own country. As I wrote in the Preface to another book with which he had helped me, his death robbed those who knew him only by his work of a distinguished American scholar of recent English history, and those of us lucky enough to have known him personally of a generous colleague, and a salty, sceptical and irreverent friend.

8

SHIVA NAIPAUL

In 1964 a young man of nineteen sailed from Trinidad to London. Shiva Naipaul later re-imagined the scene in his first novel *Fireflies*:

Bhaskar left at midday the following day. Mr and Mrs Khoja were at the docks to see him off. Mrs Lutchman wept profusely when the ship slipped its moorings.

'What you crying for?' Mr Khoja said. 'Just think, he going to come back home a doctor. Dr B. Lutchman. What you always wanted him to be. You should be laughing, not crying.'

'I know. But all the same, you know, when you spend years bringing up a child, is not an easy thing for a mother to see him leave she. He going to come back a man.'

Shiva did not go back. He was on his way to England, to Oxford to take up the Island scholarship he had won from St Mary's College in his native Port-of-Spain. His journey had in a sense begun earlier, explaining why a writer called Shivadhar Srinavasa Naipaul came from the West Indies. His family belonged to an odd, isolated community, the East Indians of the West Indies whose forebears had migrated in the nineteenth century to work on the sugar plantations as indentured labourers; part of what Shiva called 'the desperate litany of place bred by our Indian diaspora', the internal migration within the British Empire which took Indians to South Africa, Malaya, Kenya as well as Trinidad. Shiva was the sixth of seven children and the younger of two sons. When he was seven his father, a journalist, had died suddenly, a formative event in his life. Soon afterwards his elder brother Vidiadhar left for England and one day for fame and fortune as V. S. Naipaul, the novelist. And so for the best part of ten years of boyhood and adolescence Shiva's upbringing among his mother and five sisters was feminine; in consequence he liked the company of women, was 'responsive to the tidal motions of their moods – their curious gaieties and darknesses; and without consciously intending it, I see that they have had a major role in my fiction'. Perhaps the embrace of family life was almost too warm: he did not return to Trinidad for years and only briefly when he did, with a fear that 'having arrived here, I may never be able to get out again'. But then again, a sense of apprehension was one of his marked traits.

At any rate, Oxford changed his life. I scarcely knew him there – oddly enough his college, Univ., sheltered a number of people who only later became friends of mine – though we had hard-drinking friends in common like Robert MacDonald who shared lodgings with Shiva in Wellington Square. Shiva's undergraduate career was uneventful. He was a striking figure in long black hair and long black boots, he acquired a taste for whisky and cigarettes (which was to be awkward years later on a visit to Morocco during Ramadan when 'it was my misfortune to look as though I should have been a Muslim'), he had, in a characteristic phrase, 'sordid sexual encounters with girls whose faces I cannot now remember', he changed subjects on a whim, reading Chinese without much success for his final Schools. His life was changed also when he

met Jenny Stuart; they were married in the summer of 1967.

He described the donnée for his first novel. He was working in his room at Oxford, as the Chinese ideograms 'danced meaninglessly across the frail paper ... when, for no reason I can fathom, a sentence came into my head. "The Lutchmans lived in a part of the city where the houses, tall and narrow ..." I pushed away the books and paper in front of me, wrote down the sentence and started to follow it.' This sentence became the opening of the second chapter of his first novel, which was published in 1970, when Shiva was twenty-five. *Fireflies* won three prizes, was showered with praise, and deserved everything said of it. It is the story of the Khojas, 'the acknowledged leaders of the Hindu community in Trinidad'; of Baby, an unimportant cousin of the family; of her marriage to the hopeless Ram Lutchman; of their sons; of Ram's death; and of the boys' failures. Bhaskar goes to India to study medicine but breaks down and comes home defeated; Romesh goes to the bad, to prison and to New York where he marries a Puerto Rican, 'a little coloured girl'. *Fireflies* is a dazzling portrait of a society, describing with painful accuracy life on the island, where Indians called Negroes 'niggers' and are called 'coolies' in return; where a prosperous Indian family could keep a servant called Darkie, granddaughter of slaves, allowed a day's holiday a year. It is a society where 'if any member of the clan had gone so far as to contemplate marriage with a Muslim, the ensuing scandal would have been no less than if he had wished to marry a Negro', where one girl does indeed finally lose caste: 'Just imagine Renouka going about with that nigger.' *Fireflies* is also a story of struggle and loss, told with Turgenevian feeling, control, and delicacy.

And it is very funny. Shiva had a crystal ear for dialogue: ' "Huh! You hear the latest one Govind? Rheumatism and diabetes too low-class for she. She say is she eyes giving she trouble." Eye troubles were, in Mrs Khoja's opinion, an infirmity visited on only the more select people.' In 1973 – the year Shiva's and Jenny's only child was born, their son Tarun – he published a second novel, *The Chip-Chip Gatherers*, also set in Trinidad, still funny but darker in tone, down to the people of its title who gathered tiny, barely edible shells on the beach, 'filling the buckets and basins with the pink and yellow shells which were the size and the shape of a long fingernail. Inside each was the sought-after prize: a minuscule kernel of insipid flesh. A full bucket of shells would provide them with a mouthful.'

Shiva published no further novel for the next ten years, to the perplexity of his admirers. It was during those years that I came to know him well, and I was perplexed also. I don't think he suffered from a 'block' in the hackneyed sense; he was certainly not lazy, though he was a perfectionist of an almost neurotic kind, the despair of editors and publishers, a writer who could spend a morning perfecting one sentence and then decide to discard it in the afternoon. He had to earn a living, and fiction is notoriously no way of doing that (it should be said that Jenny helped to support them all those years; she became the secretary of Alexander Chancellor, editor of the *Spectator*, and remained with the magazine). He did not want to be typecast as a 'comic novelist'. He could not go on writing about Trinidad for ever from exile. He wrote journalism not just because it paid, but because he enjoyed it and was good at it, as can be seen by his collection of articles and short stories, *Beyond the Dragon's Mouth*. And in fact he worked intermittently on a novel for those ten years.

Besides he wrote two books of reportage. *North of South* was a sour description of a journey through Kenya,

Tanzania and Zambia in the mid-1970s, three independent countries north of 'South', that is, South Africa. There is a peculiarly haunting quality to Naipaul's travel writing. 'All travel is a form of self-extinction', he wrote, but travel was for him a form of self-exploration and self-discovery as well. He was acutely intelligent, and acutely sensitive, prickly, thin-skinned (about himself, that is; like many such people, Shiva's skin could sometimes be on the thick side when it came to others). Things kept happening to him. Encounters with officials turned nasty, the most quotidian exchange developed aggressive overtones. *North of South* contains an unforgettable meeting with a shoeshine boy in Nairobi who, after the job, demanded a preposterous sum and then turned hysterically nasty. I was far from finding this implausible as something like it had happened to me also in Nairobi.

For Shiva it was worse. His weakness and strength here was that he was, in a ridiculous expression, 'non-European' (try saying 'non-Asian'). Like his brother, he was thus free from the white, especially 'white liberal', hang-ups of colonial and racial guilt, which make it so hard for anyone of European descent to be honest about the 'Third World'. Quotation marks are in order: one of Shiva's best essays was on 'The Illusion of the Third World'. Blandly to subsume, 'say, Ethiopia, India and Brazil under the one banner of the Third World is as absurd and denigrating as the old assertion that all Chinese look alike.' In his memory I try to refer to it as the Tropics, which is an almost exact geographical description of what is meant. Shiva saw through the absurdity of independent Africa with its tragic figures from that bootblack to President Nyerere with his 'ujamaa' or socialist road; the 'hopeless, doomed continent ... swaddled in lies – the lies of an aborted European civilization; the lies of liberation. Nothing but lies.'

There is more to it than that. Both brothers excited admiration because they were frank and honest about what was wrong with Africa, or the Tropics in general; both caused an undercurrent of concern that they were something more than just brutally honest. The Trinidadian writer Derek Walcott came out with it: V. S. Naipaul, he has said, does not like Negroes. Were they not using a larger stage maybe, as well as their literary genius, to settle old scores against the coolie-baiters in the streets of Port-of-Spain? Shiva would have denied the direct charge, but I wondered. When I showed him once a passage from a facetious essay of Evelyn Waugh's about the unwisdom of freeing the slaves – 'The sugar plantations have been ruined or mechanized, and the Negroes, instead of following the example of the indentured coolies and becoming small proprietors, working long hours in the country, drift to the intermittent employment of the towns. They have proved quite unfit for retail trade: they are clumsy mechanics, a superstitious and excitable riff-raff hanging around the rum shops and staring listlessly at the Chinese, Madeiran and East Indian immigrants, who outstrip them in every branch of life' – he just said, 'True enough'. He himself sometimes and without resentment said that all Africans were mad (he also sometimes said that all women were mad: 'They can't help it. It's a phase in their historical development').

That may suggest contempt, which is a fairer charge than dislike. He had not gone to Africa with hostile preconceptions, was not one of those he mentions, with their aggressive Indianness, 'the kind of atavism which turns young men into "pundits" and "Negro-haters"'. But then, apart from his sharp-eyedness, he was well aware of the tension between black and brown, from Trinidad, to South Africa where black gangs kill Indian shopkeepers, to Uganda whence Amin expelled the Asians en masse. His relationship with the West Indies was tense. Some of his childhood memories were affectionate. He used to explain to me the words of a Mighty Sparrow calypso record I had, having quoted a Sparrow song in his Jonestown book. Then we went one summer's day to Lord's to see the West Indian tourists playing Middlesex and for reasons I cannot now remember washed up at a party afterwards. Meeting Deryck Murray, the West Indian wicket-keeper, Shiva reminded him that they had been at school together; the conversation did not prosper. Then again, although he was affectionate to the Indian diaspora he did not want to spend much time in its embrace. And although fascinated by his ancestry, he was appalled by the reality of India: 'Sometimes we Hindus have to weep.' He was no more impressed by those who made a profession of their Third-Worldliness than by European racists; he did not admire Salman Rushdie.

All the same, it should not have surprised him that *North of South* was disliked by professional Africanists. He would have been more amazed to learn (as I have read) that he had become 'a cult figure among discerning South Africans', sc. less than half-witted whites. He had no time at all for the South Africans, either the Afrikaners – 'a bad people with a bad culture' he said when I explained their history – or the white liberals.

He ran into trouble again with his next book. After a series of bibulous farewells in pubs and restaurants, Shiva left with Jenny for the United States where they spent 1979–80: he was working on what became *Black and White*. This was the story of the mass-suicide in the middle of the Guyanese jungle by the deluded followers of the Californian heresiarch Jim Jones. It is a book written in bitter rage, highly personal, not what his publishers had expected – 'They've got a horse of a different colour', he told me with glee – and not designed to mend Shiva's reputation in bien pensant circles. (He said to me at the time, 'I'm trying to repair my liberal image,' to which I replied not very consolingly that there was a good deal of repairing to be done.) You may say many things in this liberated age but you do not describe Californian feminists as aggressive and hirsute, even if they are. The progressive Third World experiment is epitomized in a showpiece school modelled on a World Bank blueprint:

> The chickens did not look very well. One was lying on its side.
> 'What's the matter with that chicken?'
> 'It's just having a little rest.'
> 'Are you sure? It looks sick to me.'
> He went into the coop. He tickled the chicken. It remained motionless. He brought it out of the coop. Its head lolled. It turned out that the chicken – all the chickens – were starving.

Black and White was published under the significantly different title *Journey to Nowhere* in the United States where one reviewer, in the *Washington Post*, I think, complained that Naipaul did not seem to care for American optimism or utopianism, as embodied apparently (even if in degraded form) by Jones's colony. Indeed he did not, if that was what they meant. His real contempt here was reserved not so much for Jones, still less his pathetic victims, as for the background which produced them, the California which 'sucks in America's loose ends. It twists and tangles them in a hundred different ways'; for mountebanks like Buckminster Fuller or Huey Newton or Mark Lane; and for Jones's radical-chic admirers who might have seen that he was a crook and a charlatan before he became a murderer. The fraudulence drifted like a cloud to Guyana, where 'the lies fell like steady rain'.

Someone described Guyanese politics in terms of Bolsheviks and Mensheviks; but 'there were no Bolsheviks and Mensheviks in Guyana. There are transported Indians and Africans, locked into poverty, resentment, ignorance and delusion.'

Another reviewer was Martin Amis who admired the book but wondered when Naipaul was going to provide what only he could, one of his novels. It came at last in 1983. 'Block' as I say is a trite and foolish word, but Shiva had complications which he needed to work out. He was obsessed with style, with the art which conceals art, with the need, in another sense, to remove all artifice. He had told me how he wanted to cut down to the bare bones of language and the manner of his third novel, *A Hot Country*, is simple and spare. Maybe for that reason the book was underrated when it came out (one or two reviewers had by then scores to settle). Shiva had ill-advisedly laid a false trail by calling the hot country (no longer Trinidad) 'Guyama', which he insisted was not Guyana. His characters, most memorably the high-minded liberal Aubrey St Pierre sitting in his bookshop in a distant country where no one reads books, were original and remarkable creations. It was entered but not shortlisted for the Booker Prize; Vidia rang Shiva to commiserate. The brothers' relationship was complicated. Shiva had followed closely in Vidia's steps: England, Oxford, fiction, English wife, London, even the same literary prize – the John Llewellyn Rhys – for their first novels. Shiva was on his guard where his brother was concerned. He had begun his literary career just as Vidia had reached a peak with his, winning the 1971 Booker Prize with *In a Free State*. But they were not rivals. Vidia dedicated his novel *The Enigma of Arrival* to his brother's memory.

Shiva was to some degree on guard with most people.

He was difficult, hypersensitive and blundering at once.
He caused social havoc without quite realizing why. In
1984 he visited Australia to write a book about the
country. On his return he described his visit over lunch
as a series of social disasters into which he stumbled as if
by accident. Was it really accidental? Did he really not
know about the whole series of Australian complexes he
was treading on; that in certain areas of polite, progressive
Australia you cannot refer to the Aborigines, however
accurately, as a primitive people, still less say to their self-
appointed guardians, 'You are the sort of people who
want to keep them primitive'? A couple of anthropologists
'had taken exception to my remarking over dinner in
a Chinese restaurant that the Aborigines could not be
considered to have created a culture as sophisticated –
say – as the Chinese or Greeks or Indians or Egyptians
had done'. As a result of this indiscretion he was banned
by the Northern Land Council from its territories.

His personal relations were complicated as well. I have
spoken of his thick and thin skins. He could be mag-
nificently brusque at one moment, disrupting many an
afternoon or evening, morbidly sensitive at the next. He
noticed the smallest slight, consciously intended or not.
Had I noticed, he once asked, how a journalist who had
just left the pub always made some boisterous reference
to colour in his presence? The man in question was notoriously hairy-heeled, but he liked Shiva and I don't think
he wished to hurt him. On another occasion Shiva rang
to ask if he could come and see me that evening. I said
yes, of course, though I could not imagine why it could
be so urgent. What he explained as we sat for several
hours emptying a bottle of whisky was that he had visited
two women whom I knew. Or rather, he had visited one
of them, with whom he had an amitié amoureuse, a
flirtatious friendship (it was an odd conjunction). The

other woman had joined them, and something had been said. Long as the evening lasted, I never fully understood what it had been; I tried to reassure him and, I think, succeeded. Of course, he may have been right: hypersensitive people are sometimes just that, not imagining atmospheres or nuances where they don't exist but detecting them where others miss them.

This sensitivity, mutatis mutandis, was the key to Shiva as a writer, to all his books including the Australian book he set to writing on his return. As ever, the work on his book went slowly. Shiva was still a trial to his publisher (he showed the beginnings of his book to the ever-tolerant Christopher Sinclair-Stevenson, who gently asked whether after several months he might not have got beyond Ceylon on his outward journey). He suffered as he wrote. He would ring up to say that he had cabin fever and wanted a drink or lunch, when he would shamble into the pub like a bear and shout my surname and stare around him, myopically, half-aggressively. And then we would go to lunch until Victor at the Gay Hussar* brought the third slivovitz and we realized that it was nearly four. Occasionally I took him for a last one at the Garrick; once we went to Muriel's but after one drink he said, 'Could we go? I find this place infinitely depressing.' And then he would make his way home.

For years Shiva and Jenny lived in gloomy rooms in Warrington Crescent. At last they managed to move, to an airy first-floor flat in Belsize Park. His fortunes were turning. He had scarcely been a penniless author in a garret, but he needed to make his mark beyond the critical success he had enjoyed early. There was every sign that it

* Shiva had trouble with the menu there. He ate neither beef nor, because 'Hindu and Islam got mixed up in Trinidad', pork; and because of Hungarian memories of the Turk, the restaurant did not serve lamb.

was coming. He was commissioned by the *New Yorker*, his publisher awaited another novel eagerly, agreed to another travel book tolerantly. Shiva had a party in his new flat early in 1984 before setting off for Australia; I made him a frivolous present of a pre-war guidebook to Australia. When he returned we lunched and drank together again. In February 1985 he had another party for his fortieth birthday, ten months before mine. In July I myself had a party, for the publication of a book; the Naipauls did not come because, Jenny told me later, they had had a succession of bruising evenings where Shiva had as usual provoked quarrels without seeming to want them. A few days later Dick West rang the *Evening Standard* where I was working to say that Shiva and he were in a pub in Soho and why didn't I join them; I could not. A few days after that a message was left on my answering machine in the evening but I did not return home and did not learn until I was rung at the office the following morning that Shiva had died of heart failure the day before. He had always been afraid of death. At least it came to him suddenly. We saw him cremated, by Hindu rites but in less romantic circumstances than Ram's in *Fireflies*, at Golders Green crematorium.

When he died *The Times* ran a fatuous obituary, speaking of 'unfulfilled promise'. That was untrue as well as stupid. Truer was to say, as his father-in-law Douglas Stuart did in the preface to Shiva's posthumous collection, *An Unfinished Journey*, that to speak of waste is otiose. Truest of all, I thought when sitting at the memorial meeting for Shiva, would be Grillparzer's epitaph for Schubert, whose art buried with him 'einen reichen Besitzt, aber noch viel schöneren Hoffnungen'. My feelings at his death were a mixture of grief and grievance. There was sorrow at the loss of a friend with whom one had hoped, without thinking about it, to stroll into middle age, and there was irritation with a capricious providence for removing a writer whose future books one wanted, again without thinking about it, to read.

In a Diary paragraph, written in ten minutes when I heard of his death, I called Shiva 'a lovely man and a great writer', and at his funeral another novelist said something about appropriate hyperbole. But Shiva was at least an imminently great writer, in pursuit of a great subject in our race-made age, when the obsessions of the anti-racists sometimes match those of the racists. Shiva hated racism and intolerance but, unlike many who would say the same of themselves, he looked around him with burning honesty.

It is not hindsight to see that all he wrote is of a piece. He was acutely perceptive about personal relationships: his three novels testify to that acuity. But he had another perception. He understood, cut to the heart of, one of the great questions of our time, the clash of cultures, them and us. Are cultures different? Of course they are. Are some superior to others? That depends what you mean by superior, but of course so if you are initially thinking in Eurocentric terms. A tribesman in the rain forest may be the moral equal of the neurotic don or drunken journalist or other flower of our civilization, but he is not likely to be their intellectual or cultural equal, not in their terms. To pretend in the manner of Basil Davidson that the achievements of tropical Africa can be favourably compared, in Europe's terms, with those of Europe is absurd, and the comparison does Africa no service. We must see people as they are, in *their* terms, to be fair to them. Lumping them together – as Shiva said, treating Ethiopia, Brazil and India as if there were no essential difference between them compared with their common colonial inheritance – is insulting and misleading. The attitude of many white Australians towards the Aborigines is patronizing and idiotic, at its most idiotic in the claim of those intellectual Australians who think that the Aborigines enjoyed the original socialist society. We – the West, the North, what passes for European civilization – have done quite enough harm to other peoples, from corruption to extermination, without, on the one hand, proselytizing them, first with Christianity, then capitalism, then Marxism; or, on the other, treating them as scientific curiosities, dear little things, primitive people who must be kept primitive.

Shiva saw equally the humbug of Blackness and of Third Worldliness. 'People only look alike', to continue an earlier quotation, 'when you can't be bothered to look at them too closely.' The two cant ideas went together: 'Being Third World meant being *Black*. To be Black was to be *oppressed*: to be a constant hurting casualty of the twin evils of slavery and colonialism.' But 'the Third World is an artificial construction of the West – an ideological Empire on which the sun is always setting.' And so, 'In the name of the Third World, we madden ourselves with untruth.'

Although he was conspicuously sane, Shiva sometimes seemed to be maddening himself with truth. He was working out his subject, and how he would deal with it. He was supremely well-equipped to do so since, 'The longer I live, the more convinced I become that one of the greatest honours we can confer on other people is to see them as they are; to recognize not only that they exist but that they exist in specific ways and have specific realities.' He did not live long enough to explain this as he might have. Like Schubert, Shiva left a rich possession but still fairer promises. He had much more to say.

9
MARGARET FITZHERBERT

Most parents have their favourite child. This need not matter to the others: it does them no harm to learn that life isn't fair. And in large families, I think, the favourite child of the father or mother is often the hero and inspirer of his or her brothers and sisters. So it was with Margaret FitzHerbert. I did not meet Meg until we were both nearly thirty but there is no secret about her childhood and her relationship with her father. It is all most delightfully set out in the books by and about Evelyn Waugh: the increasingly numerous biographies, the Diaries and above all the Letters. Meg seems to have been her father's favourite almost from the time she was born in 1942, his locust year of wartime frustration referred to in his dedication to her of his masterpiece *Unconditional Surrender*. As she grew up she commanded more and more of his attention and affection; 'as a result of these accidents' – of her removal from the nursery where she disliked her nanny and from her first convent school where she disliked the nuns – she herself later wrote, she became official favourite, 'a position neither resented nor sought by my siblings and one which carried with it the risks of disproportionate disfavours as well as the advantage of privilege.' There was more to it than that. Her elder brother Auberon★ has explained that she was

★ For clarity's rather than genealogy's sake, there were seven children of Evelyn and Laura Waugh: Teresa, b. 1938, m. Professor John D'Arms 1961; Auberon or Bron, b. 1939, m. Lady Teresa Onslow

the only person who 'could humour him when he was disgruntled, cheer him when he was melancholy, amuse him when he was bored'. Since by his own account and others' Waugh was a martyr to the point of derangement to ill-temper, boredom and melancholy, this gift was important.

The whole family were high-spirited, and tough. Evelyn described the motto

Quisquis amat dictis absentem ridere vitam
Hanc mensam indignam noverit esse sui

which his grandfather displayed in the dining-room: 'Backbiters are not welcome at this table', adding that it was 'a precept to which those I have known of his descendants have not proved notably amenable', and all of Evelyn's children could be sharp-tongued. This was a reaction. A phrase in which he described himself as seeing his children for 'ten, I hope awe-inspiring, minutes a day' tells perhaps more than he intended. He was, of course, part monster and part mad – though a great deal more than that – and scarcely the sentimental drooling modern parent. Meg was the exception. Their relationship as it can still be followed in print is not only funny but deeply touching. He wrote to her regularly through her exile at school and their subsequent separations, and they are much the most human, loving and lovable of all his letters.

Not everyone finds the personality revealed in his published letters as winning as I do, and by no means everyone who knew him liked him. But no one could fail to be moved by his letters to Meg: 'I really am very worried that you should be unhappy, darling little girl ... I am unhappy that you should be unhappy ... Sweet Pig [his

1961; Mary, b. and d. 1940; Margaret, b. 1942, m. Giles FitzHerbert 1962, d. 1986; Harriet or Hatty, b. 1944, m. Richard Dorment 1985; James, b. 1946, m. Rachel Green 1976; Septimus, b. 1950, m. Nicola Worcester 1976.

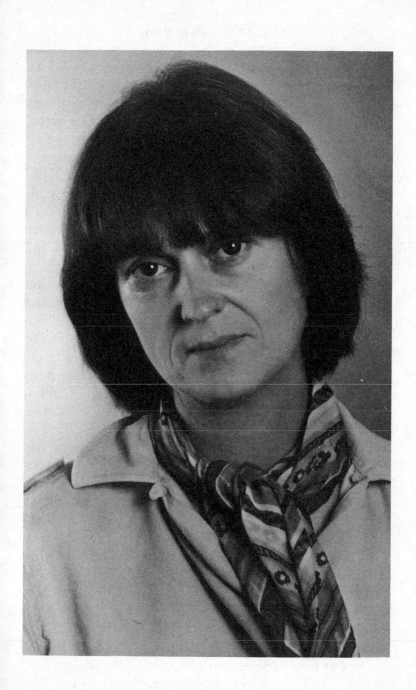

name for her] of course I am not angry with you . . .' To
a nun at one of the convents which Meg passed through,
he wrote that she was 'very pretty, very stupid, with
abounding charm'; this at much the time that he wrote
to his friend Ann Fleming: 'My sexual passion for my ten-
year-old daughter is obsessive. I wonder if you'll come to
feel this about your son. I can't keep my hands off her.'
She was obviously a tricky as well as attractive and beguiling girl who was in a series of scrapes at school. He cajoled
her and cosseted her, with nonsense letters – 'pious Hatty
[aged eight] has given up rum and cigars for Lent' – and
tender advice: 'You do not have to tell me that you have
not done anything really wicked. I know my Pig. I am
absolutely confident that you will never do anything
dishonest, impure or cruel. That is all that matters.'

He urged her, as he urged his rebellious son Bron, to
put up with the boredom and drudgery of school in the
hope of something better, which was to say Oxford. In
the event, Meg did not get in. Instead, she went to London
to work as secretary to the Jesuit Father Philip Caraman
in the Office of the Vice-Postulation for the Forty Martyrs.
As far as a Protestant can understand this esoteric work,
it was to collect miraculous and other evidence for pro-
moting these forty Catholics who had been put to death
under the Tudors and Stuarts from their Blessed state to
Sainthood. Another Catholic priest I know was similarly
engaged with regard to Newman, and said that every
year he became less enthusiastic about the cause. Father
Caraman and Meg were more successful. Their pamphlet
in support of the claim had a first printing of 100,000,
Meg's father noticed, and, in due course, canonized the
Forty were.

Living in London, Meg formed a circle of friends of
whom her father affected to disapprove. He was perhaps
jealous. The funniest and most touching letter of all was

written, ostensibly by 'Teresa Pinfold', to Father Caraman whose secretary Waugh knew would see the letter, recording 'a signal favour granted to me through the intercession of the XL Martyrs'.

> I have a daughter to whom I was tenderly attached and who in her youth seemed to reciprocate my affection. I obtained highly responsible employers for her in London & highly responsible lodging with a Catholic family. In spite of these advantages she soon gave me cause for anxiety. She took to the use of tobacco & spirits and fell into low company and despite generous wages has repeatedly had to be rescued from debt. Her appearance is slatternly. She gave up writing to me, though she had solemnly promised to do so frequently.
>
> I took my sorrow to the XL Martyrs asking for a change of heart for this girl, but without result.
>
> I then changed my prayer & asked that I might become detached from her and indifferent to her ingratitude & lack of natural affection. This petition has been answered. I no longer care how dirty her fingernails are or how disorderly her habits. I no longer have the wish to visit her. I hope you will see fit to include this favour in your bulletin.

Before long Meg fell in love with one of her low company, a dashing Irishman called Giles FitzHerbert, at that time undecided on a career. His prospective father-in-law eyed him with a certain reserve, based on undisguised jealousy: 'Twenty-seven years old and has not done a hand's turn ... A Catholic of not very pious disposition, father killed honourably in the war, a brother I haven't been allowed to see, whom [sic] I suspect is a skeleton in the cupboard (as is mine, and also Laura's for that matter). She had a number of suitors of a kind an old-fashioned father would have preferred, but she must have Fitz-Herbert, & so she shall. She wants children & that is a thing I can't decently provide for her.' And again, 'It is, to me, a bitter pill and ungilded. I would forbid the marriage If I had any other cause than jealousy and snobbery. As it is, I pretend to be complaisant. Little Meg is ripe for the kind of love I can't give her. So I am surrendering with the honours of war – without war indeed.' And once more to Diana Cooper, 'I suspect him of being a crook but I cannot doubt the sincerity of his love for Meg – nothing to be got from her or me.' And, referring to an earlier letter, he added, 'When I said "gentleman", I meant of respectable ancestry. He has rather a common way with him.'

They were married in the autumn of 1962. Giles stuck with commerce for a year or two. Evelyn remarked that he 'gets more like P. G. Wodehouse's "Ukridge" daily [and] believes he can make his fortune by importing tropical fish'. It nearly took Ukridge's eccentricity and optimism to make a stab at politics as Giles did in 1964 in one of the great quixotic gestures of the age, standing as a Liberal in Co. Fermanagh where he was roughed up by Protestant bullies. Before long he forsook trade for the Foreign Service and although they had bases in England they spent most of their time en poste, in Rome, Kuwait, Cyprus and then Rome again.

For years Meg's time was occupied with her five children and with diplomatic life. Sadly as it seems with hindsight she did not begin to write until her thirties, and she published only one book. But it showed her quality. She was highly intelligent as well as independent-minded and fearless, even if her mind was largely unmolested by formal education. When she began to work on a life of her grandfather Aubrey Herbert she had to acquaint herself with the background to his times as well as his life;

I remember her asking me who the Hughligans* were. The book which she finally produced was worth the wait. Meg did not only have an hereditary gift for expression, she was original. I thought when reading the book that she showed a genuine and unusual talent: it was no mere piece of family pietas, she had got into the period and inside the extraordinary character of Herbert.

Although I say that she was not formally learned, she understood people. She was a voracious novel-reader, often buying three new books a week. It is banal to divide life into those who think and those who feel, the reflective and the instinctive, but education does not just mean a Gradgrinding accumulation of facts. During the 1988 presidential election, Kitty Dukakis said that her husband Michael ('the liberal-governor-of-Massachusetts') had never read a novel in his life. It was meant as part joke, part affectionate sigh: crazy kind of guy, only wants to read about Swedish land usage. It struck me as one of the most tragic things I had ever heard said of anyone. The novel is one of the great sources of moral education in our civilization. It teaches how life is more than any number of statistical compendia, and on any serious subject I would always trust the judgement of a Meg to that of a Mike.

Not that our tastes were the same. I have written warmly of Meg and her family and what used to be called her connexion, but in truth the words 'West-country Catholic' chill the blood. This is well caught in Ferdinand Mount's novel *The Selkirk Strip*, where a gruesome snobbish couple recite Belloc together. Belloc was the cause of a sharp exchange with Meg. I said, unoriginally, that he was a wonderful writer, especially in the children's

---

* The young Tory ultras or Die-hards, or Ditchers, led by Lord Hugh Cecil who conducted a violent resistance in the House of Commons to the Parliament Bill in 1911.

verse (the religious poetry gives me the creeps) but an awful man. She snapped at me, 'Don't be silly. Of course he was a nice man.' There was no point in making priggish noises about her nice man's Jew-baiting, it occurred to me at the time, and it occurred to me again when reading her book on Herbert with its cold-faced descriptions of the parasitic Jewish hangers-on of London society.

This came in part from the upper-class toughness, mimicking which was an important element of her father's make-up. It was inherited on the other side, too, the Herbert hardness which even in Meg's case I saw underlying her gentle character. A friend who came to know the whole clan of Herberts and Waughs well said that dealing with any of them was like touching wire wool, and I knew what she meant, even with Meg. Though I greatly enjoyed her company I was not always at ease. Like all of the family, she had sharp eyes and ears as well as tongue, and pounced on anything foolish or pretentious. And of course they were much given to the humour known as teasing, which some have suggested is a symptom of unhappiness.

'I expect that in ten years time she will be back at my doorstep with a brood,' Meg's father said frivolously before she was married. That did not happen, but in the end her marriage did not prosper. She returned to England and the large, untidy, attractive house she had bought in one of the crumpled little valleys of Devon, where she could see her children and her brothers and sisters and her friends, and write. In January 1986 she was in London for the evening with two friends. They had gone to a vernissage at a gallery in Camden Town, had just left, and were crossing the road when Meg was hit by two cars and killed. She was forty-three.

Any death at that age is a waste. Meg's was as sad as any. When I heard the news I found it impossible not to think of her father: 'You see, I feel that with Meg I have exhausted my capacity for finding objects to love.' He once wrote her a letter of reproach when she was playing up at school: 'Don't get it into your silly head that anyone hates you or is unfair to you. You are loved far beyond your desserts, especially by your Papa.' Beyond her desserts I don't know, but she was loved. She would have written more books; she was just coming into her own as a writer; as Bron Waugh has said, she might have written a memoir of her father which would have been cherished as long as anyone reads anything. But that was not why Meg was mourned. Behind her intelligence and sharpness was a personality of autumnal melancholy and gentleness.

10

PHILIP LARKIN

Great artists have always been less and done more than the public wishes to believe, Hans Keller once said. He had England in mind, I suspect. Other countries have their chers maîtres and their Goetholatry but in England there are more insidious traditions of literary biography, of obsession with artists' personal lives, of Rowsean nonsense about Dark Ladies, of the cult of the author, from Johnson to Waugh, as personality. But the purist attitude on its own will not quite do, either, because there are some who really are both interesting as people and as writers, and the attempt to separate one from the other is false.

Four years after his death, Philip Larkin still looms large over the imagination of literary England. Our interest in him as a man is not diminished by his own cult of privacy, rather the opposite. There is that handful of work, two novels, four slim volumes – they really were slim – of poems wrought with enormous effort, other bits and pieces; the sphinx-like smile staring from the dust jacket; the impassive courtesy with which he put off interviewers who wanted to meet him or parried them if they could not be put off; the lifetime spent in the most respectably unglamorous of professions as a librarian, and lived in towns chosen as if by instinct for their remoteness and lack of glamour, Belfast and Hull. Still, Larkin could not and did not quite say, Here are my works, complete and as external to me as a cabinet-maker's chairs. How could he? Lyric poetry is the most personal and intimate of all the arts; the author of 'Talking in Bed' or 'Wild Oats' could not claim that they were as abstract as a string quartet. In fact, Larkin conspired gently with the cult-worshippers, out of good nature more than vanity, I suspect; he was kindly to his acolytes, even though he must have found some of them a trial; and, because of this cult of Larkin and the danger of Kinbotean presumption and projection, I should say straight away that I barely knew him. But I liked him as well as admired him, and little as I knew him I felt (presumptuously and project-ively, perhaps) that I understood him. His voice spoke to many people; it certainly spoke to me.

The outline of his life is easily drawn. Philip Larkin was born in 1922 and grew up in Coventry where his father was City Treasurer. His social circumstances are worth mentioning because they are often misunderstood. In the 1950s Philip was portrayed as a type of a generation, grammar-school if not red-brick, who were supposed to be working their way up from the lower-middle to the upper-middle class. This was quite false of Larkin. As he said himself, he remained all his life as the solid bourgeois he was born, with 'a succession of maids and that sort of thing' in his childhood, exactly middle-class, in fact. For the class below, private education was impossible, for the class above anything else was impossible. For the class into which Larkin was born, the choice between a minor public school and the local grammar school was a nice but not an urgent one; the only difference was that the grammar school was likely to be better academically. Philip went to the Henry VIII School in Coventry, where there were no aesthetes reading Firbank and Pater and no little press to print his poems, a point he makes in 'I Remember, I Remember'. Its last line became one of his most famous: 'Nothing, like something, happens anywhere.' This is true rather than morose: more child-

hoods are empty than unhappy, especially for someone like Larkin who suffered from short-sightedness as well as a stammer and was in any case solitary by nature (which is not a mental illness).

In the autumn of 1940 he went from school to St John's College, Oxford, an eminent and respectable foundation if one with, at that time, a reputation for heartiness and college spirit, where he was joined the following spring by Kingsley Amis. Whence, then, the subsequent hostility of Maugham and Waugh towards these plebeian upstarts, unless it was the nervous violence of men not wholly secure in their own social position? Amis had been at the City of London School, a public school, 'minor' to be sure; it is not Eton, but then neither is King's School, Canterbury, or Lancing. Amis soon met and made friends with Larkin, whom he described as a normal, hard-swearing, hard-belching undergraduate. A clue, here: the 1940s generation were in conscious reaction against their predecessors, both the political Thirties – Philip recalled Kingsley's mimetic gallery including the local comrade: 'Eesa poincher see ... assa poincher see' – and the camp Twenties. They were beery not crême-de-menthey; after the war, Philip was back in Oxford, saw a youth in long hair and gently flowing cloak, and thought, Oh, God, *that's* all started again. The reaction was mock-philistine, despising not merely aesthetic languor and ivory-tower preciosity but, rather in proto-Pseud's Corner spirit, any expression of enthusiasm for Art.

But mock-anything can become the real thing. Amis's line about filthy Mozart, Larkin's 'Books are a load of crap', were written on a level of irony, but – a fairer and more perceptive criticism of Waugh's was that, while his generation had struggled through the Classics and turned to English Literature for delight, the younger men studied Eng. Lit. as their subject and learnt to hate it as a consequence. Kingsley Amis nearly confirms this. Not only did Larkin and he loathe Old English; not only did Philip inscribe at the foot of the last page of a college volume, 'First I thought *Troilus and Criseyde* was the most *boring* poem in English. Then I thought *Beowulf* was. Then I thought *Paradise Lost* was. Now I *know* that *The Faerie Queen* is the *dullest thing* out. *Blast* it'; but Amis has 'no recollection of ever hearing Philip admit to having enjoyed, or again to being ready to tolerate, any author or book he studied'. A joke? Or a sad truth in jest? Forty years later, an exasperated interviewer from the *Paris Review* ('Have you tried any consciousness-expanding drugs?') asked him what he had learnt from his study of other poets, and Philip said, 'Oh, for Christ's sake, one doesn't *study* poets! You *read* them.' But studying was just what he had done at Oxford. Although this generation's contempt for airy-fairy l'art pour l'artisme was not entirely wrong, it is hard not to think that it led them astray, if only to their adulation of low-brow books, to sci-fi and thrillers and to the ludicrous belief that Ian Fleming was a good writer (or indeed could write at all). Even their passion for jazz seems undiscriminating, loving New Orleans as a species and failing to see the difference between Armstrong who was a genius, and Pee Wee Russell, who was if not the dullest thing out then not in fact very good.

When he left Oxford with his First, Philip kicked his heels at home. His eyesight kept him out of the Forces, and he sat and wrote until a letter from the Ministry of Labour asked what he was doing. Without it seems reflecting on what sort of police state he was living in where this could be asked, he quickly applied for a job as a librarian and found his career for the next forty years. Librarianship suited him, he used to say, with its order and calm. He had no special feelings for books as objects, never collected them, kept at hand only those he wanted to read, but he took his duties seriously. 'They' – the undergraduates – 'call me a fascist,' he once said to me. 'That's because I don't think they should steal books.' He was proud of his work; he once sent Barbara Pym as an affectionate greeting a photograph of the new building – 1970s hideousness – of his Hull Library; as she said, one of the strangest messages ever from a man to a woman.

This was his external, professional life. His writing was his other life, and a curious story. He wanted to be a novelist rather than a poet – Kingsley Amis wanted to be a poet – and always claimed that the novel was the more important form. In fact he wrote two novels. During an astonishing spurt of youthful productivity in 1943–46 he wrote his first book of poetry, *The Night Ship*, published in 1946, then *Jill*, which came out the next year (both of them published at his own expense), and then *A Girl in Winter* in 1947, which proved to be his last novel. Both novels are excellent and touching works, but I never thought they showed that fiction really was his missed métier. Nor was it easy to guess from the first book of verse, heavily in the shade of Yeats and Auden, what he would become as a poet. He published a pamphlet, *XX Poems* (of which I have never seen a copy) in 1951 and another five three years later, but it seems to have been in his early thirties that he discovered himself as a poet. People still remember the thrill of reading 'Church Going' when it was published in a magazine in 1954, and when the collection which included it appeared the next year as *The Less Deceived* Larkin was established as the poet of his generation. He achieved and maintained this position on an exiguous output. That book was followed by two more, *The Whitsun Weddings* in 1964 and *High Windows* in 1974, which both really were slim volumes, fewer than thirty poems each. He then retreated into silence. He had tried to write another novel after *A Girl in Winter* but could never finish it. Twenty-five years later he found himself unable to write any more poems, which was sad for us to whom his poetry meant so much.

Why did it? The popularity of his poetry is almost as interesting as the poems themselves. They appeal to many people, many that is who don't read much (or any) other contemporary verse. They are simple, or rather they are lucid while being also technically ingenious to a high degree. Larkin's poems illustrate his own throwaway definition of writing poetry – 'playing off the natural rhythms and word-order of speech against the artificiality of rhyme and metre' – which was true of all English verse until quite recently when poets abandoned not only the artificiality but the natural rhythms and word order.*

But it was neither the lucidity nor the technique which held readers, I think. It was the subject; or the mood. As a man and as a poet Larkin presented himself as a conservative, insular depressive. His literary journalism is intelligently conservative, his jazz criticism is more petulant. This was the one regular column that he wrote, for the *Daily Telegraph* in the 1960s, and it became a long plaint at what he had to listen to: 'I dislike such things not because they are new, but because they are irresponsible exploitation of technique in contradiction of human life as we know it. This is my essential criticism of modernism, whether perpetrated by Parker, Pound or Picasso: it helps

---

*Perhaps I should say here that my own ear for verse may easily be judged. In 1977, Philip published 'Aubade', his magnificent poem about the fear of death, with its first line, 'I work all day, and get half-drunk at night'. A couple of years later in a *Spectator* column I quoted this from memory as 'I work all day and go to bed half-drunk'. A friendly postcard of reproach from Hull asked me how many rhymes I could think of for 'drunk'.

us neither to enjoy nor to endure.' Perhaps I reacted unfavourably to this in the precise context since, although I had long got over any admiration for Pound and Picasso which I had affected at seventeen, I still admired the bop musicians of the 1940s, and later jazz also. And I was always uneasy about the cult which Larkin's generation made of New Orleans jazz. Not only were we (jazz) modernists in the 1960s scornful of the preposterous 'trad' revivalism, but I could entirely understand the post-war jazz men's wish to distance themselves from what jazz had represented socially a generation before. The Modern Jazz Quartet were a slight joke (or were when I still followed jazz), but I had some sympathy with their dressing in tail coats and comporting themselves like a string quartet. What they – to Larkin's scorn – were putting behind them was the caperings of Armstrong's generation, which itself was not many steps away from the Chocolate-Coloured Coons.

The conservatism took literary expression also in *The Oxford Book of Twentieth-Century Verse* which he edited. The anthology shocked some critics with its perversity, but its real weakness was spotted by John Gross: Larkin should have ended his selection at least ten years earlier than he did, rather than include a token sampling from his juniors, with whom he had no sympathy. Gross detected 'a vein of positive cynicism in the book' and I cannot believe that the last poem which it prints was included in anything other than a spirit of scornful irony, to show without comment what English poetry had come to.

What England had come to he found just as dejecting. His only conscious political poems are sourly despondent, like 'Homage to a Government', not to say the 'Unwritten Poem on the Queen's Jubilee' which he sent to friends in 1977:

Along with Healey's trading figures
Along with Wilson's squalid crew
Amid a rising tide of niggers
Who could look as good as you?

though perhaps it is necessary to say that this is meant to
be funny, ironical as well as satirical. Likewise, he was
direct with interviewers: 'I adore Mrs Thatcher.' 'I've
always been right-wing.' He identified the Right with
certain virtues, 'thrift, hard work, reverence, desire to
preserve', and the Left with 'idleness, greed and treason'.
Not a reactionary ogre merely, he lived to pose as a
xenophobic one. 'Oh no, I've never been to America, nor
to anywhere else, for that matter ... Who is Jorge Luis
Borges? ... *Foreign* poetry?' A lot of this was as it were
to tease the *Paris Review* and he expanded on this last
plausibly if not quite correctly to the effect that one can
never really know a foreign language as one knows one's
own.

Then again, if he thought that abroad was bloody and
foreigners were hell, he was scarcely at home in his own
country. He was all of England, but an England which
had ceased to exist, if it had ever existed. He was old-
fashioned, in his attitudes, his values, his conduct, a man
of very scrupulous standards (something which those who
criticized him from, as they supposed above, like Edith
Sitwell who was shocked by the line about removing his
bicycle clips in 'Church Going', did not grasp). I remember two letters to the Editor he wrote. One deplored
Bernard Levin's repeated use of his newspaper columns
for his personal, domestic purposes. The other raised a
matter of delicacy: he had written to a colleague in the
University whom he did not know personally as 'Dear
Smith', or as 'Dear Warlock-Williams' (see his 'Vers de
Société'), or whatever, and had been taken aback by the

offence it caused. What was the correct form? He had not realized he was touching on a real raw, class nerve, the vocative use of surnames in speech or letters being much resented by lower-class people as upper-class patronization.

And he was out of place among other people, or so he claimed. It was his stock in trade, the socially crippled bard of unhappiness: 'Deprivation is for me what daffodils were for Wordsworth', for whom 'Life is first boredom, then fear'. The particular form depression took was amorous, a better word here than sexual. He never married and it is yet another reflection on our age, when the bachelor is a disappearing species, that this caused so much speculation. As is well known, he had a long-standing attachment to a lady whom he alluded to in print but did not discuss ('We'll talk about anything except sex,' he said to me once when I had an interview with him). I suppose I speculated too. A friend of Philip's whom I asked once said that he thought he had never married for fear of sexual failure. I may have said I thought that was why people got married; at any rate, it struck me as far-fetched. Larkin could be semi-jocose on the subject. 'Sexual recreation' seeming to him 'a remote thing, like baccarat or clog-dancing'. Some of his most famous lines dealt all too accurately with middle-aged sexual resentment, of those who have seen

> Bonds and gestures pushed to the side
> Like an out-dated combine harvester
> And everyone young going down the long slide
> To happiness, endlessly

and for whom life, sexual life above all, has become

> A brilliant breaking of the bank
> A quite unlosable game.

But the heart of what he had to say on the subject is not embittered or curmudgeonly. When talking in bed

> It becomes still more difficult to find
> Words at once true and kind
> Or not untrue and not unkind

or when parting on an agreement

> That I was too selfish, withdrawn
> And easily bored to love.
> Well, useful to get that learnt

represent something more general than the experience of a shy and reclusive librarian. In fact these poems, and

> Sex, yes, but what
> Is sex? Surely, to think the lion's share
> Of happiness is found by couples – sheer
> Inaccuracy, as far as I'm concerned

are an intelligent commentary on what may one day be seen as the really curious thing about the present age: not its sexual-revolutionary licentiousness but its belief that everyone has a destiny to be fulfilled with a perfect other, physical and spiritual union between Tristan and Isolde who become Darby and Joan; a belief which to say the least is not supported by everyday observation.

Was Philip really the poet of unhappiness? And was he really the monster of misanthropy he sometimes pretended to be? The answer to the second question is easier. He hated children, he said; when he was a boy he thought he hated everyone but when he 'grew up I realized it was just children I didn't like'. He loathed Christmas shopping, which reminded him of how much he disliked everyone. He often got letters from fans or poems sent by young hopefuls, he said. What did he do with them? I asked. 'If there's no stamped envelope they go in the waste-paper basket. If there is I tell them to fuck off.' It is necessary once more, I wearily suppose, to point out that irony and exaggeration take many forms. If we really believed that Kipling thought cigars better than women, then 'A woman is only a woman ...' would not be funny. And, anyway, who hasn't felt that about children, or Christmas shopping, or uninvited correspondents?

The point is that Philip was, as I think anyone who ever met him would agree, a charming, courteous and companionable man. His misanthropy was in a sense a literary red herring, like Evelyn Waugh's snobbery or Shiva Naipaul's sense of exile. He was, I do hope it is by now clear, very funny, on and off the page. The title of the poem 'Vers de Société' was not an accident: one of the dozen poets he kept to the left of his working chair was Praed, and Larkin kept alive the tradition of skilful comic verse as much as of the introspective lyric. The disappearance of verse like Praed's or Calverly's is as grievous a loss as the love poems or nature poems whose absence from young poets Larkin lamented.

His wit was as sharp as it was subtle. It could be simple: I received a flyer for an evening, to which Philip had contributed, commemorating the opening of the Humber bridge. 'World première' was printed at the top; alongside was written, 'And dernière too, I imagine'. Or it could strike home: we were talking about a common friend whose marriage had broken up. 'Tell me,' Philip said, 'did Jane leave him for someone else? Or just as a general comment?' He was oblique and laconic. Charles Monteith still looks uneasily at the inscription on his copy of *XX Poems*. 'To Charles, most efficient of friends and kindest of publishers.' And he had the rare authentic gift of self-mockery, not least in résumés of his own work. 'Aubade' became:

When Philip gets pissed off with death
He turns all prophetic and saith,
  'Fuck death, and fuck dying,
  The Cosmos ain't trying
– And Christ, all this gin on my breath!'

His consciousness of unhappiness was not so much overdone as misplaced, missing the point. In his fulminations against modern jazz he looked back to the 1920s and 'the music of happy men'. But was it? Schubert was once asked at a party to 'play some jolly music' and replied, 'There is no jolly music, dear lady. All music is sad.' In the sense that he meant, perhaps that is true not only of music but of any art.

If Philip Larkin ever said anything true about himself it was his reply to a woman (who can she have been?) who said to him that she didn't like his poems: 'I don't like them much myself, but they are the only ones I can write.' Whether they were about the impossibility of love or the fear of death, which came to him of cancer far from unawares in 1985, his poems were completely true. And, in fact, they were the man himself.

I I

HUGH FRASER

Of all myths, the most persistent and enticing is the myth of the golden age: things were better once. It applies to public life as well as to music or architecture. Once we had greater, wiser statesmen; once politicians were honest. Of course, a myth may be true. The reactionary fallacy – that everything is getting worse – is no more logical than the progressive fallacy that everything is getting better, but some things do get worse. I cannot think any music-lover believes that European music is at a higher state today than two hundred years ago when Mozart was in his last years, Haydn in his prime and shortly to take on (not very successfully) the young Beethoven as a pupil. Nor can there be many people who think that English architecture is more attractive today than three centuries ago in the days of Wren and Hawksmoor.

A century and more ago the House of Commons was full of unimaginative people; for centuries the characteristic Member of Parliament was a not very intelligent country gentleman who came to London for social as much as political reasons. He did not work, not that is in an office or at a job: he lived off the rents which were collected for him. Although he was disdainful of trade it is not true, as is sometimes said in detraction of him, that he was ignorant of commerce or industry since he was closely connected with what was in a sense the most important business in the country, agriculture. He did not think of politics as a full-time occupation and indeed it only took up part of his time, from when shooting ended to when the harvest began.

These gentlemen legislators were by definition drawn from a tiny section of the population. By the end of the nineteenth century fewer MPs were landowning gentlemen of leisure: many of them had to work to keep alive, as lawyers or even as journalists. But it was almost impossible for the poor – the great majority of the population – to become Members of Parliament. This was not fair, or so at least many people came to think. And so a fateful and baleful step was taken: Parliamentary salaries were introduced. Strictly speaking, these weren't salaries but fees; MPs were regarded as self-employed for purposes of income tax, and the sum did not compare favourably with what middle-class people earned in the professions or in business. But the principle was established.

What happened subsequently was a classic illustration of the law of unintended consequences. Certainly it was easier for poor men to sit in Parliament, as was intended; but what no one foresaw was the creation of a new class of professional politician. This if anything weakened the intended effect: the early Labour MPs were all working men and, as both Labour's friends and foes have tended to forget, the party was from the beginning not a specifically socialist organization but just what its name suggested, a party – originally a Labour Representation Committee – whose purpose was to give a voice to the labouring classes and their representative institutions, the trade unions, in national politics. No sooner had this been done than Labour began slowly to lose its class character and with each successive Parliament more prominent Labour politicians were bourgeois. And with each successive Parliament more and more Members on both sides of the House saw themselves as full-time professional politicians, some of whom indeed had never known any other trade.

The Commons sat for longer and longer sessions and passed more and more laws. 'Parliament cannot go on legislating for ever', Palmerston had said, but recent parliamentarians have seemed determined to prove him wrong. While the number of working men and union officials decreased on the Labour benches, so did the number of landowners or merely gentlemen on the Tory benches. By the 1970s they were an endangered species. The Conservative Party had taken fright at its own image, grouse-shooting and White's-bar-hopping. By a mysterious process of consultation in 1957 Macmillan had succeeded to the Tory leadership and prime ministership instead of the middle-class and capable R. A. Butler; in 1963 he engineered the same process to ensure that Butler did not succeed him but rather the landed, Etonian Earl of Home. This episode and the 'magic circle' which had arranged it were denounced by Iain Macleod in a furious article in the *Spectator* in 1964 and in the next year, following a defeat in the general election, the Tories chose the utterly plebeian Edward Heath as their leader. Eight years later, after Heath had won one election but lost two, they understandably ejected him. Their choice of leader in 1975 was the most surprising since Disraeli became leader in 1868: Margaret Thatcher. She had defied convention by challenging Heath, but once her challenge had been thrown down, she was joined by one of the last remaining authentically patrician Tory MPs, Hugh Fraser. Hugh in fact could be said to have altered the course of British politics. On the second ballot, Mrs Thatcher won as she needed to an absolute majority of Conservative MPs' votes (she won 146; William Whitelaw, who had not stood against his leader on the first ballot, 79; Geoffrey Howe and James Prior 19 each; John Peyton 11); but on the first ballot, her majority over Heath was only 11 (130: 119), and Fraser won 16 votes which in theory might have tipped the balance back in Heath's favour.

Hugh Fraser was a Scotchman, a Highlander and a Roman Catholic; he would have listed them in the reverse order. The family were Norman adventurers who had settled in northern Scotland, acquired Lovat near the Beauly river in Inverness-shire in the early fourteenth century and been ennobled in the fifteenth. The twelfth Lord Lovat was condemned to death in Scotland in 1698 while still in his twenties after his abduction of a female cousin and was in fact put to death on Tower Hill in 1747 when he was almost in his eighties because of his role in the Forty-Five. This setback to the family lasted a couple of generations, after which the title was restored. In the nineteenth century Highlanders ceased to be terrifying tribesmen who threatened to charge down from their hills and glens and tear the country apart and became amusing, pawky fellows in kilts (usually of fake tartan), chastising English anglers and stalkers for their incompetence. Hugh descended from the Highlands to Ampleforth and Balliol. He was, I imagine, a shy as well as a charming young man. In Joan Wyndham's wartime amorous memoirs there is an amusing pseudonymous portrait, written with female unfairness, of an attractive but inhibited young officer, still too much in the thrall of his priests for the satisfactory pursuit of pleasure.

The Frasers had a family regiment, the Lovat Scouts, first raised during the Boer War, which Hugh joined when the World war broke out but through some military obtuseness the Scouts were sent off to garrison the Shetlands. That war threw up its own special units, of varying degrees of respectability: considering that they were largely recruited at the bar of Whites it is perhaps surprising that they were so effective. Hugh's was Phantom, a reconnaissance unit composed of racehorse owners and actors and budding journalists and other loafers, from which he transferred to the SAS and parachuted into Yugoslavia. Years later, after his death, a colleague of his said that she and others were unaware of Hugh's war service but that was characteristic of him. Hugh was a younger son, which conditioned his life. He was never of course poor as the poor are, but he never had much money, and he never showed much inclination to make any.

The war over, he went into Parliament, winning the Stone division of Staffordshire, the only one of seventeen seats in that county held by the Tories in the 1945 Labour landslide. He sat in the Commons for almost forty years, during a period when the quality of Members of Parliament steadily deteriorated. Is that romantic fantasy, another illusion that things were better once? I think not. It may not be itself an argument against democracy, but it is a fact that when the United States came into being, created by patrician republicans, it had presidents like Jefferson; now that it is a true democracy it has presidents like Bush. When English politics were still confined to a small aristocratic class and their hangers-on we had prime ministers like Peel, Gladstone and Salisbury. Now we have democracy, and Wilson and Heath. There were nasty elements in the House forty years ago, reactionary bigots on the Tory benches, envenomed fellow-travellers on the Labour. But even then there was a leavening of Members who were not in the full, new sense professional politicians, who worked still in their union or who spent their days at the Bar and only came to the House late in the evening (the young David Maxwell Fyfe would take the sleeper to Manchester and after a day in court would take an evening train to London for the ten o'clock division, day after day). And there was room for someone like Hugh, 'the one hope of the Tories' during the Attlee years. Hugh had had political ambitions from boyhood; his family assumed that he would be prime minister one day, the first Roman Catholic premier. In the event, his political career did not take the form he had hoped; he only climbed a few feet up the greasy pole, holding junior office under the first four post-war Tory prime ministers, Churchill, Eden, Macmillan and Douglas-Home. His last and highest rank was as Minister of State responsible for the Royal Air Force. He never reached the Cabinet, never knew office again after 1964. There were several reasons for this, almost all of them creditable to Hugh. He was his own man, and he was a romantic. When the critical vote was taken to end capital punishment Hugh voted against retention, despite very heavy pressure from the hangers in his constituency. (I was disappointed when he subsequently voted to reintroduce capital punishment for terrorists and other carefully selected categories: there may be a better moral argument for hanging political murderers than domestic, but the practical argument is a good deal worse.)

He took up causes. Two will always be associated with him. In 1967, after communal massacres, the south-eastern province of Nigeria broke away and declared itself the independent state of Biafra. This struck a chord with many of us: a small nation justly struggling to be free. It also struck alarm in some quarters. Since the colonial territories of Africa began to be granted independence in the 1950s their territorial integrity had been a touchstone for their rulers, enshrined in Organization of African Unity declarations at Mogadishu and elsewhere. The reason for this is not far to seek. More than fifty African countries have been granted statehood in the image of European nation-states but they are not nations at all, nor, many of them, in any serious sense states. They are completely artificial constructs, the arbitrary results of the partition of Africa by the European Powers, whose borders run through national groups – the Ovambo, for example, who live in northern Namibia and southern Angola – or incorporate several groups uneasily.

The Ibos were a highly distinct people with their own language and culture, and their own religion: they were Catholic. That might suggest that the cause of Biafra was no more than a function of reactionary Catholicism. In reality it was supported by men of the Left as well as of the Right, and another Biafran partisan, Auberon Waugh, says that he found it surprisingly difficult to drum up support among his fellow papists. Anyway, the Ibos lost. They were sometimes called 'the Jews of Africa' and the other people to whom Hugh gave his heart were the Jews themselves. He was a lifelong philo-Semite – not a disposition often found among the Catholic aristocracy – and an unswerving friend of Israel. He did not live to see the Palestinian uprising of 1987 onwards; I think that both the drop in Israel's esteem and the conduct of the Israeli government would have dismayed him.

This friendship for the Jews was all of a piece with Hugh's romantic chivalry, which made him a man out of place in the 1960s and 1970s. It was not to be expected that someone like Heath would find room for Hugh in his disastrous government of 1970–4 (Hugh took his revenge in 1975, not that he ever thought consciously of revenge). The woman who defeated Heath did not offer him office, either, although he was at least knighted. It was then, in the late 1970s, that I came to know Hugh, first of all as a friendly face at political or journalistic parties and party conferences. I found his quietly dashing charm cheered me up, and political conferences and parties are places where cheering up is needed. He was a regular guest at the *Spectator* lunches, especially the annual lunch held wherever the Tories were conferring. At lunch in

Brighton the American girl sitting between us turned and whispered that Hugh had his hand on her knee. When a girl said the same thing to Mr Balfour on her left about the man on her right he asked how long it had been there and, when told since the fish, replied, 'Then it must stay there.' I forget my reply.

We then discovered that we had a common interest, in the South African mining magnates. My interest was strong enough to make me leave my job and write a book about them, in which Hugh encouraged me. I was pleased with my proposed title, *The Randlords*, under which it was eventually published: for reasons which I never fully understood Hugh disliked the title, but I stuck to it. He himself had become involved with a book on Barney Barnato, about whom we would talk over lunch. It was not quite clear to me what the book was to be, or Hugh's part in it, but he was diverting on that as on other subjects. I still followed his political career with admiration, for his independence of spirit and mind. There was one sad moment: in 1983 Hugh was one of the rebellious MPs who voted against the Government for a higher increase in parliamentary salaries. To be fair, I suspect that Hugh's contribution to this wretched – and successful – initiative sprang from chivalrous motives, because other Members seemed poorer than he. All the same, it was a deplorable episode.

To eulogize Hugh as an independent aristocrat in politics may sound snobbish; the simple truth is that he was a Christian gentleman of a kind now rarely found in the Commons, or anywhere else. His life was not pure happiness, quite apart from his political disappointments. He married Lady Antonia Pakenham in 1956 and she had six children, but the marriage did not prosper and came to an end in circumstances wounding to Hugh. But he bore these sorrows privately and with great dignity. He was a good and admirable man, as few professional politicians are or perhaps by the nature of their trade now can be.

To be a Member of Parliament was once a duty and a responsibility: it was not a 'job'. Tories had once a profound scepticism of the power of government to change life for the better – 'How small of all that human hearts endure, The part that kings or laws can cause or cure' – and radicals for that matter were suspicious of government and supposed that money spent by it would be used incompetently at best, corruptly at worst, a belief inherited by the Labour Party in its early years. Since then we have been conditioned to think that the more legislation passed the better, the more money spent by the government the better, the more power exercised by the State the better: a close look at the actual achievement of Mrs Thatcher's supposedly radical government which was going to roll back the State shows how deeply engrained this belief has become, and how hard it is to do anything about it.

With this growth of government politics has grown also and it is difficult to exaggerate the degree to which professional politics as a concept and professional politicians as a class have instinctively taken on a new realm and power, if only to justify it and their existence. Little as they might like it, most people passively accept this. Why? To say that professional politics and politicians are inevitable in modern societies seems incontrovertible. It is controverted in practice. Switzerland is the best-defended country in Europe but does not have an army at all in a conventional sense. Switzerland is the best-governed country in Europe, and does not have politics or politicians in the conventional sense. Members of the Swiss parliament receive no salaries. They are elected, they meet from time to time to perform their exiguous duties and pass the occasional law, and they go back to real life while a handful of full-time ministers and civil servants run the country to the very limited extent that it needs to be run.

The conventional thing to say of Hugh would be that he was a man of another age, which in one sense is true enough, but it seems to me as it were defeatist. Why should Hugh's virtues, of chivalry and gaiety and romantic independence of spirit, have vanished – even in politics? Why should we be condemned – be resigned – to political life conducted entirely by hacks and mediocrities, by exhibitionists and buffoons and persons of the basest character who see in public life no more than the opportunity for working out their own irrelevant spites and inadequacies by bossing other people around at the same time as filling their pockets with 'consultancy fees' and other bribes; eighteenth-century corruption without the excuse of eighteenth-century taste when spending the money? The real truth is that politics should not be treated as a profession, perhaps not as a 'career' at all, because in the end politics are not important enough. There, Hugh Fraser had something to teach.

12

DWIGHT MACDONALD

Literary biographers nowadays give us as much detail as we could want about their subjects' sexual lives but neglect what is even more important, their financial lives. How much did they earn, when, and how? For journalists, money is the truly ever-interesting subject; 'The economics of journalism', a book still to seek. Not every journalist has had to write entirely for a living, and a still-further neglected area of the neglected subject is the influence of private income. Lady Bracknell claims that Gwendoline has been attending a lecture on 'The influence of a permanent income on thought', and the subject is not entirely a frivolous one. Two of the most remarkable magazines of the century owed their existence to their creators' financial independence. Karl Kraus could not have published the *Fackel*, the extraordinary one-man journal which excoriated Vienna from 1899 when he was twenty-five until his death in 1936, if he had not been a rentier.

Less famous but in its way a scarcely less remarkable magazine was *politics*, published in New York from 1944 to 1949 by Dwight Macdonald. Macdonald was an upper-class American, born of well-to-do parents and educated at a famous prep (anglice, public) school, and at Yale; he once said that when he resigned from the editorial board of the *Partisan Review* in 1943 he was graduating 'from the third and last of the educational institutions that have been important in my life – the other two were Phillips

Exeter Academy and the Trotskyist movement'. As a schoolboy in the early Twenties he was a self-conscious aesthete, founding (with two other members) a club, the Hedonists, which proclaimed 'Cynicism, Estheticism, Criticism, Pessimism' and produced two numbers of 'Masquerade', 'a magazine of extreme preciosity', whose members revered Wilde and Mencken, wore monocles and purple batik club ties at meetings, and 'carried canes as much as we dared'. It sounds curiously like English school life at the time as described by Cyril Connolly and Evelyn Waugh.

As an undergraduate his political rebellion was confined to writing an editorial asking whether the ancient Professor William Lyon Phelps honestly thought he was competent to give a new course on Shakespeare, by complaining about compulsory chapel in a letter to the President of Yale (who thought it disrespectful of Dwight to have written on both sides of the sheet of paper), and by organizing the 'Hats Off!' campaign by the lower classes – undergraduates in their first three years – against the exclusive privilege of the seniors not to wear hats on the campus. (American colleges have changed in these sixty years.) When he left Yale Macdonald became an executive trainee at Macy's Department Store until he quickly realized that he was in the wrong place, or would have realized it anyway if he hadn't been offered, on graduating as a trainee, a job at the tie counter for $30 a week. He resigned and kicked his heels until a job came his way. It was gloomy kicking, as he had no money of his own.

Then through a Yale friend he found a job on *Fortune*, the new magazine which Henry Luce was creating for his *Time* stable 'to celebrate the saga of American business'. It appeared, Macdonald later remarked, shortly after Wall Street collapsed in October 1929 when 'many entrepreneurs would have given up, but Luce had the Sta-

lingrad spirit and persisted'. Dwight remained there until
1936, increasingly sceptical about American capitalism
as he saw it at close quarters. As sometimes happens, the
magazine attracted a group of gifted young writers out
of sympathy with its ostensible aim, who wrote about the
New Deal rather than about business. For a few years
there was a compromise, 'a pastiche of mildly liberal
articles on social themes and reluctantly written corporation pieces dealing with enterprises that had somehow
managed to make a profit', until Dwight wrote a series
on the U.S. Steel Corporation which became increasingly
critical until its last instalment which began with a quotation from Lenin that monopoly was the last stage of
capitalism leading inevitably to socialism. Not very surprisingly, the piece was heavily cut and Macdonald
resigned. His decision was made easier because of his
financial position: he had been able to save some money
from his salary – a huge one in those days of $10,000 –
and he was now married, to a woman with a private
income.

In his late twenties he had for the first time become
involved in politics. He read Marx and the Marxist classics
and 'as much of a pragmatist as the next American – fellow
by the name of Luce – I leaned towards the Communists
because they alone on the American Left seemed to be
doing something'. He became an enthusiastic fellow-
traveller, supporting all the right – that was, Left – causes,
and accepting the Party's direction when a section of the
Newspaper Guild was formed in the *Time–Fortune* office.
So it was, mutatis mutandis, for many of the brightest
and best of that generation who fell for Communism
when a century earlier they might have undergone
religious conversion.

Their gods failed as (to borrow Malcolm Muggeridge's
phrase and garble pious metaphors) they passed their sta-

tions of the cross: the Molotov–Ribbentrop pact in 1939, the Prague coup in 1948, Hungary in 1956. I suggest in my chapter on Goronwy Rees that the 1930s and 1940s intellectual fellow-travellers misrepresented their motives for supporting or joining the Party. If they joined for the wrong reasons, they left in a sense for the wrong reasons also. All those landmarks were episodes of foreign policy, as Stalin or his successors partitioned Poland for the fourth time, absorbed Czechoslovakia, reconquered Hungary, and so on right down to the unhappy Afghan adventure. It is no consolation to Poles, Czechs, Hungarians or Afghans, but in each case Soviet Russia was doing no more than act like a Great Power. (Even in 1979 I thought that it was scarcely for us English to reproach anyone too loudly for invading Afghanistan: in the nineteenth century we did it three times.) The reason for leaving the Party or its thrall was the same reason for not joining in the first place: the character of the Soviet regime since 1917, and especially during the height of Stalin's Terror – which was also the heyday of Western fellow-travelling, and not by coincidence, I believe.

The way in which Dwight's eyes were opened was most unusual, but should not have been. Browsing in the Party bookshop in early 1937 he came across *The Case of the Anti-Soviet Centre*, the verbatim transcript of the Second Moscow Trial. After reading it he still believed for a time that some sort of conspiracy had taken place, until he noticed all the contradictions and lack of motivation and absence of supporting evidence. 'But even a first reading, with a pro-Soviet bias, convinced me of the absurdity of the trial's main political thesis: that Trotsky had conspired with the representatives of Hitler, Mussolini, the Mikado and most of the surviving Bolshevik leaders to kill Stalin and restore capitalism in Russia.' He was both amazed by the way in which the Stalinists had so lost touch with reality as to circulate this document, which could only arouse grave doubts in most people who were not Party members, and disgusted by the behaviour of the 'liberal' weeklies, the *New Republic* and the *Nation*, which reserved judgement while actually endorsing the prosecution case. He joined the Committee for the Defence of Leon Trotsky and, having begun writing for those liberal weeklies, soon fell out with them: 'The speed with which I evolved from a liberal into a radical and from a tepid Communist sympathizer into an ardent anti-Stalinist still amazes me. It was much the quickest of my political transformations – which some have seen as indicating an open mind, others of levity – probably because the Soviet myth is least able to bear close inspection.' This is from the closest thing Macdonald wrote to an autobiography, and it is a pity that he never wrote full-length memoirs. He knew 'everyone' in New York – though he once pointed out that this intellectual circle was a restricted one by English standards, including no politicians or businessmen – and he had an acute eye turned on his friends. He complained for example of Mary McCarthy's 'absurd need to be ultra-smart', and also said of her that her smile is 'not what it seems. It's a rather sharkish smile. When most pretty girls smile at you, you feel great. When Mary smiles at you, you look to see if your fly is open.'

In 1936 the American Communist Party suspended the Partisan Review, its literary front, rightly suspecting that the faith of its editors Philip Rahv and William Philips was wavering. Dwight and his friends approached them the following year and revived *P.R.*, to defend the autonomy of culture above politics though with a clear anti-Stalinist line. They were accused by the Communist press of social-fascism, Trotskyism, dilettantism and infantile ultra-leftism and were boycotted by Party-liners like

Howard Fast and Albert Maltz, but 'we were able to rub along with Dos Passos, Farrell, Gide, Silone, Orwell, Mary McCarthy, Delmore Schwartz, Meyer Schapiro, Edmund Wilson and T. S. Eliot'. Dwight helped to edit *Partisan Review* for five years, as well as writing for the *New International*, the organ of the Socialist Workers Party. In 1939 he joined the American Trotskyist Party, more from an emotional or moral than an intellectual impulse. He opposed not only capitalism but Soviet communism, and the World war. He resigned after a comical disagreement about an enormously long article on National Socialist Germany, which the journal only published a small part of, followed by a letter of remonstrance, not quite as long, from Dwight to the editors. It was comical, as he saw himself in retrospect, because of the discrepancy between the huge intellectual labour which he invested in the dispute, which still impressed him many years later, and on the other hand both the insignificance of the occasion and his chances of success, which did not exist: 'After all, I was trying to persuade Bolsheviks to tolerate free thought so that I could remain in the party, in *their* party.'

In 1943 he had another row, with the editors of the *Partisan Review*, which he left. Dwight was argumentative rather than quarrelsome, I think, easily provoked into a letter to the editor, or a colleague, or anyone else with whom he disagreed. His style was punchy, as well as witty and salty. It was highly individual, reflecting his own personality and utterly original mind, just as it was with Kraus, however little they otherwise resembled one another.

He needed somewhere to make his voice heard. In February 1944, *politics* began with Dwight as editor, publisher, owner, lay-out man, proofreader and chief contributor, with his wife Nancy as business manager and angel: it lost almost $1,000 in 1945, in other years between $2,000 and $6,000. The magazine began with a circulation of 2,000, stuck at 5,000, was published monthly for three years, quarterly for the last two. There were a number of distinguished contributors, Simone Weil and Bruno Bettelheim, more regularly Andrea Caffi, Nicola Chiaromonte, Paul Goodman, Peter Gutman, Victor Serge, Nicola Tucci and George Woodcock; only one of them, Macdonald noted, an American. But much the most important contributor was Dwight Macdonald himself: it was his *Fackel* in that sense also. A collection of Macdonald's writings was published in 1957 as *Memoirs of a Revolutionist*. Some of the pieces in it had been published in other magazines from the *Partisan Review* to the *New Yorker*, but most of them were the intensely personal heart of *politics* written by its editorial inspirer. Never having heard of Dwight Macdonald, I came across a paperback of these *Memoirs* in a bookshop by chance. I should remember where and when even without the sentimental bookmark, a San Francisco cable car ticket dated 1965, the summmer before I went up to Oxford. It affected me as deeply as any book I had ever read, as much as Orwell's essays – and there is an obvious comparison between the two. I wanted to know about the author, and to meet him. So I did, though not for another sixteen years.

Why did *Memoirs of a Revolutionist* have that effect, why is it still a remarkable book, and why was Macdonald one of the outstanding American writers of his time? The years of his most creative engagement with politics (and *politics*) were the central years of this century, morally as well as chronologically. 'Mankind's worst century' has become a hackneyed slogan of self-regarding and self-pitying intellectuals. It is almost (but not quite) too obvious to need stating that the second half of the century has for most people on earth been much the best time in history; and even for those of whom that is not true the more drastic obsessions of nuclear catastrophists and eco-doomsayers do not apply: if you are starving to death in a village in Mali or Bengal, the prospects of nuclear war and the destruction of the ozone layer are not your chief concerns, they really aren't.

But the 1940s truly was a terrible decade: the greatest war in history, Hitler's murder of the European Jews, Stalin's continuing terror, the destruction of so many cities (and their inhabitants) by bombing, adumbrating the threatened complete destruction of civilization, the replacement of National Socialist Germany by Soviet Socialist Russia as the enemy of the Anglo-Saxon allies and the imminent coming true of Orwell's prophecy (the accuracy in that respect in *1984* is rarely given its due) of a world divided among superpowers fighting petty wars by proxy in the Tropics. These were Macdonald's subjects. He dealt with them scintillatingly, and profoundly. And amusingly: he was a much funnier writer than Orwell, whose blokey qualities of honesty and decency made it difficult for him to be witty. An aside from Macdonald could send up the absurdity, or horror, of what he was describing. In the winter of 1939/40 the Red Army invaded Finland. That presented no problems for Communists and fellow-travellers in the West, but it did for American Trotskyists whose already minute party split into two fragments. Those following James P. Cannon – 'backed (alas) by Trotsky' – supported Soviet Russia as a 'workers' state' ('degenerated') which was bringing social-ism (degenerated) to Finland, and those led by Max Schachtman opposed the war as imperialist aggression. Macdonald was in the second group, though ' "support" and "oppose" had no practical meaning, of course', he later wrote. 'The Schachtmanites did not go off to fight for Baron Mannerheim, and the Cannonites didn't volunteer for the Red Army (which would have shot them).'

Politics had larger issues than that to deal with, though 'large' is misleading: the question of scale, of human proportion, was in a sense Macdonald's driving concern. He wrote at length on 'the responsibility of peoples' at the end of the war when it became known what was the nature and the extent of what had been committed in the name of National Socialism. And of Germany: he took Marx's phrase, 'Germans have thought in politics where other peoples have done', and pointed out that it had been reversed: the Germans had done things others had only dreamt of. On this question of collective responsibility or guilt, Macdonald was sometimes wrong in the detail. But if he underestimated the depth of popular enthusiasm for Hitler among the Germans, to almost all of whom he had something to give, Macdonald recognized the character of the National Socialist state and the way in which it had drawn from deep wellsprings of human cruelty in a way unmatched by any of the other nations engaged in the war. He was right on a deeper level, not because he picked up Hannah Arendt's theory of totalitarianism which must always become more intense of its own momentum regardless of any plausible excuse for oppression (the theory is demonstrably false) but because he saw that to blame the Germans collectively was in a sense to cede the argument. They were all tainted by the blood of Cain, eternal conquerors and barbarians, Vansittart and Rex Stout argued during the war; *Das Schwarze Korps* agreed: 'There are no innocents in Germany', the newspaper of the SS wrote in late 1944. 'Nobody after all, has preferred a democratic death to a National Socialist life.'

Macdonald saw that the Allies were in effect colluding at the collective idea of the Volk with their policy of unconditional surrender – giving the Germans no opportunity to dissociate themselves from Hitler even if they had wished – and still more with the campaign of strategic bombing or, as its victims more accurately called it, terror bombing. There were critics of bombing during the war – his criticism cost Bishop Bell of Chichester the Archbishopric of Canterbury – but none more eloquent than Macdonald. 'It is like living in a house with a maniac, who may rip up the pictures, burn the books, slash up the rugs, at any moment', he wrote as another historic European city was razed.

He saw here something significant: it was not by accident that the totalitarian countries, Russia and Germany, had neglected mass bombing as an instrument of war while the Western democracies had perfected it. The neglect was not of course from humanitarian qualms or merely because they lacked the industrial resources but because Hitler and Stalin realized the military inefficacy of bombing. The bombing campaign was a publicity stunt for the democratic peoples of England and America.

The apotheosis of bombing came in August 1945 with the destruction of Hiroshima in the twinkling of an eye. Very few people grasped at once the full meaning of the atomic bomb. Writing as a conservative Roman Catholic, Ronald Knox in his brilliant little book *God and the Atom* saw the bomb as a triple blow against faith, hope and charity. Writing as a socialist-pacifist, now of more a libertarian than a Trotskyist colour, Macdonald said that 'this atrocious action places "us", the defenders of civilization, on a moral level with "them", the beasts of Maidanek. And "we", the American people, are just as much and as little responsible for this horror as "they", the German people.' The concept of progress was now obsolete, the technical aspect of war, as Simone Weil had said, had become the evil regardless of political factors. And Macdonald observed that just as only the Western democracies had had the industrial resources for the 'conventional' bombing campaign, so the atomic bomb was 'the natural product of the kind of society we have created. It is as easy, normal and unforced an expression of the American Way of Life as electric iceboxes, banana splits, and hydromatic-drive automobiles.'

From 1945 on Dwight's dejection deepened. He still rejected Western capitalism but was, again with Orwell, in the small and uncomfortable minority who did so while loathing Soviet despotism unremittingly. After Stalin's conduct at the time of the Warsaw rising in 1944 he had written of Soviet Russia, 'Our slogan must be, once more: Écrasez l'Infâme!' He mocked Stalin, whose speech of 9 February 1946 'may be summarized briefly, since he always says everything at least three times ("moreover, after this war no one dared any more to deny the vitality of the Soviet state system. Now it is no longer a question of the vitality of the Soviet state system, since there can be no doubt of its vitality any more"). On the evidence of Stalin's barbarous oratorical style alone, one could deduce the bureaucratic inhumanity and the primitiveness of modern Soviet society.' He deplored injustice, including the Nuremberg trials: 'the difference between justice and vengeance is that justice applies equally to all.'

And he saluted independence of spirit, in whatever form. In 1948, the judges of the Bollingen Prize, twelve distinguished American writers including Eliot, Auden, and Lowell, gave the award to Ezra Pound, who had spent the war broadcasting from Italy, and who was then under arrest in a Washington mental hospital and who was awaiting trial for treason. Nor were his prize-winning *Pisan Cantos* 'by any means free of its author's detestable social and racial prejudices'. Macdonald said that he was not competent to judge the book as poetry (it would almost have reinforced his point to have conceded that, with the possible exception of Brecht, Pound is the most overrated writer of the age). The point was that when the judges claimed that they were not making a political gesture they were wrong, and that upholding 'the validity of that objective perception of value on which any civilized society must rest' *was* a political statement: 'We have a committee composed of eminent American writers and appointed by a high Government official giving an important literary prize to a man under arrest for treason. I think there are not many other countries today, and certainly none east of the Elbe, where this could happen, and I think we can take some pride as Americans in having as yet preserved a society free and "open" enough for it to happen.'

This was written in early 1949, and the dying months of *politics*. Apart from despondency, rising costs had taken their toll – printing firms and printers' unions have much to answer for in the faltering world of the little magazine – and presumably Macdonald's savings had run out and his wife's income could no longer cope. He published *Wallace, the Man and the Myth*, a short, sharp book (Dwight's copy of which I still seem to have) about Henry Wallace, Roosevelt's former vice-president: he who coined 'the century of the common man', who stood as a 'progressive' third-party candidate for the presidency in 1948 with support from the fellow-travelling milieu, and whose air-headed waffle Macdonald brilliantly analysed as 'Wallese', the dialect 'as rigidly formalized as Mandarin' in which forward-looking, freedom-loving, clear-thinking progressive people battled against reactionaries and red-baiters, clarified issues, faced problems at the grass roots or on the horizons. 'Perhaps the greatest sentence ever composed in Wallese is the following, from the hand of the master himself: "New frontiers beckon with meaningful adventure."'

Macdonald wound his magazine up 'and went back to

writing for my living (and my children's) after a thirteen-year sabbatical'. He joined the *New Yorker* from 1951 to 1965, which was ironical in view of what he had written about 'the *New Yorker*'s suave, toned-down, underplayed kind of naturalism (it might be called "denatured naturalism" . . .)', this apropos of John Hersey's 'Hiroshima', and in view also of his later 'impression I'm better known for *politics* than for my articles in the *New Yorker*, whose circulation is roughly seventy times greater'. This seemed curious, but should not be surprising. A 'little magazine' is often more intensively read (and circulated) than the big commercial magazines, being a more individual expression and so appealing with special force to other individuals of like minds.

He wrote as wittily about the young William Buckley on the Right★ as he had about Wallace on the Left. And in the mid-1950s he came to London where he worked for *Encounter* and where a number of people still remember him. He later wrote a piece, 'Confessions of an Unwitty CIA agent', which does not read quite plausibly. As A. J. Ayer has said about the earlier denials of where *Encounter*'s money came from, the source was too obvious to take the denials seriously, and in any case 'there were many worse uses to which the CIA might and indeed did apply its funds'.

Not everyone in England remembers Dwight with unmixed affection. I imagine that drink sometimes made him cantankerous, and the notoriously bad-tempered and quarrelsome atmosphere of New York intellectual life is not the same as the more sly and courtly tone of literary London. On the other hand he was an anglophile, not as immoderate as some Americans can be but admiring the

★ How many people, by the way, would correctly date unseen the words 'leading spokesman for the neo-conservative tendency that has arisen among the younger intellectuals' to May 1952?

cultural cohesion of Europe. Dwight was clear-eyed about some English nonsense. Thirty years ago you had to be outside the English pattern of class resentment and class guilt immediately to see through a piece of piffle like *The Outsider*, which had been rapturously praised by Cyril Connolly and Philip Toynbee before it was taken apart by Macdonald.* He also remarked that *Look Back in Anger* was a tedious play, consisting largely of self-pitying harangues by the unattractive hero, and that the success of *Lucky Jim*, although a very funny novel, could only be explained in terms of the cult of youth.

What Dwight liked about England was the relaxed, educated self-confidence of the weekly papers – he wrote a piece on them called 'Amateur journalism' – and of the old Third Programme. What saddened him was that thirty years ago literate cultural standards were already falling. A lifelong unbeliever ('even in late adolescence'), he wrote a marvellous review of the New English Bible, exposing its numbing banality and genteelism. Through-out, he noticed, 'harlot', which is not in current colloquial use, had replaced 'whore', which is; the only trick the translators had missed was 'Jesus burst into tears'. It was at this time that he coined 'Masscult' and 'Midcult', to describe the popular culture of tabloids, Hollywood and pop music on the one hand, and on the other hand the if anything more insidious culture of middle-brow kitsch.

Back in New York Dwight wrote on films for *Esquire*, and for the *New Yorker* again, and for the *New York Review of Books*. He may have been depoliticized, as it were. In 1953 he had written that the realistic choices during the World war had been to back Hitler, back the

---

* And Ayer, who later observed that Connolly and Toynbee had been led astray by their unfamiliarity with abstract ideas combined with a middle-class sense of guilt confronted by the work of an autodidact.

Allies or to do nothing, but that none of these 'promised any great benefit for mankind, and the one that finally triumphed has led simply to the replacing of the Nazi threat by the Communist threat, with the whole ghostly newsreel flickering through once more in a second showing. 'This is one reason I am less interested in politics than I used to be.' And four years later, 'I now think no one has a duty to interest himself in politics except a politician.'

In the 1960s he was repoliticized, protesting verbally and physically against the Vietnam war and even supporting McCarthy (Eugene, not Joe) for President. 'I now call myself a conservative anarchist,' he said at the time. When the *National Review* had first appeared and he had ruthlessly exposed its inadequacies, he said that 'we have long needed a good conservative magazine' (characteristically adding 'we have also long needed a good liberal magazine'); and when I met him twenty-five years later he said much the same, that principled conservatism had a great deal to be admired, perhaps under the misapprehension that because I was writing for the *Spectator* I was a principled conservative. He never made the notorious middle-aged shift to the right, the path so many of his contemporaries followed. (It is interesting, by the way, to read him quoting Sidney Hook on 'the new failure of nerve' in the mid-1950s.) He never doubted that imperfect Western democracy was superior – in every way – to perfect Communist tyranny, but he conspicuously did not follow those youthful Marxists who turned into elderly supporters of American military adventurism, unable to see that they had been wrong both times: Dwight was as tough-minded a pacifist in 1967 as he had been a quarter of a century earlier, more so indeed in terms of advocating civil disobedience.

But having once been a Kulturbolshevik, he became a

Kulturkonservativ. He hated the vulgarization of language evidenced by the New English Bible or the 'permissive' Webster's New International Dictionary, or by that signal phenomenon of our time, intellectually pretentious shlock, 'a feeble "highbrow" novel like, say, *Under the Volcano*', or James Gould Cozzens's ludicrous *By Love Possessed*, now forgotten but an enormous critical and popular success on its publication until Macdonald pointed out its nakedness. Wearing his movie critic's hat, he also observed that 'One of the less fortunate effects of the post 1945 upgrading of our culture is that the "art film" is beginning to influence Hollywood. One gets the worst of both − the pretension of the one, and the superficiality of the other'. He was, I had forgotten until rereading a disintegrating paperback collection of *Dwight Macdonald on Movies*, a marvellous critic, particularly good, an English film-goer must admit, on the worthlessness of the Anderson−Richardson New Wave of the 1960s. I had forgotten also just how bad *This Sporting Life* and *The Pumpkin Eater* and *Morgan!* and *Tom Jones* were.

He engaged in one other controversy. Nothing Macdonald ever wrote was more powerful than his reaction to the terrible last years of the World war and especially to the fate of the Jews of Europe. He remained on this as on other subjects conspicuously independent-minded. I was taken aback after Dwight's death to read Colin Welch's description − confirmed by someone else who had been there − of Macdonald at a party in London in the mid-1950s, baiting a woman who had been in a concentration camp. I think this must have been an aberration in his cups; he was, as I have said, cantankerous and disputatious by nature. He was also in one respect in a minority. By the Thirties, the first-generation 'New York intellectual' whose parents had come from East Europe had passed through school and college (usually the City

College of New York) and into the literary and political movements on the periphery of American life, to give them their noisy and brilliant character. Macdonald and a few other Wasps fellow-travelled with this movement, not on sufferance quite but as tokens, whose position was sometimes uneasy.

This may explain Macdonald's tone, aggressively defensive and edgy on occasions. When he reprinted an essay from 1945 on the horrors of the World war, including 'the greatest of them all: the execution of half the Jewish population of Europe [in] "death factories"', he added a footnote: 'By an ironical twist of history, the victims have now become oppressors in their turn. Since 1948, some 800,000 Arab refugees, who fled from Palestine during the fighting, have been living wretchedly in camps around the country's borders maintained by UN charity. The Israeli government – opposed by no important Jewish group that I know of – refuses to let them back and has given their homes, farms, and villages to the Jewish settlers. This is rationalized by the usual "collective responsibility" nonsense. The expropriation cannot, of course, be put on the same plane as the infinitely greater crime of the Nazis. But neither should it be passed over in silence.' This was not less admirable for the fact that in 1953 in New York such views were (as they say in Dublin) neither profitable nor popular. And he later remarked that *Ben Hur* falsified the Bible by making the Romans and not the Jews responsible for Christ's martyrdom: 'But there are no ancient Romans around and there are many Jews and $15 million is $15 million.'★

★ He concluded the review on 'a more positive and American note': '*Ben Hur* makes a real contribution to international amity. All the Romans are played by English – or at least by British Commonwealth – actors, while all the Hebrews except Miss Harareet of Israel (using her for Esther was a really inspired bit of public relations) are Americans. MGM attributes this to "Mr Wyler's determination

This passage provoked a spate of angry letters, he recalled two years later when reviewing another Biblical shlock-epic, *King of Kings*. One Jewish periodical accused him of 'ugly bigotry'. Another, 'a normally sensible magazine called *Midstream*, asked why I favoured the inclusion of a "Christ killer scene" merely "because the Gospels say there was one",' and also found it sinister that Macdonald had been a member of the advisory board of the by then defunct Jewish *Newsletter* 'which specialized in uncovering Zionist conspiracies'. To which Macdonald replied that he preferred to call it muckraking, something for which he had a penchant; that if muckraking is 'directed against OK targets like Tammany or Standard Oil or the Grand Mufti, then all Men of Good Will are on your side'; but that there were secular as well as sacred cows, and Israel was now as much one as Soviet Russia was in the Thirties. He replied bluffly to his critics. 'We live in a time when the pendulum of social justice has swung too far, when certain racial groups are sacrosanct.' He had also been accused of anti-Negro prejudice for saying that Harry Belafonte was not a thespian genius and for criticizing the acting in *Come Back, Africa* (more than twenty-five years later it is still difficult and dangerous to be objective about black actors).

All of this is to set the scene for a more serious dispute. In 1963 the late Hannah Arendt published her book *Eichmann in Jerusalem*, which provoked a bitter reaction from Jewish writers. From the 'Jewish community'? But that is to beg the question. At any rate, Hannah Arendt's critics all agreed that she had been harder on the victims than

---

not to have a clash of accents", but I suggest that MGM, in a more tactful gesture, gave the colonial parts to the country that is now acquiring an empire and the imperial parts to a country that recently lost one.'

she should, gentler on the culprits. The accusation was blunt: 'Self-hating Jewess writes pro-Eichmann series' was a headline in the *Intermountain Jewish News* while the book was appearing in the *New Yorker*; or sober: Eichmann 'comes off so much better in her book than do the victims', Lionel Abel put it in *Partisan Review*. 'In place of the Jew as virtuous martyr, she gives us the Jew as accomplice in evil; and in place of the confrontation of guilt and innocence, she gives us the "cohabitation" of criminal and victim', Norman Podhoretz wrote in *Commentary*.

The controversy was painful because it divided friends and still more because it divided them on Jewish–Gentile lines, as Mary McCarthy pointed out while defending Hannah Arendt, though Macdonald observed in turn that several Jewish writers had in fact taken Arendt's side, including Bruno Bettelheim, 'the best treatment I've seen'. Macdonald's own treatment (in the Spring 1964 *Partisan Review*) is intensely interesting. Like Mary McCarthy, he observes that the divide over the book had seemed to him even more pronounced in private conversation, where he had had 'the same experience of feeling "like a child with a reading defect in a class of normal readers" when discussing the book with Jewish friends. We often disagree even on what the book is about: Eichmann and Nazism, I'd thought, but they talk, and write, as if it was equally about the Jewish Councils. Yet out of 256 pages, less than fifteen are devoted to this question. Abel devotes half his space to this one-fifteenth of the book.'

Elsewhere, Macdonald says 'I find it depressing to talk about "Jewish friends" and "Jewish critics" when after all these years I'd thought we'd gotten beyond such labels in serious discussion', though he recognizes that this was the heart of the matter, rather than Hannah Arendt's contention, with which it is superficially hard to argue, that if the Jewish Councils had not co-operated with the

National Socialists, 'If the Jewish people had really been unorganized and leaderless, there would have been chaos and plenty of misery, but the final number of victims could hardly have been between 4.5 and 6 million'. He makes the fair point that to criticize the Jewish leadership in central Europe is not to criticize those whom they led, 'unless, of course, [it is] thought wrong, per se, to criticize Jews. Although some of Miss Arendt's more violent denouncers cut their eyeteeth on Marxist theory, they in this case identify the Jewish masses with their leaders, writing as though European Jewry were a classless utopian community. They actually seem to have forgotten more Marxism than I have'. Fairly as well, he points out the logical nonsense of saying that those like the Jewish Councils who passively co-operated with the National Socialists – or those like the Pope or the Western Allies who, as some say, did less than they might to condemn the crime while it was taking place – were as guilty as the active murderers.

All the same, I do not think that Macdonald won a clear knock-out in this context; perhaps a points victory. He was wrong about Hannah Arendt: wrong generally in his estimate of her as writer and philosopher (*The Origins of Totalitarianism* is one of the most over-praised and wrong-headed books of the age, and as falsified by events as Marx himself) and wrong in particular about her book on Eichmann. The logical arguments do not tell the whole story: there is such a thing as tone of voice, and such a thing as human understanding. What Hannah Arendt missed – and her critics too, oddly enough – is that the European Jews, leaders and led, behaved as they did not only from a long tradition of passivity in the face of persecution and the hope that if they sat tight and did not struggle it would go away. They were dazed in the face of their fate, unable to believe what was happening.

They could not believe it, because it was unbelievable. (Others from Pius XII to Churchill were dazed also, as can be seen again and again in the incredulity which greeted reports of the death camps.)

He was more right to criticize Hannah Arendt's critics. They were, he concluded obviously enough, 'writing more as Jews than as critics', and he deplored 'the Semiticist reflex' the book provoked. Even if Dwight's own response was rather bluff and thick-skinned, he was right to say that this was no way to conduct an intellectual argument. Whether the critics were coarse ('self-hating Jewess') or gentle ('In the Jewish tradition there is a concept,' Gershon Sholem wrote in *Encounter*, 'we know as Ahabath Israel: "Love of the Jewish people". In you, dear Hannah, as in so many intellectuals who came from the German Left, I find little trace of this'), they were not dealing with her arguments, good or bad, so much as reproaching her for lack of team spirit.

But most of all he was right about one of the central points at issue, more right than Hannah Arendt herself. As long before as 1947 when he still called himself a pacifist Dwight Macdonald had written with greater sensitivity or profundity than she: 'Pacifists are often asked: what would you have advised the Jews of Europe to have done after Hitler had conquered the continent – to submit peacefully to the Nazis, to go along quietly to the gas chambers? The odd thing about this question is that those who ask it have forgotten that this is pretty much what most of the Jews of Europe did in reality, not because they were pacifists, for they weren't, but *because they, like most people today, had become accustomed to obeying the authority of the State: that is, essentially, because they recognized the authority of force*.' My italics, his words, everyone's lesson.

It was, as I say, more than fifteen years after meeting Dwight Macdonald on the page that I met him in person.

Not having the taste or the face for gate-crashing heroes out of the blue and without pretext, I waited until 1981 when I noticed that he was approaching his seventy-fifth birthday, which was a suitable peg for a short profile, and when I was going to be in New York. I wrote to him and went to see him and his second wife Gloria at their apartment on the Upper East Side. We talked about his life, and about his time in England. I gently hinted that extreme American anglophilia had always seemed to me more sinister than the good old anglophobia of Colonel McCormack's *Chicago Tribune*, though of course in the context of the Angry Young Man and the New Wave, Dwight's enthusiasm for things English could be distinctly temperate. Afterwards, he wrote me a kindly and flattering letter, before my kindly and flattering article had appeared, saying that I should look them up when I was next in Manhattan or East Hampton. We did not meet again; he died in 1982.

He once used a quotation from Marx, 'The Root is Man', as the title of a book in which he distinguished between the 'Progressive' and the 'Radical':

The Progressive makes history the centre of his ideology. The Radical puts man there. The Progressive's attitude is optimistic both about human nature (which he thinks is basically good, hence all that is needed is to change institutions so as to give this goodness a chance to work) and about the possibility of understanding history through scientific method. The Radical is more aware of the dual nature of man; he sees evil as well as good at the base of human nature; he is sceptical about the ability of science to explain things beyond a certain point; he is aware of the tragic element in man's fate not only today but in any conceivable kind of society. The Progressive thinks in collective terms (the interests of society or of the working class); the Radical stresses individual conscience. The Progressive starts off from what is actually happening, the Radical from what he wants to happen . . .

The Radical admits the validity of science in its own sphere, but thinks there also exists another sphere that is outside the reach of scientific investigation, one in which value judgements cannot be *proved*, though they can be demolished in the traditional terms of art and ethical teaching . . .

The Marxists still hold fast to the classic Left faith in human liberation through scientific progress, while admitting – some of them – that revisions of doctrine and refinement of method are necessary. This was my opinion until I began to edit *politics* . . . The difficulties lie much deeper, I now think, than is assumed by the Progressives, and the crisis is much more serious.

That was the opinion in which I had been brought up until I first read that magnificent passage in 1965. To say that a book or a writer 'changed one's life' is perhaps affected if one has not become a missionary or a publicist. *Memoirs of a Revolutionist* made me nothing of the sort. All the same, few books have ever affected me as much, and I have rarely been touched so deeply as by the writing of this great and wise man.

13
SAM WHITE

'School of Hemingway journalist, you know,' a friend of mine would say of some Australian confrère, intending a larger-than-life, legend-in-his-own-lunchtime character, boisterous and garrulous, an old man who forgot nothing that had ever happened to him or forgot to tell every-one about it, determined (as the racecourse joke goes) to make a complete cult of himself. If you had not met another Australian, Sam White, you might have thought that he too fell into the category, the parody foreign correspondent, holding court in Paris where he was the *Evening Standard*'s correspondent for more than forty years.

Sam was a legend both to his contemporaries and even more to younger journalists, and he enjoyed reminiscence. As with most raconteurs, the stories sometimes needed a pinch of salt or at least needed decoding. In the summer of 1985 I took him to Lord's for the Test, my side against his, and as we were watching we talked about the 'Body-line' tour of Australia in 1932–3 when the English fast bowlers captained by Jardine had tried to intimidate the Australians. Sam said that not only did he remember the tour vividly but he had been present to witness the very ball from Larwood that felled Woodfull. I was deeply impressed and even mentioned this in the 'Londoner's Diary', but later I remembered that the Test where that happened had been in Adelaide. What was a Melbourne student doing there? Perhaps it was true, perhaps on this occasion old men did forget, perhaps in any case it didn't matter.

Although not one of those self-promoting newspaper legends, Sam was a romancer who did not mind a certain air of mystery which hung about him. The first mystery was simply, what was he called? Sam was a Jew, born in the Ukraine in 1911 when times were hard. Somehow or other – and he was only partly forthcoming here – his family managed to escape in the turbulent years following the October Revolution. They made their way to the Argentine and finally to Australia, where Sam was Australianized and grew up speaking English and loving cricket. I never discovered if he could still speak Yiddish or Russian, and he positively refused to say what his family name was; probably no more than Weitz. Australia suited Sam as much as England did Hans Keller (except that they were both Jewish exiles, I cannot think of two more disparate characters), to begin with at least. He went to school and university in Melbourne and then, while he was knocking about, 'politics bit me'. He joined the Australian Communist Party and wrote for little journals of the Left. But Sam could have borrowed Dwight Macdonald's words: they 'were a highly esoteric audience, while I was a highly exoteric writer' – or personality would be more to the point in Sam's case. And so while his friends in the party were purged for the usual crime of Trotskyism, or ultra-Leftism, Sam was expelled for 'bourgeois bohemianism', and it must be said that the comrades were right for once. He was, not quite a sybarite but at least an extreme non-puritan, a lover of wine and women.

The second of these loves brought him to Europe: he took up with the daughter of an Australian press magnate and they ran away together, so that he was in England when war broke out in 1939. Sam wanted naturally to return home and join the Australian army but when he

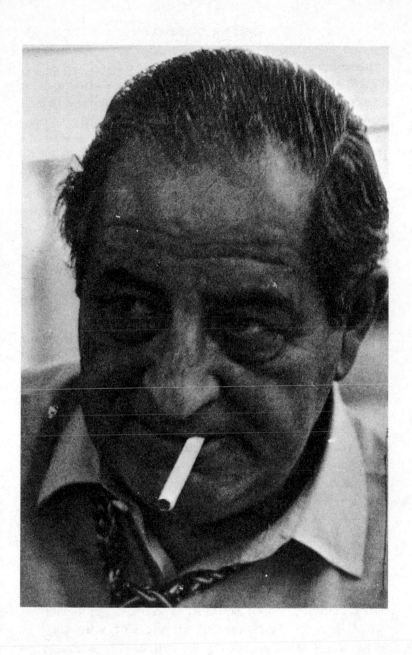

applied for a travel permit he saw – or thought he saw –
a look of contempt in the clerk's eyes for someone who
was running away. And so he stayed and joined the British
army instead. His career as a despatch rider ended with a
serious accident and an injury for which he drew a 40 per
cent disability pension for the rest of his life. When he
recovered, he joined the *Sydney Daily Telegraph* as a war
correspondent, filing for some London paper also, I think;
at least, he caught the eye of Ronald Hyde of the *Evening
Standard*. He covered the Normandy campaign and
entered Paris with the American army. Before 'liberating
the Coupole' Sam had only once and as a day-tripper seen
the city where he was to spend most of his life.

Once the war was over, Sam returned to Australia and
to what he called 'the usual Aussie treatment' for anyone
who was thought to have done well abroad, which for
this successful war correspondent meant being sent to
report from the Sydney North Police Court. He was
unable to take this work very seriously and was sacked
for not turning up on time. By now he had some savings,
and staked them on a one-way ticket to London. In 1947
he heard that the *Standard* needed a Paris correspondent.
He applied and three weeks after what he thought had
been an unsuccessful interview he was offered the job. He
was asked about his command of French and answered
honestly that it didn't exist. This was relayed to the *Standard*'s owner, Lord Beaverbrook, who said, 'At least we'll
have someone in Paris who won't let himself be bam-
boozled by the French.'

Like a few others of the old rascal's observations, this
had a canny grain of sense in it. Sam never became a
'great foreign correspondent' of the sort who used to
write for *The Times*, from Russell to Wickham Steed
to Louis Heren. He often did not write about politics at
all. Admittedly, his first decade in Paris saw the pro-

tracted tragi-farce of the Fourth Republic, when as he once put it even a reasonably well-informed man might have some difficulty remembering who the prime minister was that day. He turned for his copy instead to the gratin and the criminal classes, not to say the overlap between them. London in the bleak post-war years under the Attlee Terror did not have much glamour of its own to enjoy, and vicariously relished the round of ostentatious balls given in Paris. His readers also learned about the flourishing black market and the racketeers who ran it.

In those days Sam's haunt was Jimmy's night club. It may have been there that he came to know another Jimmy, the young James Goldsmith. Goldsmith had fallen for a Bolivian girl, Isabel Patino and eloped with her. This gave rise to a memorable exchange between Goldsmith and his father-in-law, who said, 'In our family it is not the custom to marry Jews,' to which Goldsmith replied, 'In our family it is not the custom to marry Red Indians'. It gave rise also to one of Sam's great scoops, the news of the runaway match. Or rather it should have been a scoop had the newspaper's cowardly lawyers not insisted that it should be spiked. Sam had other scoops. He made an enemy of Lady Diana Cooper when her husband Duff was Ambassador in Paris, by writing about her face-lifts, and when the Coopers were replaced by the Jebbs he vexed Lady Jebb by publishing the startling news that she had ordered the removal of the bidets from the Embassy.

All of which suggests that Sam was, if not a self-created legend, little more than a Winchell or Castlerosse, an expensive gossip columnist. Those of us who grew up reading his weekly *Standard* column and came to work with him know that he was more than that. He did not take life seriously, not always or all of it; but some of it sometimes. Any charge of frivolity against Sam is answered by not the one great scoop but the great insight of his career. Sam was convinced that the man who could and would rescue France again was de Gaulle. He predicted the General's return in 1958, and what is more he predicted that de Gaulle would grant independence to Algeria, this at a time when such opinions were regarded by most sage Parisians as little better than deranged.

Sam was ever a Gaullist. In the early 1960s he took de Gaulle's line over the blackballing of England from the Common Market. This unfashionable attitude was made easier by the fact that his proprietor Beaverbrook was in the same minority, but it was not mere calculation on Sam's part. He shared de Gaulle's suspicion that England was not, not then at least, a sincere European. As part colonial, part continental, he may have instinctively disliked the way in which British statesmen – or statesman, the posturing Macmillan – were trying to have it three ways at once, retaining the conveniences of the Commonwealth connection and 'special relationship' with the United States (albeit both of them illusory) while getting stuck into what looked a nourishing European trough. Years later in 1984 a collection of Sam's despatches was published on *De Gaulle* and is better value for someone trying to understand postwar France than many academic studies.

Sam was both unpopular and popular. He did nothing, as I have said, to ingratiate himself with a succession of British Ambassadors to Paris, including Sir Christopher Soames, or with successive châtelaines of the Ambassador's residence. It was typical of them both that he made friends with Mary Soames, who gave a touching address at Sam's memorial service in London. He made one enemy who could answer back. In 1960 Nancy Mitford published *Don't Tell Alfred*, a novel containing her usual mixture of implausibility and perceptiveness, about a newly arrived British Ambassador and his wife. When Evelyn Waugh reviewed it (in the *London Magazine*) he asked disingenuously why the character of Amyas Mockbar was so curiously drawn, without any recognizable physical characteristics. This slippery trouble-making journalist was of course a portrait of Sam: 'Amyas' as Mitford girls' back-slang for 'Sam', Mockbar the Russian name for Moscow in allusion to Sam's origins.

Although I never asked him about this episode, I knew that it had upset him. This was uncharacteristic, perhaps, though it has to be said that many journalists show a disproportionate sensitivity when it comes to what is written about them rather than what they write about others. He wanted to sue but was dissuaded by Beaverbrook who said that he expected his employees to have thicker skins.★

This sensitivity on Sam's part was real but the more surprising for being concealed in his bonhomous exterior. He knew sorrow. After one marriage, by which he had two sons, he married again and had a daughter. In the 1970s his wife contracted cancer and was treated at expensive length in the American Hospital in Paris. Sam had assumed, perhaps too lightly, that the paper would see him right financially but on top of his grief as she slowly died he found that he had misunderstood, that the paper knew no obligation to him on this score, and that he would have to bear the crippling financial burden himself. And so in his last years Sam was often in low spirits, no longer found at the bar of the Crillon, where for so many years a corner had been kept for him with his own telephone bearing his name, but at the Travellers' where

★ Beaverbrook did not dissuade another group of *Express* journalists from successfully suing the BBC when a broadcast on *Any Questions* said that all Beaverbrook's employees were hirelings.

I would meet him amid the bridge and backgammon players. His own health began to fail: there was an impressive array of medicines he took for his heart condition on a shelf in his flat, and he swore by the French health service to which he had finally subscribed after discovering the drawbacks of private treatment.

Every summer he came to London, on the pretext of attending the annual *Spectator* party in July. I can still picture him there, dishevelled and deflated, his huge and impressive head slumped, and feeling with a twinge of sorrow that his life was seeping out of him. He still wrote lively copy, for the *Spectator* which had shrewdly taken him on as well as for the *Standard*, but he was low, and tired. Each time I picked him up from Brooks's there were still flashes of the old Sam but less of the sparkle was there.

'They don't make them like that any more,' the old boys in the bar sigh, and in one sense they are right: 'make' is the operative word, rather than are born. There are many things one could have imagined Sam White doing, but not attending – or teaching at – a School of Journalism. What indeed did they teach at those American academies? There are technical arcana to the business of bringing out newspapers, but that can be learned in a few weeks. 'Journalistic ethics' cannot be taught: being honest is quite a good idea, but you don't need a lecturer to tell you that, and some of the ideologically-committed journalists most given to lecturing others on the subject are themselves dishonest in a quite different and more dangerous way. Again, some 'amateur' journalists can write well instinctively, while others spend a lifetime of toil without even acquiring the knack.

Sam was a reporter born not made. He understood that journalism means entertaining as well as instructing the reader, and that excessive seriousness is death to good reporting as much as excessive frivolity. In a life which, as his own showed, has as much to be endured as to be enjoyed, he showed that journalism can help with both. It can be fun.

14

PHILIP HOPE-WALLACE

In the Fleet Street bar El Vino (or 'El Vino's public house', as Lord Beaverbrook used to call it), there are one or two mementoes. One chair has a brass plaque screwed on to say that it is Lord Northcliffe's chair, which is puzzling. Is this, like those bedrooms where Queen Elizabeth once slept, the mark of a single visit? Can there have been a time when Northcliffe (or Harmsworth as he had been before he was ennobled and went mad) regularly drank in that dingy room? The bar was originally frequented by barristers' clerks, I believe, who unlike their masters had no clubs or Inns to go to but who felt themselves a cut above the surrounding pubs. Now that Fleet Street has all but disappeared in its synechdochic sense, perhaps the bar will revert to its former role, with only the occasional rheumy-eyed journalist dropping in for old time's sake.

When I first visited El Vino around 1970 there were a number of eminences installed there, but only one whom I was really pleased to meet. El Vino was Philip Hope-Wallace's home from the years after the war when he and Gerard Fay and James Morris shared the tiny London office next door of the *Manchester Guardian* as it then and more happily was. Twenty years later, Philip had his own little court, the centre alcove on the left at the back, where he arrived at 11.30 to hold his levée. He would already have stopped at a pub which opened earlier on the way from his home in St John's Wood. At El Vino he would sit until after two, entertaining whoever turned up apart from his regular drinking companion, the ancient book-trade gossip-columnist Eric Hiscock. Then he would lunch in the stuffy restaurant downstairs, potter about the Fleet Street drinking clubs until El Vino reopened at five, when he would return until the opera called. It was an impressive timetable; I realized that later when I came to attend the opera professionally and sometimes had difficulty remaining awake in complete sobriety.

As a young man Philip had been abstemious and frail. His schooldays at Charterhouse were clouded by ill-health, and I think that his days at Oxford were quiet. Already his personality must have been formed; his tastes were. When the Balliol pansies asked him who his favourite composers were he shocked them by saying Handel and Verdi (the correct answers were Mozart and Schubert) – 'and I haven't changed my mind since'. Well, as Hans Keller used to say, taste has nothing to do with art, and at least he didn't say Vivaldi and Bellini. Philip's tastes were not reactionary but they were often unfashionable. Sir William Glock was head of music at the BBC in the 1960s, an influential and knowledgeable proponent of modernism. During a performance of *Don Pasquale* decades ago, Philip had noticed the 'rictus of dismay' on Glock's face: 'it must be hard to imagine the contempt in which Donizetti as a composer was held in the Twenties and Thirties.' Nor with Donizetti alone was Philip both behind and ahead of his time: 'in those days I was still innocent about Massenet. I did not know that the very mention of his name in my own country was enough to set the table in a roar; to make lady members of the Bach Choir turn pale with disapproval; to induce apoplexy in the most bloodless cathedral organist.' When I read those words eighteen months after Philip's death in September 1979 I was amused to reflect that he had lived to see *Manon*

in the repertory of one of the London opera houses, *Werther* of both. In fact, I owe him a debt of gratitude, for loosening my own Anglo-Puritan suspicion of French opera, even when it was idiomatically performed. (Badly played Massenet sung in Churchillian French – still the norm at the Royal Opera – remains a torment.) Before its London revival I once asked Philip if he had ever seen Charpentier's *Louise*. 'My dear boy, I've seen it dozens of times in Rouen and Tours.'

This was one happy consequence of his chequered career before the war. Coming down from Oxford with a Third when the slump was at its deepest (its effect on the upper-middle classes, though not often the cause of destitution, should not be forgotten), he scavenged around for jobs and found one as an 'uncle' at Radio Fécamp, not far from Rouen where he had first learned French as a schoolboy. Returning to England, he worked even less appropriately for the Gas Light & Coke Co. as press officer, and sometimes selling appliances from door to door. Or so he later claimed, I don't know with what truth: both jobs became the grist of anecdote and article.

Luckily enough he was given the opportunity to review song recitals for *The Times*, and discovered his métier. He was living in Pimlico at the time; he did not write overnight notices but walked home from the concert, woke early, wrote the piece and posted it in the morning knowing that from SW1 it would reach EC4 that afternoon for the following day's paper. He mentioned this in passing, not as some cosmic lament about the way everything was going to the dogs or the devil. Though no radical he was a rational conservative without illusions, just as ready to acknowledge how some things – general standards of pianism, for example – were better today than in his youth as to lament change and decay.

He was not a scholar, not a musical historian, not thank

God a musicologist, in one sense not even a critic: it was not for him to tell composers how to write music, and he never displayed that mixture of superiority and obtuseness which gives 'criticism' such a bad name. He was a critical journalist, who possessed three essential gifts: style, a fault-less ear (and eye) and, what is rarest of all, even among celebrated critics, the gift of communicating enthusiasm. Not a scholar – but how much more he knew and felt than some dons. His knowledge of French and German and their literatures was (and is) unusual for an English-man. He went abroad for *The Times*, first to review the première in Zurich of *Mathis der Maler* in 1938, then to Frankfurt for *Faust* in August 1939, of all dates. He reflected on the temptation 'to draw comparisons between the supreme wisdom of this great play and the supreme unwisdom of the hour'. French flu had an effect on his writing in terms of idiom and syntax. Absence often of main verbs. And to say that the music 'was given a most vivid eloquence' is itself eloquent, but not quite English. Not that, whatever idiom he employed, there was ever anything slipshod in Philip's prose. He had a marked contempt (to express which his own paper gave him ample opportunity) for all that was inaccurate or meretricious or slovenly, in the written and spoken use of language, that is: Philip's attire can rarely have given much pleasure to the editor of the *Tailor & Cutter*. But I shall return to his appearance, and his attitude to the *Guardian*.

He spent the war as a press officer at the Air Ministry, 'censoring parish magazines', he claimed. I suspected that someone of his ability would have been given more scope, though with military departments you never know. After the war, he wrote for the *Daily Telegraph* and *Time and Tide* (which writeth for no man, according to George Orwell who contributed to it a few years earlier) before he landed in his berth at the *Guardian*. He was a general or all-purpose critic, for many years chief dance critic, but most of all opera-lover. Philip's only book was *A Key to Opera*, written before the war with the music critic of *The Times*, Frank Howes, and this was the subject on which he always wrote best.

He was not writing for posterity. Critics who think they do deceive themselves. Kenneth Tynan thought so, and few now read or even remember him. Philip's notices were not careful literary compositions, but extemporisations from a draughty telephone box to a bad-tempered copy-taker, a few scribbled notes in hand. At the Royal Opera House, he would tear out the cast list to use as his note-sheet and throw the rest of the programme away: he knew the story and did not need to read the lucubrations and exegeses of commentators.

When I came to read for review his posthumous anthology *Words and Music* I was struck by how good these pieces were, not only under the circumstances in which they were 'written' but in any case. He could be sharp. He recognized that with all his technical mastery Solti lacked sincerity, he said early on that Pavarotti had a 'long way to go until he gets into the Gigli or Schipa class' (he never has, or anywhere near it), and he had no illusions about Callas's technical imperfections. All the same, he summed her up over the wine glasses: 'Sings like a cat and looks like Anthony Lejeune – but what an artist!' Nobody caught her magic better than Philip: 'Mme Callas never fails to hypnotize her audience. She takes the stage as Rachel must have taken it. Visually she is magnificent. Musically she exerts so much will-power and bends art when fashioning it in such an imperious manner that even if she were to whistle the music ... she would still make us hang upon her every phrase.'

Philip used to lament that he lacked Tynan's knack of

the dazzling phrase. But some of his own lines could not be improved on. 'I think the most magical high note I ever heard was the C in the first aria of Gigli's Rodolfo in his *Bohème* here – right at the back of the gallery, it enveloped you in its beauty, as if the tiny frog-shaped figure on the stage had reached up and stroked your ear.' He was marvellous too on my heroine Caballé: 'The strong voice is so perfectly placed in the mask that loud notes and soft ones ring out like the strokes of a bell ... Mme Caballé looks like a portrait by Ingres and draws a vocal line like that of this painter; not overcharged with colour but riding on the invisible breath like the bow of a violinist on his string.' Many self-proclaimed enthusiasts for the opera might wish that they could write like that.

And the *Guardian* might have appreciated him more than it did. His last years on the paper – the 1970s when I knew him – were not entirely happy. He still went to the opera after he had ceased to be chief critic. He spoke of the new *Guardian* of illiterate Trotskyists and feminists with genial contempt (though he delighted in the names of some of his younger female colleagues, rolling them round on his tongue: 'Angela Neustatter, Mandy Merck, Nikki Knewstub. And, ah, yes, Linda Christmas, comes but once a year'). When I asked him why the *Guardian* had had no obituary of a singer, it may have been Lauri-Volpi, he replied with an almost impassive face, 'They say at the *Guardian* that young people find obituaries depressing.' Although the ever-increasing flow of Grauniadisms exasperated him they also perversely delighted him. He claimed to have intercepted an arts sub ('Why must they always employ young women from New Zealand?') sending down his account of Christoff as Doris Godunov. With the copy-takers he was less lucky. He once finished a notice which he was putting over: 'The programme began with an admirable performance of

Elgar's overture "In the South". Ends [i.e. that's the lot].'
This appeared as 'Elgar's overture "In Southend"'. A
notice of *Traviata* said that 'the music-hall direction was
in the capable hands of Mark Elder'. And in his straight-
theatrical days, Philip read his own description of *The
Merchant of Venice* with Olivier as Skylark.

In this there may have been the hand of an ironical
providence: when he first joined the *Manchester Guardian*
his father had warned him, 'Never work for a liberal
newspaper, my boy. They'll sack you on Christmas Eve.'
To be fair, the *Guardian* granted him some licence. In
the 1970s he was given a Saturday column where he
reminisced. Some of these columns came off, not all, as I
recall. It must be said that I have always had an abhorrence
of 'light' pieces. The causerie, the Chestertonian Essay on
Nothing in Particular, *The Times* Fourth Leader – all lay
leadenly on English journalism, and Philip as a man of his
generation was too much under their influence. He had
in fact a true lightness of touch, which showed itself in
another medium. He used to say, 'The most damning
thing you can say about someone is, "He was an excellent
broadcaster",' but he himself was just that. His enchanting
programmes on Sacha Guitry and Yvonne Printemps
should be repeated regularly.

Philip was a man in whose company many of us
delighted, but if he was droll he was not joyful. His
gaiety sparkled against a sombre background. I sometimes
thought that this might reflect on Auden's apparently
sweeping observation that 'Few, if any, homosexuals can
honestly boast that their sex life has been happy'. This
was a subject on which Philip was neither reticent nor
anguished: he was not hung up (as he would not have
said) about being queer (as he would have said), even
though most of his life had been spent when homosexual
Englishmen lived in the shadow of a stupid and cruel law.

But then again homosexuality had not yet become a substitute religion or nationality in the recent manner. One long-standing friendship was with a policeman; I think that he may have had few successful liaisons with people of his own class.

But in any case, the roots of his melancholy went deeper. It reflected perhaps his Jewish blood, a small part, but of which he was proud; it also reflected his intermittent ill-health. Not that he took much care of himself. The years and his habits of life took their toll on Philip's appearance. He was a striking, formerly a handsome man, tall and imposing with a high-domed head over a cherubic face. Prime ministers are supposed to look like bishops or bookmakers; Philip could have been either, a squarson or a bookish bookie. I have remarked on his dress and his fondness for wine. His clothes became shabbier and shabbier, scarcely reputable indeed: on one evening at the Opera House his trousers seemed to be in the process of falling down, a part of that negligence in material matters which was his characteristic (he sometimes complained about the water coming through his ceiling, but dismissed the idea of having anything done to repair the roof as too far-fetched to be worth discussing). And it might be said that the amount he habitually drank was also negligent, though it did not do him drastic harm. He lived after all to be sixty-nine and might have lived longer but for an ill-advised visit with a friend to a health farm where he fell and broke his leg, from the complications of which he died two weeks later. On the other hand, I am not sure that he would have wished to live much longer; his gloom was deepening.

There is another memento in El Vino, a plaque commemorating him, put up next to his table while he was still alive. To his delight, his Christian name was misspelt 'Phillip': 'They checked with the *Guardian*.'

15

WILLI FRISCHAUER

Vienna looms over the twentieth century like a bad dream. It was thence that half of modern European culture sprang: Freud, Mahler, Wittgenstein, Schoenberg, Kraus. Less often remarked is that half modern European politics also sprang from Vienna. If you look back a century and more at four men who were all originally Viennese liberals, their careers illustrate the death of liberalism, and what happened to us all. Adler became a socialist, Schoenerer a pan-German nationalist, Herzl a Zionist, and Lueger a 'Christian Social' or proto-National Socialist. The city in the last decades of Franz Josef's reign has taken on a mythic quality and anyone who can remember it has – soon anyone who can remember it before Hitler's return to Vienna in 1938 will have – an audience among those fascinated by the myth.

A good many people I have known knew Vienna between the wars, few before 1914. Sitting once in El Vino in Fleet Street I was talking to Philip Hope-Wallace about Bayreuth. Philip remembered performances he had attended there in the 1920s. He described Cosima Wagner as he had once seen her plain, by then nearly ninety. At which Willi Frischauer who was sitting with us cut in to say that in 1913 he had heard Caruso at what was then the Court Opera, an irrelevant piece of capping though an interesting one. If, that is, it was true. He was seventy-two at the time of his death in 1978, and so must have been a precocious five-year-old opera-goer. Or perhaps he meant 1923; except that Caruso was dead by then and had not sung in Vienna since the war. Perhaps, as with so many of Willi's stories, it was not designed for close examination.

That he was born in Vienna I am fairly sure, though not when. I say he died at seventy-two but one paper gave his age as seventy-five and Willi was not in *Who's Who*, though he was a good deal more interesting than some who are. That Viennese world at the turn of the century was partly Jewish; so was Willi. One of the rare occasions on which I heard him speak without levity was in describing how his gentile father had chosen to stay behind with his Jewish mother to die under National Socialism. Willi grew up in Vienna and then in the Twenties joined a newspaper with which his family was connected. He led at the time the life of a playboy as much as a journalist, and was comfort-loving if not sybaritic all his life. He loved food and wine and by the time I knew him in his sixties was enormous, one of the fattest men I have ever met. Like some other fat men he managed not to be gross; he was delicate in his movements and always smelt sweetly of good soap. As a young man he was an athlete, hard as that was to believe a half-century later, and keen on girls. Nor was that all. At one time – no, for years – Willi spoke of writing his memoirs. He talked about them, talked them away as it may have been. He had decided to be frank about his sex life, he told me, and added gravely that there had been a homosexual side also. 'Really, Willi?' 'Yes. You do not know what went on in the Austrian national water polo team in the 1920s.'

This magnificent revelation interested me if anything less than his journalistic and political career. He dealt with the subject in his book, *Twilight in Vienna*, but his own role remained shadowy. He was a democrat and of course an anti-Nazi, but he was an associate of both Dollfuss,

who was assassinated in the abortive National Socialist putsch of 1934, and of Schuschnigg, the last Chancellor of the first Austrian republic. He also claimed to have made the great discovery which he published in his paper in 1932 that Hitler's real name was Schickelgruber. In the 1930s he made more than one visit to London as a representative of the Austrian government. He returned from London to Vienna in March 1938, learned that the Anschluss had taken place, and turned round and took the next flight to London, where he spent the rest of his life. During the war among other services to his new country his help was enlisted by Bomber Command in planning its raids on Austria through his knowledge of Vienna and other Austrian cities.

This did not endear him to his former compatriots. Years later there was a reconciliation marked by the Austrian government's bestowal of the curious, not to say risible, honorary title of 'Professor' on him. He wrote as well for the *News Chronicle* and after the war he began to write books. By the time he migrated he was in his thirties: like other, younger emigrés he never lost his accent. 'I speak English without a trace of an accent – an English accent, that is' was a regular joke and indeed the accent was so strong after forty years in England as to suggest the deliberate playing of a part, a Viennese Maurice Chevalier. But in fact, and unlike the younger refugees – Hans Keller, for example, whose English was inhumanly good, better in a sense than an English native's – he never acquired a completely idiomatic command of English.

Not that a command of language would have made his books more eminent. Books on Vienna in the 1930s and *The Nazis in War* were one thing: they were followed by books that make me blush for Willi as I list them, on Brigitte Bardot, Onassis, Jackie Kennedy, David Frost and the Aga Khan. When I first met him he was an author with the publishing firm I then worked for and it was not my place to say anything against this gruesome collection of subjects, not over lunch at Wheeler's to which he with characteristic generosity had taken me. I later found that Willi did not like being teased about his books and their reverential treatment of their subjects. Behind this slight prickliness was a sense of disappointment. Willi could still quote Schiller and Grillparzer at length; he was a source of endless anecdote, printable and otherwise, about a European century; and I think it was, perhaps inappropriately, from him that I first heard the name of Karl Kraus, scourge of all cheap journalism. He could have written something better than he did, and he knew it: not necessarily a great biography or novel, but he could have composed some highly entertaining as well as intelligent memoirs, or even a serious history book. Though I learned other things from him, I learned that professional cynicism is a mistake because it eats away at the heart and soul. No one but a blockhead ever wrote except for money, Johnson said, and in a sense that is true. But Pushkin's advice was better: write for pleasure and publish for money.

Willi was not a cynic in his private life. He was deeply devoted to his wife Nicki, and also to his daughter Ann. In the summer of 1978 Nicki died. As was appropriate for Willi's wife, she was a marvellous cook, who kept him contentedly well fed. After her death his decline was visible: he actually began to lose weight. He was utterly cut down. 'When my mother's life ended,' Ann said, 'I think he thought his had too. She was his wife, confidante, secretary and researcher', apart from cook, that is. Willi began to talk of suicide. This places a certain degree of strain the conversation: does one say, I know how you feel, or, Pull yourself together, or, Don't do anything silly, or, like 'Miss Lonelyhearts', Go ahead and jump? I humoured Willi, saying I knew how he felt, and we facetiously discussed methods. I quoted Dorothy Parker's 'Gas smells awful, Nooses give ...' which he had not heard before; he copied the line onto a packet of cheroots. He went in fact to Beachy Head but there were too many trippers and so he turned back and into a hotel and drank a bottle of champagne. He held out for a few months. The Austrian government was proposing to honour him, or so the Austrian ambassador said at Willi's memorial service. The honour was too late. At the beginning of December Willi was found dead – pregnant phrase – at his flat. It was sad, though also touching, when one person finds that he cannot live without another. Willi would not have enjoyed a long, lonely old age.

16

T. E. UTLEY

As Fleet Street disappears, the 'Fleet Street' which throughout the English-speaking world was instantly understood to mean journalism; the Fleet Street in or near which nearly a dozen daily papers were once published, not to say the Sundays, and the London evenings, three of those when I was a boy; the Fleet Street of pubs and drinking clubs and gossip and backbiting and back-stabbing; as all of that fades into the past, and journalists from papers now published in Kensington or the Isle of Dogs or Battersea bump into each other in Soho restaurants; as that happens, many of us feel a sentimental pang in thinking of dead days and about the places where we once drank and talked. But I do not believe that the most reminiscential or nostalgic sentimentalist will ever claim that he misses the King and Keys.

This pub stood – still stands – to the west or left-hand side of the old Telegraph building, and was the paper's local until the two newspapers, *Daily* and *Sunday*, moved to Essex in 1986. Quite why the King and Keys was so horrible is not easy to say. Many other pubs in or off Fleet Street were grim in their ways as, after all, London pubs tend to be: malodorous, crowded, dirty, the ashtrays never emptied. Added to that in the King and Keys was the strange atmosphere created by the Telegraphers them-selves, the staffs of the papers. Strange because of a contrast. Here was the *Daily Telegraph*, the straightest arrow in the Tory press, staid, middle-brow and middle-class, candid friend to the Conservative Party and more generally the upholder of private enterprise and Victorian values, Christian family life and thrift. Look here upon this picture, and on this: the men and women who wrote the paper, as idle, spendthrift, dissipated, and raffish a bunch of adulterers and dipsomaniacs as you could meet in a day's march. About several of them there hung an air of barely suppressed violence: a saleroom correspondent drunkenly cursing the effing Rembrandts and blinding Ming vases he was supposed to write about, a diplomatic correspondent who fell into violent rages, on one occasion ending an argument with a colleague, 'If I was you I'd go home and cut my throat', and then, remembering that the man was gravely maimed and had no hands, adding in triumph, 'Only you couldn't, could you?'

Different members of the staff had their corners of the bar reserved by custom. Halfway down was where Michael Wharton ('Peter Simple') would arrive at half past two for his lunch of sandwiches and brandy, nearer the door might be John Moynihan standing in silence (it is said that he once described someone, perhaps thinking that the phrase was original, as 'the Sphinx without a riddle', to which a friend replied 'That's funny. You're known as the enigma without any variations'), or Colin Welch conducting a one-man cabaret, singing a large stretch of *Die Walküre*, perhaps, with his spectacles as the only prop. Nearer the door still at half past six in the evening might be Bill Deedes, very unusual among Fleet Street editors in regularly taking a drink with his troops and surveying as it were the carnage on the battlefield as he genially looked around him. Behind the door on the right were two tables. At one of them you would find seated in the evening and also surveying the scene – as it were, in a different sense – the chief assistant editor of the *Daily Telegraph*, T. E. Utley; as it were – because, in his

serene face, one eye was covered with a patch, one was closed.

Although his Christian names were Thomas Edwin, he was always known as Peter; for that matter, Utley was not the surname he had been born with. His father was a research chemist from Liverpool who died when his son was an infant: Utley was the name of the maiden aunt who adopted him and who liked to call him Peter. He had a happy childhood in the Lake country. And then, when he was nine, he contracted a disease and lost the sight of both eyes, one after the other. He had been an avid reader and soon learned Braille; he was a brilliant pupil at his school for the blind, and went up to Cambridge to read History at Corpus. Because his intellect was matched (not an invariable combination) with great charm and courtesy, he had no difficulty in finding willing readers, usually nurses. With their help he took an easy First.

It may sound perverse to say so, but Peter's handicap was in some ways an advantage. The art of memory has been in decay ever since the invention of movable type. Knowing that we can always look something up easily, we do not have to commit it to memory. Every subsequent technical innovation has dealt a further blow. When the young Lord Holland made the Grand Tour, his uncle Charles James Fox wrote to him (in the language of whichever country the boy had reached, French or Italian) describing the pictures he was going to see: paintings in Paris or Florence which Fox had seen once only in his life but remembered in detail more exact than those of us can who knew every picture in the Louvre or the Uffizi from colour-plate books long before we visited the galleries. Musical children used to learn Beethoven's symphonies by playing them in piano duet, and they could capture and retain a piece of music after hearing it once. Now we all hear great music incessantly on radio or record; we hear it without listening to it, we are familiar with it without knowing it. Peter did not have the opportunity for casual familiarity with books. If one had been read to him, he knew it.

After working briefly for a group concerned with post-war Anglo-French relations at the Royal Institute of International Affairs, whose grave tone cannot have suited him, Peter joined *The Times* as a temporary foreign leader writer because, he said, everyone was away at the war and 'there was no one else to do it'. He moved to the *Observer* and the *Sunday Times* (both very different papers forty years ago from what they have since become) before returning to *The Times*, where he stayed until 1954. Meantime he had become a well-known figure in the esoteric circles where political ideas are taken seriously, as an intelligent voice of romantic conservatism. 'Romantic' may not have been quite the right word; 'Burkean' was more accurate, and the several books he wrote in the 1950s following *Essays in Conservatism* and *Modern Political Thought* included one on his revered Edmund Burke. Peter's attractive voice was often heard in those days on the Third Programme. It was Frank Johnson who once described Utley as an itinerant Tory philosopher – bard or even troubadour might have been better – and he was much in demand as speaker or pamphleteer.

His natural home was the *Daily Telegraph* and he spent most but not all of his last quarter-century there. He was chief leader writer for sixteen years, then chief assistant editor for seven. Most of those years were happy, especially under the editorship of W. F. Deedes from 1974 to 1986. Peter and Bill Deedes were not soul brothers, were indeed in some ways opposites, but established a rapport, Utley the thinker, sometimes dreamer, Deedes the empiricist who understood how politics worked from the inside and knew what was going on in the minds of 'the colleagues' in the Tory party, if minds they could be called.

Peter's professional happiness at this time was increased also by the young journalists he brought up on the paper. In the late 1970s and early 1980s the *Telegraph* was in some ways the most stylish of the London papers, quite apart from its news coverage. There were the dazzlingly witty Parliamentary sketches of John O'Sullivan, later editor of the *National Review* in New York, and Frank Johnson, later chief associate editor of the *Sunday Telegraph*. Both also wrote the paper's deft and often funny leaders, where they were joined by Charles Moore, later editor of the *Spectator*. These youngsters were inspired by Colin Welch, deputy editor and tunesmith, but they made a special cult of Peter and some or all of them were to be found at his table in the 'K & K' at 6.30 in the evening. Peter sat making laconic jokes, his dark suit only slightly dishevelled, ash falling on his trousers from the cigarettes which he happily chain-smoked for fifty years while he sipped whisky, his glass constantly replenished by one of his succession of dazzling girls (he had an uncanny aptitude for picking beautiful secretaries). He was attractive in a roguish way; with the patch covering one of his sightless eyes he was almost piratical, only needing, a friend once said, a parrot on his shoulder. Or he might have been an old courtier, a survival into the 1830s, say, who had known Prinny and the faro table at Brooks's fifty years before. Apart from political wisdom, the young men looked to Peter as a source of idiosyncratic worldly advice. Frank Johnson was a member of the Reform Club and was taken with the looks of a young waitress who worked there. He wondered whether he could ask her out and sought Peter's guidance as to whether this was within the conventions. 'Dear boy. Only if you fuck her.'

This happy age came to an end. One by one the boys left and in 1986 Max Hastings arrived as editor of the *Daily Telegraph*. He was in many ways just what was needed by the paper, whose dire financial condition had only become fully apparent when the Berry family lost control the year before, but he was no respecter of political or other traditions and he and Peter were a light year apart in personality. Things soon went wrong between them. The particular cause of friction was Ulster. Peter was a firm Unionist, a friend and ally of Enoch Powell's, the author of *Lessons of Ulster*. Hastings was one of those Englishmen with little time for the troublesome Unionists. He had covered the Ulster troubles in the early days of 1968–9 and had been so disgusted by the oppression of the RUC and of the unlamented B-Specials as to conclude that the answer was that chimera called a United Ireland. Peter made no fetish of democracy, but he saw that the undoubted and sometimes appalling injustices suffered by the Catholic minority in Northern Ireland could not justify forcing a million Protestants out of one country and into another against their will (an act which was in any case not much likely to benefit the Irish state). He was not a religious bigot – a High Anglican married to a Roman Catholic – and he exactly demonstrated his sympathies in the February 1974 general election by standing as an Official Unionist against Ian Paisley in Antrim.

This demonstrated Peter's courage and independence and clearsightedness, in some fields. I did not find the rest of his political philosophy so captivating. Partly that is to say that his politics were not mine, as he would have been the first to agree. Because we both wrote for Tory papers, disliked Labour governments, repudiated socialist doctrine, seemed to place us objectively (as Marxists say) on the same line. But here again our description is distorted by that false spectrum of Left and Right. A valid political term of description should be two- or even three-dimensional: there is as much room between Peter's patriotic, paternalistic Conservatism and liberal individualism as between either of them and socialism.

He began writing at an interesting moment, when the Tories were fretting under the Attlee regime but still more under the apparent moral and intellectual dominance of the Left. A small beleaguered intellectual Right tried to rethink its position, in academic terms with Michael Oakeshott, practical with R. A. Butler and his young team. What was Conservatism to be if it was not merely a defence of privilege speaking to base passions, more than the Tory party of A. J. P. Taylor's cruel phrase, 'an alliance of the City and the mob'? Peter Utley saw the problem. Has Conservatism merely 'assigned to itself the unheroic function of maintaining a fair balance between its opponents' principles?' (Yes, would be the honest answer to that in terms of everyday politics at the time.) He asked the question, and then tried to answer it. He certainly gave an unambiguous statement of his position, and would not have minded being told that the position was as much prejudice as principle: what else was the conservative tradition but 'the general and perpetual voice of man', in Hooker's words, voicing that is man's instincts or prejudices? And although this voice may well be general and perpetual, it is fair to ask whether it amounted to an intellectual tradition.

It may be argued as Utley did – many, perhaps most great political philosophers have argued – that human nature is 'violent and predatory, held in check by only three forces: the Grace of God, the fear of the gallows, and the presence of a social tradition subtly and unconsciously acting as a brake on human instinct'. (Peter, the least pompous and priggish of men, was not very persuasive when he wrote sentences like '[man] is free to use his sexual capacity for the natural and intended purpose of procreating a family or for the purpose of merely gratifying his desires'; why not both?) It is right to distinguish between 'those who regard politics as supremely important and those who conceive it to be the handmaid of religion, art, science' and to propound as the first principle of Conservatism that 'there are many things which historically and morally take precedence over the State'. But he will then go on to speak of Government (with a reverential capital letter, like Professor Scruton's 'State') as 'the steward of a moral system eternally and everywhere valid', without apparently noticing any contradiction.

Nor did he notice another contradiction. For thirty years he preached a brand of Toryism which was not merely distinct from economic individualism but was in many ways its antithesis. He was a strong protectionist. A nation like England 'cannot afford to neglect its agriculture. If its agriculture is an uneconomic industry it is its interest and its duty to support it out of national taxation'; cheap food is 'the choice of the traitor'. Vested interests are entitled to respect 'as such'. More than that, Tories should not share 'the left-wing prejudice against anything that savours of Fascist corporatism' (interesting, by the way, that consule Attlee an intelligent writer could identify this as a left-wing prejudice).

Well, came the 1960s and corporatism and protectionism were tried, by both Labour and Conservatives, and failed. One vested interest was the trade unions, which won the respect of successive governments, whether entitled to it as such or not. Came 1975 and the Conservative party put its faith in Margaret Thatcher, rather as a gambler makes a desperate switch of bet with his last stake. In political terms the bet paid off, like none other. Mrs Thatcher's mixture of laissez-faire economics and populist nationalism won her an unprecedented hat-trick of electoral victories. During the first of these elections, in 1979, Peter Utley was drafted in as a speech-writer and adviser and for the first time moved in from the fringe of politics (though still delighting fringe meetings at the party conference as a speaker) to become a consultant director of the Conservative Research Department. He was rewarded with a CBE, and Mrs Thatcher attended both Peter's funeral and his memorial service.

In all of this Peter seemed to have forgotten what Mrs Thatcher stood for: an attack on corporatism, vested interests, protectionism, even in an unguarded phrase of hers on the community, all in the name of the atomized individual; Hayek not Hooker. Peter might have claimed that he admired Margaret Thatcher's Anglo-Gaullism, at least, and of course her love of individual freedom was (as is the way with politicians) more preached than practised. Her real politics were those of Lord Copper: self-sufficiency at home, self-assertion abroad. Moreover, Peter was not the only Tory politician, philosopher or courtier who performed an adroit tergiversation: there were a good few books published in the mid-Seventies which in effect required corrigendum slips: 'For "Heath" read "Thatcher" passim.'

In any case, perhaps Peter's career as a Tory philosopher says less about him personally than about Tory philosophy. 'Mr T. E. Utley concealing the poverty of his thought by the incoherence of his style' was A. J. P. Taylor's side-swipe once, but poverty was not the right word. Contradictoriness, as I have said, would be better. A short-tempered reader who found Peter saying that Liberalism 'has no use for groups within the nation' (as untrue in its way as Margaret Thatcher's assertion that there is no such thing as the community); then that 'traditional Conservatism regards the national State not merely as inevitable but as the form of social organization most likely to result in the happiness of mankind'; and then again that 'the first principle of Conservatism, on the other hand, is that there are many things which historically and morally take precedent over the state', might have felt like saying, Get on with it: What *is* your philosophy of the State? Perhaps there isn't one; perhaps, despite the efforts of all of them from Professor Oakeshott to every ambitious hack backbencher with his pamphlet on 'My Tory Philosophy', there is no such thing; perhaps a Conservative Philosophy Group is what Oliver St John Gogarty called the Royal Hibernian Academy, a treble contradiction in terms.

Peter might have wished to be remembered for his writing. He should not have minded being remembered, as he is and will be, more for his personal influence. Everyone who came into contact with him learned something from him, if not about politics then about self-possession and dignity. His blindness at once did and did not matter. As Charles Moore has said, he was unique among people whether one has known them or not who have suffered comparable afflictions and overcome them with superhuman bravery. In his conquest of his deafness, Beethoven's is surely the most heroic life recorded. But there is always a tension, a sense of rage and disappointment mastered by will. Peter had nothing of that. He was completely relaxed, at ease with his fellow men and, Charles says though I cannot judge, at ease with his God. Peter's self-consciousness was confined to the printed page, not least on the subject of religion. After meeting Harvey Thomas, a hot-gospeller who had joined Mrs Thatcher's strange court of wizards and mountebanks, Peter wrote of him all too charitably, though mentioning a natural lack of sympathy between Thomas's Bible-Belting and 'my own arid Anglicanism'. The phrase struck me, if only as a Freudian slip. Did he not mean 'austere'?

No one wants to think of his faith as dry or parched, does he?

But in person he was remarkably unselfconscious. Blind people often have about them a beguiling stillness, but this was less noticeable with Peter than his wry cordiality – 'How nice to see you', was his invariable greeting – and his humorous face. He was not only without self-pity but without much sympathy for the Handicap Industry and its wilder excesses. As I write I have just seen an advert in the paper for the Royal National Institute for the Blind, an estimable body from whom Peter must have benefited – 'Attending a RNIB business training course convinced Bill he could use his experience and skill to show art galleries how to cater for blind people' – and wished I could read it to Peter; I could almost hear him laugh.*

Peter was relaxed. After two or three rounds in the King and Keys Brigid would arrive, more serene in her way even than Peter in those ghastly surroundings. Here was the secret. His marriage to Brigid made possible his engaging sloth but their deeply happy marriage was, I suspect, the heart of all Peter's calm. He was entirely unfrantic. He smoked untipped Player's heavily for the best part of fifty years, he drank the best part of a bottle of whisky a day. On this subject at least he was a true liberal. The nearest he came to anger was with anti-drink crusaders, with taxi-drivers who put up insufferable (and illegal) signs saying 'Thank you for not smoking', and with the derangedly bossy junior minister Edwina Currie. 'Sack Mrs Currie', was Peter's repeated advice to Mrs

---

* In a hallowed *Telegraph* story, Maurice Green when he was editor announced that he wanted to make Utley television critic, but that was not quite as silly as it sounds: the flickering screen is there for hypnotic effect but whether television is essentially a visual or aural medium may easily be judged by trying to follow a programme with your eyes shut, then with eyes opened but sound off.

Thatcher in his *Times* column; he did not live to see Edwina's at least temporary eclipse. But no one who knew him could have suspected that there was even a hint of desperation behind these habits, which is rare.

Peter was an example and a reproach. 'Counting your blessings', as Nanny advised, is a dubious practice: one's blessings imply other's curses, which is not far short of Schadenfreude. No one ever counted Peter's curses. It was strange to think that he did not know what his beautiful wife looked like, but not sad.* No one was sorry for Peter, and he was never sorry for himself. Apropos of his friend Peter Beatty who lost his sight and his balance and took his life, Evelyn Waugh wrote that 'the world is full of radiantly happy blind men'. 'Full' might be an exaggeration; Peter showed that 'radiant' was not.

* People often said, on hearing when Peter had lost his sight, 'You mean you've never seen her?' meaning Brigid. Denis Thatcher on hearing it said, 'You mean you've never seen Margaret?'

17

MURIEL BELCHER

What is the real vice anglais? Hypocrisy, perhaps, or bossiness. Both contributed to the birth of that uniquely English institution, the drinking club. A century ago, drinking was barely restricted despite the temperance movement and a working man could buy a much-needed glass of rum on his way to mine or mill at six in the morning. He could drink later in the day if he wished, and when during the Great War Lloyd George was looking for an excuse for the shortage of shells which was his responsibility as Minister of Munitions he found it in the supposed drinking habits of the munitions workers. So it was that the beer was watered on order of the State, the opening hours of pubs curtailed, and the afternoon gap came in: the pubs shut from 3.00 to 5.30 in London, longer in the provinces.

Oppression breeds resistance. In this case the resisters found their safe houses in the London drinking clubs. There were dozens of them in the 1950s, and still in the 1960s when I first knew them. There were Gerry's in Shaftesbury Avenue, the Kismet ('the Iron Lung') in Panton Street, and the Colony Room Club above an Italian restaurant in Dean Street. Each had its own character, as much as White's, the Garrick, Pratt's and the Beefsteak. Gerry's was full of actors – Mark Boxer's camp, self-obsessed monomaniacs; the Kismet was where villains and policemen met on equal terms in one bar while the usual Soho flotsam drank in another (it was there for

the one and only time I met 'the Roberts', the painters
Colquhoun and MacBryde, shortly before the former's
death; that must have been in 1962, and I can only have
been a precocious sixteen); and the Colony – well, Muriel's
was like nowhere else, its tone set and governed by the
remarkable woman who was its owner, châtelaine and
hostess, and after whom the club was invariably known.

Muriel Belcher was, I think, of a Birmingham Jewish
family. Of her past little was certain except that it had
been chequered. During the war she had started one club,
the Music Box, frequented by the less conventional type
of Guards officer. Then in 1948 she opened the Colony.
The name was sometimes said to have been for her West
Indian girlfriend, Carmel. Otherwise there was nothing
colonial about it. It was metropolitan and cosmopolitan
and all of Soho. The people whom Muriel attracted to
her bar were not of any one type. Of course, half of the
most famous painters and writers in London congregated
there – it became a journalistic cliché to list them, and
even now it is hard to write about the club without lapsing
into the higher name-dropping.

In the early days of the club Francis Bacon worked
behind the bar; he remained a friend of Muriel's all her
life, not only with an ever-open handbag in the club for
bottles of champagne all afternoon ('Come on, Lottie,
where's your handbag?' was a Murielism addressed to
anyone tight-fisted) but standing her and Carmel more
and more extravagant treats as the years went by and his
fame and fortune waxed. Lucian Freud was sometimes in
the club, though not regularly, less often in later years,
not at all in the 1980s after his falling-out with Bacon.
But it was Michael Andrews who painted the best of all
portraits of Muriel.

To me, the club was a place of remote glamour in the
1960s. I did not start going there until I was perhaps

twenty-four; at first someone's guest, then a regular but unofficial dropper-in, then osmotically a member. I took to Muriel, and she to me, I think: 'Here's my cup of tea' was another of her obscure phrases when I arrived. And so I enjoyed a season of favour, taken to lunch and taken on jaunts to the country. Her entourage fluctuated. There was Carmel, there was Ian Board, her as it were adoptive son and heir, whom she had discovered as a lissom lad from Devon and put behind the bar, there was Dan Farson, there was Jeff Bernard, both of them in whatever stage of inebriation (not that that wasn't true of most of us), there was Lady Rose and Barry and Sue and George and Tom. I think of them like the list of those 'who enjoyed Jay Gatsby's hospitality' in the fourth chapter of *The Great Gatsby*.

Muriel's gift as a hostess lay in striking a balance. There was a balance of the sexes, almost always a few women in the club apart from Mu herself; she was not of course hostile to women, and even encouraged a few to attend. Romantic liaisons sometimes began in that half-lit room, though it seemed a depressing place for it. There was a balance between the famous and the obscure. Some may have come to ogle Francis and Lucian, but not, I think, many: the Colony really was a club, where in its own way the convenances of equality were observed between members as much as in St James's Street. One afternoon, Francis Bacon tore apart the front of my shirt (for no reason than that he had lost his balance and was trying to break a fall), at a time when I could not afford many shirts. Late one other evening I was given the task of extricating him from the club when there was a feud between him and Ian; we went to a casino where I lost all my money, at a time when I could not afford it. Francis won, and gave me all his winnings except what he needed for a taxi home. Perhaps I was starstruck by such paltry episodes; but I think the glamour of the place was more collective than individual Big Names.

And there was a balance between normal and queer, to use once again the terms of art which we used then. The camaraderie of Dean Street was always partly homosexual, as well as wholly alcoholic. Until the late 1960s, the law had given homosexuality the danger and excitement of persecution, which lingered on in the happy interval until the rise of Gay Power. The atmosphere of Muriel's – and Muriel's own conversation – reflected this. A friend of mine caused a certain amount of surprise by getting married. A year or two later he and I were lunching in Soho and decided to take a digestif in the Colony, where he proudly announced the birth of his first child. Muriel's congratulations were succinct: 'It's amazing what a pouf can do when she tries.'

At the time I was working dejectedly for a publishing firm, which in itself explains my long afternoons in Muriel's. Having taken the job I discovered that there was nothing for me to do, except act as a shuttlecock between warring directors of the house and read the 'junk pile' of unsolicited fiction manuscripts, which no one sane could be expected to do sober. And so I crept back to the office towards the end of the afternoon. Once, my amiable superior Raleigh Trevelyan had to ask me, to his regret, where I had been all the previous afternoon. The answer – 'Talking to an author' – was only partly suggestio falsi. Indeed, I commissioned several books in the Colony. One or two of them were even written and published. One book which I did see through the press was on the Kray brothers. When proof copies were circulating, I was rung one day by a well-known solicitor who after beating about the bush and passing the time of day said that his friend – he was only speaking as a friend, not a lawyer – Tom Driberg had been distressed to find a very embarrassing photograph of himself among the illustrations. Was it too late to do anything about it?

This was interesting, as the same lawyer had read the manuscript for libel and in the process all references to Driberg had disappeared. I knew Tom slightly from Soho; he would sometimes come into the Colony with a leather-jacketed youth – 'One of my constituents' – who would be parked in a corner while Tom moved over to instruct us at the bar. I was far from disliking him, but there was something about his imposture which may have led me while assembling the pics for the book to insert, not absent of malice, as the Americans say, a photograph captioned 'The Krays entertain' which showed the brothers surrounded by boys, boxers, and the Member for Dagenham not yet assumed as Lord Bradwell. I said to the lawyer that it was too late to do anything (suppressio veri, this); and repeated my hypocritical apologies when next I saw Tom at the Colony. He was very morose, complaining that the picture had haunted him, having originally stopped him from joining a club (which? Brooks's? The Athenaeum?). Later still, I told all this even more long-windedly to Muriel, who ended the recitation, 'Well, Tom was happy enough with Ronnie Kray's cock in his mouth.'

Her one-liners were repeated by us as a revered school-master's might be by his pupils: she was very funny. There was the whole elaborate private language, partly theatrical camp, partly her own invention. In a passage in *Sodom et Gomorrhe*, Proust discusses the way homosexual men talk, their habit of speaking of each other as 'she'.* Muriel

---

*This passage has another minor interest for those interested in two languages. To describe homosexual carry-on, Proust uses the word 'chi-chi', which in English has come to mean something different. In his wildly perverse translation, Scott-Moncrieffe – who knew a thing or two in this context – translated the word as 'camp'.

developed this to its conclusion, where everyone was she, not only shrieking queens, not only my ambivalent friend, but Miss Hemingway – by which she intended the writer, not actress – or Miss Hitler. An old army hand – and there were still a fair number in the club – was 'a gallant little woman'.

And she had a superb gift of surprise. One Friday morning, Joe Scott-Clark was doing his shopping in Old Compton Street and in Bifulco's butchers shop (now fled from Soho) ordered his provisions for a solitary bachelor's weekend: 'A lamb chop, half a pound of sausages and six rashers of bacon, please,' as he heard Muriel's voice from behind: 'Giving another of your slap-up dinner parties, eh, cunty?' This was her favourite term of endearment, or merely of address. Staying in a country house in Wales once – yes, that sometimes happened – she toyed with an empty glass for a while before turning to the dowager marchioness who was her hostess: 'You're not very agile with the fucking champagne, are you, cunty?' As this suggests, Muriel was no conventional respecter of persons, but she had a shrewd grasp of reality. Dan Farson remembers her saying something disparaging about Olga Deterding one afternoon when that sad creature had been brought into the club. He explained Olga's background and that she was one of the richest women in the world. Muriel's reaction was precisely the same as Lady Bracknell's when she learns of Cecily's £130,000 in the funds: 'She does appear a most attractive young lady now that I look at her.'

She set the tone of conversation at the club as some bluestocking hostess of the eighteenth century might in her salon. Francis Bacon has said that the club was 'a place where we went to dissolve our inhibitions', and that is part of the answer. Even if you weren't especially inhibited or puritanical – and I was, rather – the atmosphere and the conversation were startling: vehement and completely unrestrained. Jeff Bernard went once to a drying-out clinic where I visited him, taking a carton of two hundred Players whipped-round for in Muriel's. He described the group therapy sessions he was experiencing. The patients sat round telling their deepest secrets and denouncing one another for being such wrecks and wastrels: 'It's just like the Colony with everyone on Perrier.' But the club was in its way a form of therapy, where retired majors of the Blues could talk about the whores they had just been visiting or girls could talk about which positions (not of employment) they liked best.

Not everyone liked Muriel's or even Muriel. Shiva Naipaul's aversion from the Colony I mention on another page. Auberon Waugh never saw the charm of the place; any nostalgie he may have is for a different kind of boue. He had a memorable encounter there with an inarticulate R. D. Laing and a prickly Bacon who said, 'Your father didn't like me. He thought I was common.' (Bron Waugh's next *Private Eye* column contained the potential candidates for some imaginary committee, with their disqualifications: 'Francis Bacon too common, Ronald Laing too drunk.') And plenty of would-be admirers were driven away by Muriel's tongue, which could be ferocious. She had a longish list of pet hates, some of them justified. Colin MacInnes was more often banned from the club than not, which I could understand as although I admired him as a writer I found his monotonously abusive, insulting conversation hard to take. But if anything more surprising than her intolerance of some was her tolerance of so many, including some who were pretty intolerable. The truth was, well-concealed though it might be at times, that Muriel was a kind and generous as well as a witty and outrageous woman.

She died ten years ago. Now, the pubs are open all

afternoon and there is no pretext for going to the Colony even if some of us weren't in middle age trying to avoid drinking uninterruptedly from luncheon to dinner. But I miss those afternoons where we misspent our youth, led lives of noisy desperation, grew old gracelessly. In the early years of the Colony Room it was a centre of resistance in several ways, what with absurd laws criminalizing homosexuality as well as telling the people when they could drink. Today a different kind of puritanism reigns: industry, efficiency and looking after your health are supposed to be our watchwords. They never will be at the Colony as long as it survives, a naughty deed in a goody-goody world.

18

GORONWY REES

Ever since Guy Burgess and Donald Maclean vanished in 1951, and Cyril Connolly wrote his memorable and unintentionally comical *The Missing Diplomats*, the 'Cambridge traitors' have held a prominent place in twentieth-century English folklore. They were a fascinating group. Caught up in the excitement of intellectual Communism in the early Thirties, a few of them were drawn into the inner circle which served Soviet Russia secretly. Who was the original recruiting officer? The Cambridge economist Maurice Dobb seems one plausible answer, though the evidence is inconclusive. When the diplomats went missing there was speculation as to the identity of a Third Man who had tipped them off when they were under investigation. In the House of Commons in 1955 Harold Macmillan gave a curious flat denial that this was Kim Philby, when he must have known that it was. After Philby's own disappearance and reappearance in Moscow, speculation turned to the Fourth Man, who had perhaps controlled the other three. And then in 1979, the new Prime Minister Margaret Thatcher astounded the nation by revealing his identity as Sir Anthony Blunt, the distinguished art historian and former Keeper of the Queen's Pictures.

Astounding news to most but not to all. Six years earlier I had sat in the French pub in Dean Street with Goronwy Rees, when after only three or four large glasses of pink gin he told me that Blunt was the Fourth Man. Perhaps I should have been more excited by this identification than I was. For one thing, it struck me that such a dark secret could not be very secret or closely guarded if Goronwy knew, and if he had told me. Although I liked him, we were not intimate friends and he was not a discreet man. For another thing, there was the historian's (and political reporter's) response to any source: why was this document written, or, why am I being told this? And what had Goronwy's own involvement with the quartet been?

Goronwy's life was a success story, and then a failure story. He was the son of a dissenting minister, a Welsh boy (boy is appropriate for most of his life) who made good by going to Oxford from his grammar school in Cardiff. After a first in PPE and an All Souls fellowship, he went to Berlin where he failed to write about Ferdinand Lassalle and succeeded in playing a Highland officer in a German film (his story; what was the movie called?) and then returned to England and journalism. He was a leader writer on the *Manchester Guardian* for four years, somewhat improbably: it is hard to imagine Goronwy writing one of those *Guardian* leaders captured in Malcolm Muggeridge's (perhaps ben trovato) recollection: 'One is sometimes tempted to believe that the Greeks do not want a stable government.'

Then in 1936 Goronwy left the *Guardian* for the easier atmosphere of the *Spectator* as assistant editor. He published two novels before the war, *The Summer Flood*, written when he was an undergraduate, and *A Bridge to Divide Them*. It was at this time that he came to know Guy Burgess. Though he was never quite – candid is too harsh, rather forthcoming – about the matter, Goronwy clearly flirted with what Dwight Macdonald would have called the Stalinist ambience; it would not be odd if he had been a Party member; he evidently knew something

of what was going on in the inner circle, and he was to learn more.

He was at least not one of those who regarded the war as an imperialist conflict, the Moscow line in 1939–41. Goronwy was a Territorial volunteer before the war, was mobilized as a gunner, commissioned in the Royal Welch Fusiliers, and had a distinguished military career. He took part in the Dieppe raid in 1942, then joined Montgomery's staff and left the army as a brigadier after serving with the British Military Government in Germany. He always spoke warmly and even sententiously of Montgomery, 'from whom I learned what I know of the art of war'. Perhaps at some unconscious level Montgomery's charlatanism appealed to him.

Or perhaps this merely illustrated Goronwy's judgement, which to say the least never matched his abilities. One of his more entertaining books was the autobiographical *A Chapter of Accidents*, and no truer title was ever chosen. He had a rare gift for landing in the soup. After a spell working in the engineering firm of Pontifex with his friend Henry Yorke (the novelist Henry Green) he went back to All Souls as estates bursar and showed a real aptitude for making money, even if not for himself. He should have stayed there.

Instead he went to be head of the University College at Aberystwyth, as inappropriate an appointment as it would be possible to imagine. He had no qualifications except early academic distinction and being Welsh, which were both irrelevant: he wasn't their sort of Welsh. On top of the provincialism and touchiness of Welsh academia (shortly to be lampooned by Kingsley Amis), Aberystwyth was ardently nationalistic, puritanical, or merely prim. It cannot have been a question of whether Goronwy would fall foul of his colleagues after his arrival in 1953, but when and how. In the event, Burgess and Maclean were the cause. Several years after the diplomats went missing, Goronwy was induced to write about them for a popular Sunday newspaper.

Almost thirty years later a television 'drama-doc' was made about Rees's involvement with Burgess and Blunt. As usual, the programme was a compendium of error. Discussing it subsequently on the radio, a well-known literary lady attacked Rees in vehement terms as a notoriously untrustworthy and universally despised person. Had she known him? I wondered as I listened. Goronwy was not the twitching neurotic shown on the television screen, and he was not a monster either. As this most disastrous of accidents into which he walked demonstrated, the whole point about him was that Goronwy was a Welsh boy on the make, a chancer, a man undone by his own charm, good looks and gift of the gab; an innocent in the world. The Sunday newspaper articles showed not so much carelessness as almost incredible naïvety. They had been published anonymously but soon Goronwy's cover was blown, as he, like Gary Bennett, should have known. He was denounced on both sides: by some on the Forsterian grounds that he had betrayed Guy and Co. who were his friends – Maurice Bowra asked him whether he was going to plant Judas trees in his college garden – and by his severe colleagues at Aberystwyth on the grounds that he should never have known such villainous people in the first place.

Just what Goronwy's involvement with the Cambridge gang had been we may never know. He understood their complex motives, as far as they can be understood, and he knew their hang-ups. Close as he was to them, and sympathetic to them politically at one time, I suspect that he saw through them.

After all, that was not so hard. Despite a certain amount of blustering about treason, the Cambridge group have had a better press than they deserved. They have been taken at their own estimate. Quite why a few men became active Soviet agents is one question, perhaps not the most important one. Blunt's reply to someone who asked him that – 'Cowboys and Indians, cowboys and Indians' – though tiresome, has the ring of truth. It was all a great game with the added frisson of danger, a taste which some of them had inevitably acquired with their other interests.*

The broader excuses were still being made less than ten years ago – by A. J. P. Taylor, for example, reviewing one of the books on Blunt after his disgrace – but now sound hollow. The Thirties Communists were worried by the rise of Fascism and shocked by unemployment. But why did Russia have the only answer? Roosevelt and the Swedish Social Democrats were both conducting state-directed experiments for ending the Depression which did not involve massacring a large part of the population. Stalin was a curious choice to combat Fascism, he who had subverted the German republic (and the Social Democrats, or 'Social-Fascists') and left it for Hitler's taking, who betrayed the Spanish republic in turn, who again and again showed no concern for anything but Russian power and security. The argument made by Taylor and others that Russia was on our side during the war is what lawyers call a bad point. Even in 1941–5 Stalin was only on the Western Allies' side in the objective sense that my enemy's enemy is my friend; and from 1939 to 1941 so far was he from being on the same side that anyone who served him was effectively serving Hitler.

Others have said that they find it hard to drum up any patriotic indignation against Blunt or Burgess, or even

* When Burgess was arrested once cottaging at one of the London main line stations, a friend said, 'Yes, I always knew that Guy would meet his Waterloo at either Paddington or Victoria'.

Philby. Those are the words of Alan Bennett, ruminating about his own plays *An Englishman Abroad* and *A Question of Attribution*: 'I can say I love England. I can't say I love my country because I don't know what it means,' he quotes Burgess as saying, and he adds, 'The Falklands war helped me to understand how a fastidious stepping aside from patriotism could be an element in characters as different as Burgess and Blunt.' But that won't do at all. The fallacy of Forster's distinction between 'my country' and 'my friend' in this context has been pointed out before. Any of us would naturally and rightly choose someone we loved (and Forster's phrase would sound less wan if he could have said, as he could not, 'my wife' or 'my children' rather than 'my friend') rather than a gang of politicians. But in this particular context to which the saying is misleadingly applied, 'my country' includes my friends, and betraying one means betraying the other both politically and personally, as Blunt and Burgess of necessity continually did.

As for stepping fastidiously aside from gross patri- otism – which many of us did during the Falklands war – the Cambridge gang did nothing of the kind. They were ardent patriots, chauvinists, jingoes; only not for their own country. Two generations earlier they would have been fire-eating empire-builders; as the Empire of their own country was in decline, they had to find another. This psychology is clearest in the case of Goronwy's friend Burgess, who has always fascinated me as much as he does Alan Bennett.★ Burgess was obsessed by Victorian England; his favourite novel was *Middlemarch*; he used to discuss the greatness, the true eminence, of the Victorians when compared with the contemptible and puny Strachey who mocked them.

★ Though we may both be wrong; Freddie Ayer once told me, 'Guy was even more boring drunk than sober'.

More than their specific excuses, the fellow-travellers – the word is appropriate for all, Party members or not; they all believed that they were travelling on the same train, drawn by the engine of History with Stalin at the controls – misrepresented their motives, having first deluded themselves. They pretended to love liberty but what they really worshipped was power (and one of the reasons for that generation's slow disillusionment with Soviet Russia was their realization that the first victims of naked power were people like themselves). After all, liberty in practice is unintellectual, unmethodical, messy, unlike a mathematical equation, and unlike the neatly planned economy and society which Soviet Russia appeared to have created.

Even to call it power-worship is putting it kindly. Many years ago Bertrand Russell noticed a positive love of brutality shown by some intellectuals. As I have said earlier, it is not a coincidence (to borrow a favourite Marxists' phrase) that the heyday of Western fellow-travelling was also the very height of Stalin's terror. To suppose that all of those who endorsed the verdicts of the Moscow trials truly believed in them as they believed in everyday, empirically verifiable phenomena insults their intelligence and ours. Nearer the truth was Brecht when he was asked about those condemned in the Moscow trials and in a moment's irritation uttered one of the great socialist sayings of the age: 'The more innocent they were the more they deserved to be shot.' At a deep psychological level he spoke for many others.

There is, as I suggest, an endearing side to Guy Burgess. He was right about the greatness of *Middlemarch* and the smallness of *Eminent Victorians*, and right also to say that Lady Gwendolen Cecil's life of her father Lord Salisbury is one of the greatest biographies in the language; it was his unfulfilled ambition to complete it. There is even something endearing about his appalling behaviour.* And in his own excuse: 'At this moment in history, how is one expected to behave except badly?'

Goronwy might have used the same words in modified form. His life was not as calamitous as his friend Guy's, but it was badly conducted in its own way. His articles on the runaways led to a débâcle. He resigned from Aberystwyth and departed from Wales, only to career into another kind of accident when he was badly injured in a motor crash, and yet another when he ventured into the building trade. The first of these at least produced a remarkable book, *A Bundle of Sensations*. Otherwise he found himself writing for his living in his last two decades, a monthly column in *Encounter* under the coy nom de guerre 'R', and several books, company histories and biographies of rich men which he must surely have felt were not quite worthy of him and which did not, one suspects, even justify themselves by making large sums of money. It was in this connection that I first came to know him. A project for a book was got up and commissioned by the publishing house for whom I worked at the time, and Goronwy and I would meet. We were supposed to be talking about the book, but I wanted to talk about Burgess, and Blunt as well once Goronwy had produced his tasty morsel of revelation, and Victor Rothschild's flat in Bentinck Street where Guy had lived, and salacious gossip about the women they all knew. He did not seem at all averse from talking about these either.

The charm was still there (and has passed on to his

---

* When he was setting off for his last disastrous posting to Washington his friend at the Foreign Office Hector MacNeill gave him some advice: as long as he was there, no Left-wing politics, no queer antics, and steer clear of the colour question. 'I think', Burgess replied, 'what you're trying to say is, don't make a pass at Paul Robeson.' But, if he never quite did that, he ignored the advice more generally.

children), but I felt that he was an entertainer with few tricks left to play. As it turned out, I had met him quite near the end of his life. His memorial service in All Souls' chapel struck an incongruous note – Goronwy had never been a don in any serious sense – though where else should it have been held? There were mocking ghosts present. They did not include Blunt, at the time still alive and still Sir Anthony. He did not come to the service in Oxford.

After Blunt's exposure, Goronwy's name was much bandied about. A. J. P. Taylor, whose views on the Soviet agents was, as I have suggested, at best equivocal, wrote a chaffing letter to the paper saying that although he had always delighted in Goronwy's company, he would never have trusted a word he said. (It is true that the author who effectively exposed Blunt did not enhance his own credibility by lifting something Goronwy had written and printing it as though it were a deathbed confession told to him by Rees.) All the same, romancer and chancer and messer-up of his own and others' lives that he undoubtedly was, I think that Goronwy was in his way a witness of truth.

19

ELIZABETH SMART

When Glyndebourne presented its first opera in 1934, a triumph in the South Downs against the odds, the conductor Fritz Busch spoke at the cast party afterwards. He could only attribute their success to the fact that even work was better than the nightlife of Lewes. But was the nightlife of London much better, and is it? The absence of anywhere to go and anything to do late in the evening has always been one of the many things which make London a disagreeable place to live. Even today there are a handful of discos masquerading as nightclubs, one very good, very expensive nightclub in Berkeley Square, and a few other places here and there where the determined can sit and drink and talk after eleven – in any civilized city, of course, they could go to a bar or café.

One of the bravest attempts to put this right was in the early sixties, when Annie's Room was opened in Covent Garden. It was not a jazz club in the sense of Ronnie Scott's where devotees went to listen to the masters through a haze of smoke, but good groups played and the eponymous Annie Ross sang. There were tables, with food and drink served, the whisky I recall in miniatures to show they were full measure. There I went when I was eighteen, why I cannot now remember. I think the connexion may have been Joe Scott-Clark, who might have been one of my subjects here; he and Liz Smart were both then working on *Queen*. I forget what had found Joe there. When I first met him he was in effect on the run. He had owned an English-for-foreigners school in Cambridge where he was a well-known figure in the early 1960s; he had not himself attended the University, though his memory was sometimes vague on the point. Joe was fat and funny, sometimes lugubrious, sometimes melancholy, often drunk. His life was a helter skelter; a manic-depressive steeplechase of ups and downs.

After he had sorted out his legal problems following the collapse of his Cambridge business he worked for Berlitz and then washed up at *Queen* where he found a fellow-spirit, or at least a drinking companion, in Liz. He later moved to a different kind of magazine publishing, working for a successful trade publishing group – he liked being in charge of a mag called *The Muckshifter*, and very lucrative it was, I believe – and then started magazine publishing on his own account with what might have been a money-spinning health mag. But Joe could never quite pull anything off for good, rather like Michael Dempsey with whom he got on, up to a point. Everything always crumbled in his hands. His personal life was absurdly erratic, a mess of booze and boys. He perked up when he discovered Marrakesh, a place I hated when I first went there more than ten years later but then it did not have the same appeal for me. But he was always near the rocks and smashed on to them again in the early 1980s when his final business fell apart and he rang me often to say that he was being persecuted by creditors and reporters. On my return from South Africa after one visit I heard that Joe was dead; not, as in the first second I assumed, by his own hand, but more shockingly still murdered, it is to be supposed by some rough trade he had brought home.

It was this fascinating and doomed character who was the link between Liz and myself, when I first met her, danced with her, and fell for her.

She was then, I later realized, in her late forties at least. She was born in 1913 into a moneyed Canadian family, and she wanted to be a writer. As all the world knows – the world which knows about literary romances – her life was changed when she met George Barker. He was, indeed is, an English poet, at least as well known for his personality as for his verse, amorous and philoprogenitive in a remarkable degree. He and Liz spent years together and had several children, but it was their early amour fou which produced her famous book *By Grand Central Station I Sat Down and Wept*. When it was first published it was not famous at all, a 'sleeper' as the book trade says. It long had a cult reputation, to use another tiresome phrase, and when it was reissued in paperback in 1966 it enjoyed a season of fame. Brigid Brophy called it one of the few great prose rhapsodies in the language, and that may be why I never enjoyed it as much as I wanted to. My loss, but 'prose rhapsody' is a phrase to chill the blood of some of us. Good of its kind I could see *Grand Central* was, though tempted to add, like the man in an old *New Yorker* cartoon, 'but God damn its kind'. It is full-hearted and written without reserve, and moving, but not a good model for any other girl tempted to pour out her heart on the page.

It is not for her book that I remember Liz, but for her person. She had 'it', not merely sex-appeal, though she had this, but a kind of personal warmth which communicated itself immediately. It had done when we first met, it did when we met again, presumably in Soho – where else? – and at the occasional publishing party. By the 1970s she was beginning to show the years. Her face looked lived-in, to use a phrase which can mean a number of things. But, although no one could have claimed that she was 'a beautiful woman' in the conventional sense in her sixties and seventies, a beauty was still there, an echo of how captivating she must have been in her youth, and how she still was when I first met her.

She survived and indeed wore better than some Old Sohovians by the simple device of living in the country and spending her time in the garden and the kitchen rather than in the pub. There is a notorious English sentimentality about the superior virtue of country life, which affects writers as much as anyone – the assimilation of middle-class intellectual into country gentleman is a long-standing joke. And yet, for some people – for some of us – a base in the country for at least part of the time is the only key to physical and mental health. Again and again I have noticed the at least less rapid deterioration of those members of the old gang who limit their life in London to brief, albeit disastrous, forays. One exception is Liz's dear friend Jeffrey Bernard who has tried country life and abandoned it and who is still with us pluckily slugging it out between Greek Street and Dean Street all week all year long, but then Jeff is an exception to most rules.

It was at his bar of the Coach and Horses that I last saw Liz; it might have been the Colony, but I recall seeing her before lunch. That is how I remember her, not for her weeping and her rogues and rascals but that mobile face and the question she always asked whenever we met, 'Do you still love me as much as ever?'

20

MARK BOXER

Decades take on their own characters, and they come in different lengths. The Twenties ended in October 1929, the Thirties as abruptly in September 1939, the Nineties with Wilde's imprisonment in 1895. When did the 1960s start and end? In 1963, 'Between the end of the Chatterley ban and the Beatles' first LP' was when sexual intercourse began, and with it perhaps the Swinging Sixties; but there is a case for saying that they began as early as 1956 with Suez and *Look Back in Anger*. And ended maybe as late as 1975, the year that Saigon fell to the Communists and Margaret Thatcher became leader of the Tory party. If the definitive man of those long Sixties had to be named it would be Kenneth Tynan, whose mixture of wit and exhibitionism and intelligence and hedonism was highly characteristic of the time.

Another and more amiable candidate is Mark Boxer. Mark was twenty-five in 1956 and on the brink of a glittering journalistic, as well as a brilliant social, career. He was the son of a Colonel Boxer, who is said to have worked in the motor trade, and was educated at Berkhamsted where, he wrote forty years later, 'I was born on the stage of Dean's Hall'. This is not strictly true. Closer reading of the same account shows that he was born at King's College, Cambridge. Another school play was *The Birds* by Aristophanes translated by the then Provost of King's, who saw the performance and encouraged the striking young actor playing Peisthetaerus to apply to the college. While he was in Cambridge to sit the scholarship exam, he saw the Marlowe Society's production of *Henry IV Part II* directed by John Barton and was captivated. His first year at Cambridge was devoted to the stage; he had spent the months before going up with a professional touring company, 'having avoided National Service'. How? There was always a mystery about Mark's health, which was intermittently poor. Maybe there is a premonition here.

Meeting actors at Cambridge and even more in the drinking clubs of Shaftesbury Avenue where he spent his vacs, he asked himself: 'Did I really want to spend the rest of my life with these self-centred, camp monomaniacs?' And so he 'switched subjects from the theatre to magazine journalism' and found his career. Then and later he wrote from time to time, but the King's don Dadie Rylands perceptively saw that this was not his true métier and advised him to draw. As a draughtsman, Mark (or 'Marc', his caricaturing pen-name) was born almost fully formed.

He had also a genius for society. In middle age Mark was very striking. At twenty, a friend remembers, he had the sort of looks which halted a party when he entered the room, turning every head of either sex. He was tall, drooping, with a mop of black curls above a handsome mobile face. He was a dandy, and a show-off. Even then Mark was distinguished by a quality of playful silliness: another contemporary has told me with exaggerated horror how one would have to flee a party when Mark decided to do his strip-tease. If no monomaniac, then and always he was camp himself. King's was sui generis among Cambridge or Oxford colleges, with a tradition of friendship between dons and undergraduates, who lunched together, and its tradition of sentimental homosexuality, 'the higher sodomy' of Keynes's phrase. Mark's first dalliances were with boys rather than girls. He remained gay

in the sense of his youth all his life, but changed tracks at Cambridge. At a party in the Gibbs Building at King's, the archaeologist Charles McBurney gave him some unexpected advice: 'My dear Mark, you are getting to the age when you are particularly attractive to women. You must fuck and fuck and fuck.' He certainly became and remained an homme à femmes; Noel Annan credited him with changing the King's tradition from homo- to heterosexual, which Mark thought far-fetched.

In his new magazine career he became editor of the *Granta* 'by some sleight of hand'. At the end of his last year he asked the eccentric Catholic writer Anthony de Houghton to take over the magazine while he revised for the Tripos. De Houghton published a blasphemous poem, the magazine was banned and Mark rusticated. This led to the first great episode of Mark's legend. He left Cambridge in a hearse attended by full funerary rites. With mild spitefulness, the rustication had been dated to end the day after the King's summer ball, but the authorities had forgotten that a ball goes on all night: on the stroke of midnight Mark reappeared, Cinderella in reverse.

For university to be the best and most memorable years of one's life is a peculiarly English affliction (some people, especially Etonians, feel it about their schooldays). Although Mark's had been the most conspicuous career of a remarkable Cambridge generation, he did not live off his memories. In London he soon joined the magazine *Queen*, under the owner-editorship of Jocelyn Stevens; and in London the Sixties soon began. *Queen* was smart, bright, sharp, frivolous. Stevens held the balance between Beatrix Miller, who 'was the one who had any sense', and Mark who 'had all the impatient brilliant ideas', according to Francis Wyndham, whom Mark took on as theatre critic, and who followed Mark to what Evelyn Waugh called 'Lord Snowdon's blindingly ugly and banal coloured supplement'. The *Sunday Times* Magazine was in fact edited by Mark from 1962 to 1965 and was his creation more than anyone's.

The magazine changed Sunday newspapers – English journalism generally – for good or ill. Partly for good: it revived a tradition of illustrated journalism which had vanished with *Picture Post*, and it created a new tradition of long, serious reportage. It had a frivolous side to it, which did not matter, and a trivial side, which perhaps did. What was irritating about the old pansy Left (Orwell's phrase, which Mark used), or about what was later and undyingly christened radical chic, was the striking of attitudes in contexts which made it hard to take them seriously: in the case of magazine journalism, earnest articles on Trotsky and compassionate photographs of starving black babies ringed by glossy ads for every kind of consumer durable or unendurable. Mark was not cynical about his work, but he could be ironical about it. He and others were talking once about different Cambridge generations when Mark said with exaggerated woe: 'And what did *our* generation ever produce? A colour magazine!'

He stayed with the *Sunday Times* as an assistant editor for another fourteen years, until 1979; was with the paper, that is, in its characteristic years of fame under the editorship of Harold Evans. Enemies of the paper and of Evans liked to picture the *Sunday Times* as a proletarian racket run by mean and uneducated persons. This missed the point. Under the amiable and innocent Harry Evans were the same gang of scheming, ambitious public-school men as were to be found on most other London papers, sometimes intriguing with their editor against other colleagues, sometimes laughing at him behind his back. The relationship between editor and staff was nicely illustrated when the *Sunday Times* obtained Jeremy Thorpe's letters to his friend Norman Scott. Evans had been and remained a doughty champion of Thorpe's innocence and showed the letters to colleagues as further evidence. Mark, the man of the world, was summoned and shown the letters which (as Evans hoped and imagined) 'totally vindicated' Thorpe: 'Bunnies can and will go to France ... I miss you.' The man of the world fell about giggling.

His work at the *Sunday Times* involved choosing books for serialization and was not a sinecure, but it left him with time to develop his real craft. Mark could write well, but no more than well. He was a brilliant editor, but his unique gift lay in one field only. Rylands had been right. Mark drew a comic strip for the *Listener* about life in NW1, that is, among the media trendocracy. Whether or not the Stringalongs were originally based on a well-known couple, they developed a life of their own, clever and busy and fatuously fashionable. They summed up 'the Sixties'. The strip was all the better because Mark was drawing quite near his own knuckle. He never strung along, but he liked the beau monde with transparent innocence, and he also knew what were the fashionable causes of the moment. For years he drew a daily pocket cartoon, first for *The Times* then for the *Guardian* (which characteristically tucked it away in obscurity, finally but briefly for the *Daily Telegraph*. Sometimes the gag (more often than not supplied by his friend George Melly) was funny, occasionally very funny. Mark could exactly catch certain types with his pen and line: the media trendy, the chinless wonder, the bimbo in the cocktail bar. But even these were not his genius on fullest display.

His caricatures were. He produced these over the years to illustrate newspaper profiles and books. There was no other draughtsman of the age to match him, perhaps none since Beerbohm, with whom he obviously compared. They should be collected in a full volume: the papers in which they first appeared do not survive, and for that matter some of the books which he illustrated are not likely to either. Mark had not only an astonishing felicity of line, he had a knack rare even among the best political cartoonists (with whom he did not compete) of getting under the subject's skin, of capturing the real, inner likeness as well as the contours of a face.

He did not have to know the subjects well, but, as he told me when we were working together, he had to have seen them moving; this would ideally be in the flesh, at worst on television. He did not like to draw people who were unknown, since like any parodist or satirist the caricaturist needs a received background to stand out against. He did not like to draw women, since an element of cruelty, even if not a strong one, was necessary for a good caricature. (In fact the Queen, Mrs Thatcher and Germaine Greer were all memorably drawn by him.) This was said from a mixture of genuine chivalry and, as he admitted, not wanting to be seen as unchivalrous.

He knew quite enough about women. Having taken McBurney's advice, he married twice and had numerous other attachments besides. Both of his wives were women of great charm and character, the ethereal Arabella, whose career as a cookery writer Mark encouraged, and Anna Ford who was a famous broadcaster when they met some time after the first marriage had ended. As a young man Mark had shocked Princess Margaret, with whom he was dancing and who asked him where he was staying the night, by answering, 'I don't know yet, Ma'am'; he once pronounced apophthegmatically, 'I do think it's the height of rudeness only to go to bed with a girl once'; one of the famous femmes fatales of her generation entangled Mark, who was very highly-strung, and drove him to attempted suicide; his funeral was full of women, as an amused friend put it, all looking mysterious and as if only they had known the real Mark.

It was not hard to see why women and men fell for him. He had as much charm as he could want when he chose to use it; more than that, he was graceful, and kind; and silly. Mark's profound silliness showed in more than merely social ways, though it is true that he was a mixture of pretty manners and you-can't-take-him-anywhere. He could behave tiresomely, sometimes rudely, looking round the room at length to see who else was there, and with all his gracefulness he could be gauche. At a *Spectator* lunch once he was describing the liaison between a well-known young beauty and an oriental diplomatist, also well known. 'I said to her I could guess what had happened: "He's got a very small cock and wanted to bugger you".' It was said in a high voice in a nervous giggling rush, and was followed by a half-second's silence as Mark realized that others at the table – a dull woman Tory MP and a High Court judge – weren't on his wavelength.

This was endearing, and it was what made him so much a man of his age. Those long Sixties could be defined so: they weren't wicked or decadent, just terribly silly. That was why a man as clever and talented as Tynan ended up as a professional pornographer. And why someone of Mark's gifts – not to say someone who called himself a man of the Left – should have spent what might have been the most fruitful years of his life editing the *Tatler*. Mrs Thatcher was right about Victorian values, righter than her critics allowed or that she knew herself. They need not be the values of Mr Gradgrind or Samuel Smiles. They might be the values of George Eliot or Newman or Leslie Stephen or Robert Blatchford: the Victorians who took life seriously.

Mark went to the *Tatler* after leaving the *Sunday Times* and after a brief and unhappy interlude working for

George Weidenfeld. As a regular contributor to the magazine, my relations with him were cordial enough. We had
known each other for years. I had happy memories of
Mark in Tuscany in, I think, 1976. Then again our paths
crossed professionally. Mark had, as I say, been drawing
for the *Observer*. The *Sunday Telegraph* tried to seduce
him but failed: the *Observer*'s progressive flavour suited
him better, he said. He was disarmingly innocent in the
old-fashioned pink politics which he stuck to through
thick of country house and thin of bridge afternoons at
the Portland Club. Anna rather than he, I believe, said to
someone at James Goldsmith's vast ball at Cliveden on
the night of the 1987 election that she and Mark must be
the only people there who had voted Labour. But the
Observer, with more rashness than sense, then published a
story about Anna and a former boyfriend, and Mark
instantly resigned. (I later said without malice to Anthony
Howard, then the deputy editor of the *Observer*, that
although it had been a good story it just wasn't good
enough to lose Mark over; he ruefully nodded.)

And so Mark joined the *Telegraph* after all. I had been
cheerful, depressed (when he changed his mind), and
elated in turn. My elation was short-lived. Working with
him was a delight, not least because of his professionalism,
but the column of mine which Mark was to illustrate
lasted all of five weeks, almost but not quite a record.
What went wrong is neither here nor there, but on the
Friday of the fifth week I was summoned to rewrite the
whole column by the editor, Peregrine Worsthorne, as
was within his rights. I had written, though I say it, an
admirably ironical tribute to Anthony Blond on his six-
tieth birthday, for which Mark had drawn one of his best
caricatures ever, a masterpiece. A charming man and a
remarkable editor, Perry Worsthorne had a whole array
of prejudices and dislikes which he wanted to project onto

others. He disapproved of Blond, and he had the same morbid obsession with the royal family as any other Belgian reader of *Paris Dimanche*. The profile of Blond was cut in half and the drawing discarded, to be replaced by a piece on why we didn't hear so much from the Duke of Edinburgh nowadays, illustrated by an uninspired Marc drawing from stock. I resigned.

In any case I had half-consciously felt that the column was doomed. Several weeks before it was to begin, we heard that Mark was seriously ill. He went into hospital for prolonged tests, came out, went back. Mark sometimes liked to quote Italo Svevo's line that life is not cruel or unfair, it is original. It did not seem merely original when the news came that he had an inoperable brain tumour.

Trying to make sense of the news, I asked a medical friend. She said that after years of witnessing every type of cancer, she was inured to most things; one still filled her with utter horror. The prognosis came and went, weeks, months, weeks again. Mark found that he could no longer draw, and add to his list of the subjects he had caught.

Formal portraiture is in decay; most portraitists are hacks, few good painters now paint portraits (an exception is Lucian Freud, whom Marc in turn drew brilliantly not long before his death); the camera often lies. And so when future generations want to know what Harold Wilson or Professor Ayer or David Gower or Lady Antonia Fraser really looked like they will do well to look at Marc's drawings. They cannot look at his versions of Steve Davis, Tom Rosenthal, William Waldegrave, Julian Wilson or Michael Grade. Those were all an interesting if ill-assorted list of 'people I would like to draw' which he had sent me before his illness was diagnosed.

In February he wrote to me, 'I'm having mild treatment for seven weeks and hope to be in pretty good shape after that. Anna is being wonderful.' After I left the *Telegraph* he wrote, 'It's very sad but I hope all goes well with you and I hope to see you soon – perhaps some bad afternoon bridge – but I may get weaker.' He did. The next time I wrote was to Anna, who said that he was too weak for visitors, and I did not see him again. He had been receiving radical treatment, drugs and radiation, which both have unattractive side-effects. And so he decided to give up the treatment. It was clear that he was destined to die soon, and he chose to spend his remaining days with his family, ever weaker but his mind unclouded by chemicals. He faced the death which he knew to be near with a courage and gaiety that were admirable to witness; although his death in June 1988 was lamentable, it was the best performance he had ever put on.

21

IAIN MONCREIFFE

Another candidate for the English disease might be snobbery. It is certainly an English obsession. Not that as some people sometimes suppose we are unique in having a class system. Anyone who knows France or Italy well, or Russia or India, will not make that mistake. Or the United States. 'Are you suggesting there's no sense of class in America? That's not the impression I get from the works of Mr O'Hara,' Philip Larkin once said to an American interviewer. But England *is* different. The English and class are like the French and sex. It is not that we do it any more than others but that we talk and think and write about it more.

Although he was called 'the world's Master Snob' by one newspaper and claimed to rejoice in the name, Iain Moncreiffe was not a snob in Thackeray's sense of 'foolish looking down'. Then again, he was not English at all but Scotch through and through. But he did devote his life to badges of rank: title, pedigree, land, pedigree, heraldry. It was through the last that I first became aware of him, as a romantic little boy who fell on his and Don Pottinger's delightful and pretty book on heraldry. At the time he wrote the book Iain had not yet inherited his sonorous title as eleventh baronet, Sir Iain Moncreiffe of that Ilk.*

* As a precocious natural pedant I did at least know that 'Ilk' does not, as so many English people think, mean 'sort': 'people of that ilk' is meaningless. It means 'same', so that 'Moncreiff of that Ilk' is no more than a way of saying 'Moncreiffe of Moncreiffe'.

His inheritance came about through a sad accident in 1957 when his cousin Sir David died in the fire which destroyed the ancestral House of Moncreiffe. Nor had Iain acquired his final office as Albany Herald, or all of his initials, as CVO, DL, QC, FSA, Ph.D. He was a young and not very successful barrister in Edinburgh, combining a little legal work with his real love, for what would once have seemed not in the least arcane research into the byways of genealogy.

He was born in 1919 in Kenya. His father had settled there but died when Iain was three. Iain was educated at Stowe, at Heidelberg – an episode about which I always meant to ask him – and at Christ Church. His ancestry was splendidly exotic: Moncreiffe is a Pictish name, his maternal grandfather was an Austrian count of French origin descended from Erszebet Báthory, the Hungarian 'Blood Countess' who is first in the *Guinness Book of Records* under 'murderer'; not to say that 'The most recent serf from whom I can personally trace my ancestry was freed by the Bishop of Zagreb in 1552'. During the war Iain served not very enjoyably with the Scots Guards. He was bullied by the NCOs at the Guards depot at Pirbright and when he was a serving soldier suffered, as he did all his life, from painful stomach disorders. He remained in the army for a while after the war. There are stories of his inviting Herbert Morrison and Ernest Bevin to lunch at St James's Palace to impress on them the necessity not to tamper with an institution like the Brigade of Guards; an interesting example of what Cobbett called THE THING. He also served for a time in our Moscow Embassy.

Back in Scotland, Iain studied law at Edinburgh University and was called to the Bar, or rather admitted to the Faculty of Advocates. He did not prosper as a lawyer, not taken entirely seriously by the haughtier Edinburgh solicitors, and he never afterwards professed much affec-

tion for the legal establishment in Scotland. When he finally took silk it was in recognition of his scholarship rather than his advocacy, his own interests having taken him elsewhere. He wrote a doctoral dissertation on the law of succession of arms and dignities in Scotland, and he joined the court of Lord Lyon King of Arms, the Scots equivalent of Garter. He spent more time as herald at Lyon Office, less as lawyer at the Parliament House, and slowly ascended a wonderful scale of offices: Falkland Pursuivant Extraordinary in 1952, Kintyre Pursuivant the following year, Albany Herald in 1961. He wanted to become Lord Lyon, to his disappointment he did not.

Although Iain was a real scholar, it is not simply as scholar that most people remember him and it was not as a scholar that I knew him, or as a countryman; I don't think we ever met in Scotland. I knew him as a clubman, or simply as a drinking companion. We would run into each other at the Beefsteak at lunch and then, if neither of us had anything better to do (we didn't), would walk to White's to dispose of the rest of the afternoon. I found Iain's company delightful, but that is an inadequate word to describe him. For one thing, like many learned people he could be fascinating or a crashing bore depending on the interlocutor's mood. If you wanted to hear about Gaelic or Georgian pedigree and if you asked Iain, he was more easily started than stopped. But that was only one layer of the Ilk (as he was often called). The scholarly obsessions were woven up with a personality of endearing silliness and playfulness or just childishness. I never knew why 'Woof, woof' was his usual greeting (to people rather than his Afghan hound), nor understood one or two other of his turns of phrase.

He could be difficult, the impossible recalcitrant little boy. He was unpredictable. Sukey Paravicini remembers sitting next to Iain at dinner somewhere in Scotland when she was eighteen and being asked whether she was wearing any knickers. Thinking the brave rather than truthful answer was No, she was then told, 'Good, we're going to hold you upside-down by your legs and pour champagne over you.' Years later Iain found himself talking to Mrs Thatcher at some gathering or other and in effect propositioned her (did she really reply that in his condition she didn't think he would be much use? It seems too good to be true). This exchange was given wider currency – much wider – when Iain's compatriot Nicholas Fairbairn told the story in the House of Commons, one of the more memorable recent interventions in the British Senate. Although Fairbairn did not mention the Ilk's name, it became known that he it was, and the episode caused him some distress. At the time he made the suggestion to the Prime Minister Iain was not wholly sober. He quite often wasn't. My recollection is of his drinking Guinness, but he drank most things at one time or another, from boredom or shyness or melancholy, I am not sure which.

In his writing also Iain could be babyish, once more in an endearing way. His letters were written in fantasy language, or with the sense of humour of: 'On my mother's side I am descended from Anton Fugger, Count of Kirchberg (1493–1560) who was then the richest man in Europe. So I hope you will take it in good part when I describe as a fugger whoever "corrected" and edited my Foreword into such a mess ...' This, as is evident, to an editor. Some of his jokes were better than that, and even had a serious point. There was a phrase of the time to describe someone's politics 'to the Right of Genghis Khan'. But as the Ilk used to point out, Genghis was nothing if not a collectivist and social engineer. And he had a serious point also when he said that who was doing what with Lady Bonkworthy was not the same when she was called Lady Felicity Bonkworthy: 'It is hard to believe the latest rumour about one's friends' private lives when the gossip columnists can't get their names right.' I tried my best with only limited success to impress this on my team when, after Iain's death, I found myself writing a gossip column. At the least, I insisted and insist, these niceties are pedantic rather than snobbish. Personal titles being got wrong in serious papers only is one thing. A few years back a by-election was held in Newcastle-under-Lyme, in Staffordshire. A story about the election appeared in the *Daily Mirror* under the headline, 'Geordie poll shock for Labour'. There was a time not long ago when most people in this country, and to be sure most tabloid subs, knew that there were two Newcastles, and that Geordies came from the one -upon-Tyne. If an age which despises academic élitism and correctitude means that these distinctions disappear, then soon language disappears as well, in the sense of a code which conveys meaning.

Playfulness was part of Iain's life through and through: life in fact was a charade. He only wore part fancy dress in London. At home it was kilts and trews, dressing gown and nightcaps; best of all was his herald's tabard. On anyone else, come to that, his would have seemed an impostor's moustache, but then in Iain's case it rarely hid any attempt at a straight face. Even his attitude to rank and title had an element of play-acting. His first wife was the Countess of Erroll in her own right, having inherited the title as Scots law allows from her father Joss, the all-too-well-known 22nd Earl whose white-mischievous murder in Kenya in 1941 inspired books and films.*

---

* She gave her family surname to her daughter, Lady Alexandra Hay. Their elder son Merlin inherited the earldom, the younger Peregrine – allusively ornithic names – remained Moncreiffe of that Ilk, giving parents and children almost as many different names as the clan of Koch de Gooreynd, Norman, Towneley and Worsthorne.

She was premier earl and hereditary Lord High Constable of Scotland and Iain decided that she should have a Slains pursuivant in the form of the Oxford don Michael Maclagan. Procession was held with banners, roasting of oxen and, I think, a falconer.

Was any of this in any sense serious? Jamie Neidpath has written that Iain 'was one of the principal pillars of the intellectual Right in post-war Britain', which is perhaps pitching it a bit high: that 'social history was the cumulation of the history of significant men, that human courage was the primary factor in human affairs, and that ancient, symbolic ceremonies and customs was the lifeblood of any healthy society' is not untrue, merely part of the truth. It is certainly true that no one ought to be ashamed of their illustrious birth (and vice versa: only in England need one say that being born poor is nothing to be ashamed of, or proud either). Nor is it shameful to be interested in meeting the Duke of Omnium; nor necessary to explain away one's interest, as Conor Cruise O'Brien did with delicate irony: 'Like most people who read history – however progressive their opinions – I was not insensitive, at a sub-rational level, to the penumbra of a historic name. (Reader: "A pompous way of admitting he is a snob.") Proust's narrator was not able, until nearly the end of his life, entirely to separate the name of Guermantes from the Patriarchs and Judges on the portal of the Cathedral of Laon, and I was in similar trouble with the Prince de Ligne.' Why not? As long as it is remembered – only in England is it necessary to say so – that kind hearts are different from coronets and that Norman blood never got anyone to heaven.

This is all by the by where Iain was concerned. To talk to or to read, he was obsessively fascinated by birth and ancestry, but then a linguist is obsessed by words, a musicologist by keys and chords. Iain's chosen field was as much a legitimate branch of scholarship as philosophy or spectroscopy, a good deal more so than sociology or Eng. Lit. In any case, again, to be as serious as that is to miss Iain's point. He summed up his view of life once when he said, 'Goodness, I feel sorry for grown-ups: chairmen of companies, social democrats, civil servants . . .'

22
A. J. AYER

His trouble, the Master in College at Eton, H. K. Marsden wrote in a report, was that Ayer did not know when he was not wanted. When he got his First, the Headmaster, Dr Alington, sent a postcard with the delphic message, 'Clever Mr Ayer'. That was unkind. But was it unfair? A. J. Ayer was of course formidably clever, but was Alington wrong to suggest that he was clever-clever, perhaps not in a very attractive way? All through his life, Freddie Ayer put some people off; not everyone took to him; he made enemies. After his death one Cambridge don described him as 'wicked', not long before it I heard another describe him as 'perfectly horrible'.

Admittedly, both belonged to the Peterhouse Right – High Church, High Tory, high camp – with whom Ayer had as little in common as possible, but all the same the phrases surprised me then and surprise me now. No one who knew Freddie could possibly have thought him faultless. His faults of vanity and self-absorption were in some ways more obvious than his virtues. As he moved away at a party once, a woman said, 'You notice how Freddie leaves us as soon as we stop talking about him?' and one of his numerous girl-friends has described his taking her round an exhibition in London (where, as it happened, she met Graham Greene, who took her over), telling her how lucky she was to be in his company. Anyone who knew Freddie will think of their own examples. More to the point is why I liked him as much as I did.

One answer was cricket, which 'brings us together', Freddie once said to a hostess who had seen us talking and, as he thought, deserved an explanation. We used to go to Lord's to watch, and do the *Times* crossword between overs, when I wasn't enjoying exquisite examples of Freddie's didacticism: 'Do you know how many members of the present Middlesex team who are not black were not educated at Oxford or Cambridge?' He was genuinely learned in cricket as in many other subjects, though it might be said that he let you know this.

Oddly enough, one of my first memories of Freddie has to do with cricket. In the summer vac of 1966 I had stayed behind at Oxford for a couple of weeks, less to catch up on work than because I had nothing better to do. The prep schoolboys of New College Choir School played an annual match against the dons of the college, who were breakfasting in hall before the match. I found myself sitting next to Ayer who asked me if I played. I said fatuously that I had not played for five years; 'That is very much more recently than most of us'. I already knew of him, of course, not only as writer but as telly-don, quick and formidable and rather frightening in argument. He later said that he had acquired at that time, the late Fifties and early Sixties, a somewhat uncritical appetite for publicity which he came to regret. He even appeared once on 'Juke Box Jury'.

Was this – was Freddie's hedonism – a reaction against his background? He was if not of puritanical then of stoutly industrious bourgeois descent, French-Swiss on his father's side, Dutch-Jewish on his mother's, she a Citroën of the family who made the French motor cars. Born in London in 1910, he was christened Alfred Jules, names which he never liked and never used – he was always A.J. Ayer professionally, Freddie to those who knew him – until he was knighted. ('Sir A.J. Ayer' was a form used

by the Victorians, I pointed out, though it would have taken courage to revive it.) He went as a scholar to Eton where, 'intellectually precocious but socially immature', he had an awkward time. He was savagely flogged by an older Colleger called Quintin Hogg, and even by his own recollection was a bumptious little boy, but he at least got his colours for the Wall Game before he went up to Christ Church. There, he took against the 'surly and unadventurous tone' of Oxford philosophy under H. A. Prichard and H. W. B. Joseph with their hostility to Bertrand Russell, already Ayer's hero. The Oxford myth is that Freddie got his First in Greats on the strength of his Ancient History papers, rather than for his heterodox philosophy. True or not, he sometimes said that he would have liked to be an historian, and he sometimes held forth on historical topics, as in the eccentric book on Tom Paine he published in his late seventies.

In 1932 Freddie left Oxford with a Christ Church lectureship under his belt and a young wife, Renée, and went to Vienna where he met the Vienna Circle of Carnap and Neurath. The result of his short time in Vienna was his first book, written rapidly on his return to Oxford. *Language, Truth and Logic* was published when Ayer was barely twenty-five. It not only made his name, it remained for half a century the book by which he was best known. This was somewhat mortifying since he wrote several other books subsequently, one of which at least, *The Problem of Knowledge*, published twenty years later, Freddie thought a distinctly better book than *Language, Truth and Logic*. In fact, they are both marvellous. That is no expert opinion. (I failed to get into King's, Cambridge, after an aptitude paper for philosophy – two questions I remember were, 'When we fall asleep at night, how do we know that our bed does not disappear?' and 'What is the difference between red and green?' – and at Oxford I fled from PPE to the gentler fields of history after a week and one philosophy tutorial.) And yet you do not have to be a philosopher to enjoy Ayer. His books belong to that quite small category which can be read for literary as well as intellectual pleasure (certainly not true of literary critics like F. R. Leavis).

There were checks to Ayer's academic career. One writer has spoken of the atmosphere of anti-Semitism at pre-war Christ Church but I suspect that this is an exaggeration, or beside the point. It was not Freddie's part-Jewishness that put people's backs up. He did indeed have a series of skirmishes with the ancien régime at the House, most notably the Canons who were then both more reactionary and more formidable than they are now. Freddie had a number of like-minded friends in Oxford, Isaiah Berlin at All Souls and Hugh Trevor-Roper at his own college. With Trevor-Roper he intrigued to laicize Christ Church, so that the Dean, like the Heads of all other Oxford colleges, need no longer be in holy orders, but this came to nothing.

By the time Freddie came to publish his second book, *The Foundations of Empirical Knowledge*, in 1940, he was able to subscribe the Preface, 'Brigade of Guards Depot, Caterham'. He was incongruously commissioned into the Welsh Guards, but was never what would have been even more incongruous, a full-time regimental officer. Like the General in *The Importance of Being Earnest*, Freddie was essentially a man of peace except in his domestic life. He became a supernumerary soldier, working for SOE in New York and West Africa and at the end of the war on a more or less unofficial tour of liberated France, from which de Gaulle tried to expel him. But the truth was summed up by a wartime file which the historian M. R. D. Foot later found in the War Office archives labelled 'No job for Freddie Ayer'.

Christ Church had recognized his patriotism by renewing his research studentship but, when he returned to Oxford, Maurice Bowra fixed him up with a fellowship at Wadham. Almost immediately, Freddie left Oxford for London to take up the Grote Chair of Philosophy of Mind (in his blokey way, his friend George Orwell asked him what non-mental philosophy was). He was in London from 1946 to 1959, when he returned to Oxford as Wykham Professor of Logic (and Fellow of New College). Freddie spoke affectionately of his years in London.

He had a good time there. On the occasion of Sir Isaiah Berlin's eightieth birthday, the reactionary political philosopher Roger Scruton published an attack on him, followed some weeks later by an attack on Freddie Ayer on the occasion of his death. In Berlin, he found 'a dearth of the experiences in which the suspicion of the liberal idea is rooted: experiences of the sacred and the erotic, mourning and holy dread', but even Scruton could not have accused Freddie of lacking experiences of the erotic. When he was trying to get a fellowship at Oxford before the war, an enemy maliciously put it about that he could not be trusted with young men; no falser accusation was ever made. Freddie married young, and his marriage to Renée effectively lasted less than ten years. From 1941 till 1960 he was a bachelor once more, and a celebrated coureur.

He was not conventionally good-looking, but that has never mattered. He had a good deal of charm when he wanted to use it, as he often did with women. He once said to me, 'I used to have the reputation of enjoying a certain degree of success in that area. It's perfectly easy. All you have to do is pay a woman the smallest attention. In this country no one else does.' As he would have agreed himself, he was a more successful lover than husband, although his third marriage, to Vanessa Salmon, formerly the wife of the politician Nigel Lawson, ended in her death rather than in divorce, and in the last year of Freddie's life his second wife Dee Wells gamely remarried him.

In his somewhat Pooterish memoirs, Freddie listed the women in his life, which he later regretted. There and in other areas there was a sense of disappointment. When he turned forty he quite wrongly had a sense of failing powers and the spent pleasures of youth. He was conscious when he returned to Oxford as a professor of having passed from Young Turk to elder statesman 'without ever having known the plenitude of office'. Perhaps he felt that he had frittered away his energies, not so much by way of wine, women and song as in the footling round of philosophical conferences from, literally, China to Peru, and in university administration. The last is to his credit. He was a most conscientious head of department at University College, London, building it into one of the most distinguished in the country, and again at Oxford an energetic and creative teacher, running discussion groups for other philosophy dons and informal seminars for undergraduates as well as lectures.

Freddie was sometimes aggressive with his contemporaries, always kind and encouraging with the young. That should be remembered when fogeyish Tories complain about his character, conduct and beliefs (or lack of them). Of course he sometimes behaved badly in his dealings with women, he was selfish, and he was delightfully vain. But these were quite transparent. He enjoyed instructing or testing others, and his company could sometimes be rather like a viva, with questions about cricket teams, or, could one name all the presidents of the Third Republic.

There were times when anyone might have understood what E. E. Cummings had meant. The two became friends and Cummings, who was painter as well as poet, painted an interesting portrait of Freddie (who once pointed to it in his house in York Street, asked if I could guess who painted it, and was nonplussed when I could: no guess, I had read Freddie's memoirs). At an early stage of their acquaintance, Cummings had asked Freddie's wife what she was doing with 'that stainless steel mind'. That was partly true. True also that Freddie could seem self-obsessed. Peregrine Worsthorne has recalled Freddie's asking him when Vanessa was mortally ill if he could join the Garrick again, as he would soon have lonely evenings to fill. To be fair, Perry himself has added that many people might have thought the same thing; only Freddie would have been brutal or honest enough (according to taste) to put thought into words. Others have recalled him saying, on hearing of the death of Philip Toynbee, 'But he admired me so much'. And when I saw him for the first time after the death of Gary Bennett and mentioned him, Freddie said, 'Yes, we were elected Fellows of New College on the same day.'

This vanity was not the same as intellectual arrogance, of which Freddie was conspicuously free. His first book was written with the brilliant blinding self-confidence of youth, but he later came to see its weaknesses, indeed the faults of much that he had written. This was illustrated at lunch one day in the Beefsteak. I said, 'I'm sorry, Perry, but try as I may I can't make head or tail of your hero Professor Oakshott.' Worsthorne: 'Oh, well, that's because he's a philosopher. All philosophers are hard to understand.' Myself: 'No, they're not. Some Germans, maybe. But not our own team. Hume isn't difficult, or Russell – or for that matter' – gesturing to my left – 'Freddie'. Ayer: 'Quite so. My books aren't in the least bit difficult. They are full of error, but entirely lucid.' It was an enchanting remark, and completely in character.

Did that mean that Freddie had recognized the emptiness and sterility of his reductionist philosophy, in which not only was God dead but the whole of metaphysics, where all value judgements were meaningless, where a proposition must either be empirically verifiable or tautologous? So his latter-day enemies on the religious (or would-be religious) Right would like to think. But then their own denunciations of Ayer are empty unless they conduct the debate in his own terms. A year before his death, Freddie had had a strange experience in hospital when his heart stopped for four minutes and in those minutes of 'death' he saw 'a red light, exceedingly bright. I was aware that this light was responsible for the government of the universe.' He later added that the episode had shaken not his disbelief in life after death – he had been an unbeliever, he once said, since his failure to get into his private school First XI persuaded him of the inefficacy of imperative prayer – but modified his inflexible attitude.

In any case, this rigid atheist (whose friends included two Jesuits, Frs D'Arcy and Copplestone) was open to more subtle charges. He admitted that Christianity had at least produced some good art, but there was still something philistine in his hostility to religion. He said that the central Christian doctrine of vicarious redemption was morally repulsive and intellectually absurd; which might be answered, Maybe so – but psychologically compelling. He never fully recognized that belief is a deep human need, though he had only to look about him. After all, Freddie came from a generation many of whose brightest members persuaded themselves to believe in the Soviet Myth, compared with which believing in the liquefaction of the blood of San Gennaro is a triumph of empirical sense. Freddie never became a Communist – he told the proselytizing Stephen Spender that he did not believe in dialectical materialism, an unique reason for declining to join the Party – but he was always a progressive of just the sort condemned by Dwight Macdonald.

In the spring of 1988 I was in New York. I knew that Freddie was lecturing at an obscure American college as a way of supplementing his pension. But when I rang his step-daughter Gully Wells I learned that he was seriously ill in hospital. We visited him with smoked salmon, off which he practically lived at that time of his life. With uncharacteristic tact I omitted to point out that it was the hospital where Dylan Thomas died, and he talked contentedly about himself, and about the sombre social and gastronomic life of New College: 'The portraits in Hall, Wykhamists, all bishops, no archbishops.' As a treat on his return to London, I arranged to take him to Lord's for the one-day international, but we were defeated by the English summer weather. Icy rain spat all day as the players came on and went off and Freddie huddled deeper inside his overcoat and scarf. A few days later I heard that he was in hospital once more with pneumonia, and I thought for a moment that I had finished the aged logician off. In the event, and after his strange experience, he recovered to live for another year. He had been cast down deeply by Vanessa's death, to the point of contemplating suicide. His remarriage to Dee brightened his last months. He died at seventy-eight, tired and ill. I wonder if he met his bright red light a second time.

INDEX

279